The Rickshaw Reveries

Ipshita Nath teaches English Literature at Delhi University. She enjoys reading Victorian literature, travel writing, fantasy, dystopian, and lately, noir fiction. For her, engaging with the metropolis is a terrible but thrilling ride, and she likes wandering in the city in search of the bewildering realities of urban spaces. *The Rickshaw Reveries* is her first book, and comes out of her experiences of walking in Delhi.

The Rickshaw Reveries

dark dazzling delhi stories

IPSHITA NATH

SIMON & SCHUSTER

London · New York · Sydney · Toronto · New Delhi

A CBS COMPANY

First published in India by Simon & Schuster India, 2020
A CBS company

1 3 5 7 9 10 8 6 4 2

Simon & Schuster India
818, Indraprakash Building,
21, Barakhamba Road,
New Delhi 110001

www.simonandschuster.co.in

PB ISBN: 978-93-86797-77-3
eBook ISBN: 978-93-86797-78-0

Typeset in India by SÜRYA, New Delhi

Printed and bound in India by Replika Press Pvt. Ltd.

FSC www.fsc.org MIX Paper from responsible sources FSC® C016779

Simon & Schuster India is committed to sourcing paper that is made from wood grown in sustainable forests and support the Forest Stewardship Council, the leading international forest certification organisation. Our books displaying the FSC logo are printed on FSC certified paper.

Dedicated to Ma, Babu and Shelly

CONTENTS

A METAMORPHOSIS ON THE NORTHERN RIDGE

The sky was overcast, and a light wind had begun raking up the crumbling earth around the ridge area near North Campus. Dust blew in people's faces as they made their way through the buzzing post-college traffic around the metro station.

Balram was feeling strangely unwell when he returned to his spot near the metro station after dropping two students off at the Gwyer Hall canteen. He wiped the sweat off his face and snatched the old bottle of water he kept tucked under the rickshaw seat. The water had little bubbles in it. He gulped it down thirstily but felt no different after drinking it. He flung it away and eyed the water vendor standing some way ahead. Should he buy a glass of cold water? It would cost him money but he badly needed it.

He strode forward and slapped some coins on the steel counter of the water cart. He would have two glasses and no more.

Students milled about as he stood gulping down the sweet refrigerated water. Right before him, a colourful row of rickshaws undulated as passengers came and went. Some rickshawwallas scuttled here and there, jumping before prospective passengers like a team of footballers in a penalty shoot-out trying to block the goal. They shouted the names of different colleges while making eye contact so that they could claim the passenger whose destination they had guessed correctly or who looked their way first. He saw his friend Harish trot after some girls, almost pleading with them to take his rickshaw, his face screwed up in desperation. Balram wondered how long had he stood at the station. Had he not found a single passenger since morning?

He returned the glass and sauntered away, still watching Harish. He had finally found a man to ferry and was excitedly walking towards his rickshaw with him in tow. On the other side of the road, he saw Rajnish pulling his rickshaw away from the station and pedalling towards the campus.

Scanning the crowd for a potential passenger as he went back to his rickshaw, he patted his breast pocket and felt the thin wad of notes. Ninety rupees. That wasn't bad at all. Maybe he would take a break before lunch.

He was about to climb up in the backseat of the rickshaw to catch a nap when a woman in tight short pants walked by. His heart gave a sudden flip at the sight of bare feminine skin and he jumped up hastily.

'Madam, Hansraj? Miranda?' He knew that such a fashionable type belonged to either a girls' college, or

Hansraj. He could profile people quite accurately after just a few years of plying around the campus area.

But the girl had earphones on and did not turn towards him. He did not mind. He stared after her, his eyes stuck on the lovely rounded ass that swayed this way and that as she wobbled away. He automatically turned to look at the exit gate of the metro station as if expecting to see a train of such nubile beauties following after her, but there weren't any. He looked back to gaze after the girl—she was already at a distance but he could still see the fair pair of naked legs between a mass of jeans and salwars. He grinned to himself. It wasn't too often that he saw such sights.

He turned to climb back onto his rickshaw again, still smiling, when another woman's voice came from behind: 'Bhaiya, Miranda House le chalenge?'

He turned to see a strikingly fair girl standing right before his rickshaw, looking at him anxiously. She too was wearing a hugging pair of shorts, revealing a glorious pair of milky white legs. Balram felt that the last time he had seen such whiteness was when he had drunk bhaang during Holi. He gulped, trying to keep his excitement in check. 'Ji…ji Madam,' he stuttered, and clambered off so that she may sit.

The girl didn't notice. She came forward and hurriedly climbed up. As she sat, he had a full view of the back of her thighs, curving promisingly at the edge of the shorts, right where the hips began. He almost felt choked with desire.

The image of the creamy pair of legs stayed in his mind as he pulled away and pedaled towards the college.

'Madam, idhar se lu, ya udhar se?' he asked cheekily at the red light, turning a tad bit to be able to catch a glimpse of her. Lucky for him, she was looking into her mobile phone and didn't bother.

'Kahi se bhi le lijiye bhaiya, bas jaldi.'

Balram chuckled to himself. He pedaled faster, eager for her to get down so he could watch her ass sway as she walked away.

He had to slow down because by the time he was crossing Khalsa, he had an erection.

✦

That afternoon, Balram saw four or five more of such voluptuous women, and managed to give a ride to three of them. Each of them had beautiful thighs of varying shades and thickness. The thickest ones with no gap in the meeting of the thighs were the most tempting, and he had had an instant impulse to kiss and bite them. Thin legs were sexy too. He couldn't decide which ones he preferred most. He was a man after all. And the young women in campus, so painfully young and provocative.

Obviously, he never let his lustful fantasies show. He remained straight-faced and earnest, and kept his legs together so that the bulge in his pants was not visible if he ever got turned on by a passenger in skimpy clothes.

✦

Balram went home that evening to his wife, now bloated with multiple pregnancies, sitting and waiting for him. She was nursing his newborn and sat with her breasts hanging down to her navel as she made rotis on the stove. He looked away in revulsion. Why couldn't she be fairer or slimmer?

Her breasts were shapeless now and flapped about stupidly when he made her sit on top and ride him. Even her vagina had become loose and shapeless, and he couldn't imagine going down on her anymore. Oh, how he wanted to taste a tight young pussy again…

Frustrated, he plopped himself on the mattress to nap facing away from her. In the afternoon, he had had to go into the ridge to relieve himself off of the massive erection he had developed as a result of imagining fucking the girls who had ridden his rickshaw. How delicious they were. Even the thought of taking them was enough to drive a man crazy.

He squirmed, beginning to get hard again. With a groan, he lay on his abdomen to catch some sleep before dinner. There was no use getting an erection now. He did not want to fuck the fat cow in his house.

✦

The next few weeks, Balram kept seeing scantily clad women in campus and went around with an erection half the time. It was getting quite inconvenient for him and he almost hoped he would not see bare skin anymore. But strangely, he kept finding women who were either dressed in revealing shorts, or absolutely fitted shirts that showed the mounds of their breasts. And so, he went about pedalling beautiful women to their destinations, with his head filled with images of the dirty things he would do to them, and his pants filled out with the inevitable result of such fantasies.

✦

Balram was a simple man with very few vices. His only weakness was college girls. But which man did not lust after young women? He was not particularly guilty about having desires of the flesh. His high sex drive was only a sign of a robust physical and mental health, and he was proud of it.

During weekends, Balram took a couple of hours off and went up to GB Road to meet Queen—his favourite of the whores who populated the dusty corners of the pandemonium. Those visits relieved him to a great extent of the tensions of the week, and the daily frustration of having to fuck an ugly woman at home.

But the weekly visit weren't enough for his high libido. He would prefer to have Queen more often—to lay his head between these legs everyday—but he couldn't afford it so frequently. She charged way too much.

And yet, the satisfaction she gave him in one night was more than he could hope for otherwise. She knew all the tricks in the trade. Every time he went to her, she dutifully told him that she had been missing him and that she had been depressed because she thought he had taken up another mistress. He, of course, knew she was bluffing and that it was all a part of her game. After all, hadn't he known prostitutes before her? If she was a good dissembler, he too was experienced in the art of kama to fall for such wiles and take her as a mistress as she obviously wanted because it would then include maintenance costs. Besides, he knew very well just how popular she was and how many men she took in a day. She probably said the same lines to each and every one of them, and moaned and writhed in the same way while being fucked. She was well practised—a true connoisseur in her profession.

But despite being aware of her trickery, the coyness, feigned and repetitive ways, it worked well for him during foreplay.

And so when Monday arrived, he managed to get back to the grind only because relief was promised for the weekend.

✦

One Monday evening, Balram stationed himself at the metro station after dropping a passenger at Patel Chest.

He sat down to relax and had just a lit a bidi when a young couple exited the gates and made a beeline for his rickshaw.

'Bhaiya...take us to the ridge,' the boy said, looking like he meant 'take us to the ridge so that we can fuck there.'

Trying not to smirk, Balram dismounted and tossed away the bidi as the boy and the girl climbed up and sat holding hands. The girl was blushing and the boy was being cocky and playful with her. Balram was truly amused at the innocent horny pair. They were definitely going to the ridge to have sex.

He began pedalling. He knew where they might want to go—not the entrance opposite the VC's office obviously, but the small gate opposite the St Stephen's back-gate. As he pedaled by the road towards the ridge, memories of the previous night spent with Queen made pangs of arousal course through his body, and collect in his member. By the time he reached the gate and the couple got off, he had a full-fledged erection.

He watched them enter the gate, and disappear inside.

His erection stood out and he waited for it to subside so he could get on the rickshaw again.

But it did not go away. He stood for a good ten or fifteen minutes, but it remained rock solid.

What was the matter with him? He held his penis and shook it around. It stayed rigid and sprung back to attack position. Exasperated, he climbed into the back of the rickshaw and positioned himself so that his cock did not rub against his pants too much. Some more time passed, and the cock remained the way it was. He was baffled, but amazed and pleased at the sudden sign of masculine vigour. Should he just go into the ridge and jerk off? He did feel the stirrings of arousal. But he was too tired and did not want to get up and walk all the way. Besides, someone might notice the bulge…

But it was already getting dark and nobody was on the street. He decided to go into the ridge after all. The erection was not going away and he badly felt like masturbating. He pulled out the photo of the naked golden-haired woman he always kept in his money pouch, and stared hard at her full, melon-sized breasts, while imagining sucking them. Then he locked the rickshaw and walked towards the gate.

It grew darker as he entered and there was no one in the clearing. Peacocks called from a distance, and the crickets in the bushes began chriping louder as he walked by. Some dogs barked at a distance. It was mating season after all.

He walked in, towards the pathway leading into the ridge, and turned towards a familiar trail. Twigs and dried leaves crunched under his feet as he walked in, careful of not tripping over a twisted root protruding from the ground. It was getting darker by the minute. He walked on, turning once again, towards the spot where he knew couples usually went to fuck. Maybe he would be able to spy on someone...

The trees above him rustled suddenly, as if convulsing under duress. He paused. Monkeys. Hopefully, he wouldn't encounter one on his way.

Just then he saw the boy and girl. They were fucking frantically on a rock next to an old Kikar tree. The sight of their grinding half-naked bodies sent a sudden shock coursing through him. He ducked behind a tree and pulled out his throbbing penis, and began jerking it, watching the boy's organ entering the woman from behind as she stood with her legs wide apart, her jeans pulled down to her ankles. Her ass vibrated as he thrust. How he would love to pound that pussy...

He slowed down, enjoying the view. He could take his time.

The trees above them were still rustling. Somewhere, a male peacock bellowed. Balram's eyes remained on the boy's cock thrusting into the girl. They were breathing heavily, and the girl kept yelping as he penetrated her.

Balram began jerking harder. The boy was on his knees now, licking her ass as she whimpered in pleasure. Balram thrust out his tongue to lick an imaginary ass in the air, jerking faster. He would ejaculate any moment now.

The chattering of monkeys filled the air as he slumped sideways on the tree, his hand sticky with his fluids, his chest heaving with the effort.

He was still in the middle of the orgasm when the boy

and girl dressed hurriedly and left, passing dangerously close to the tree behind which he stood. He would wait for them to gain some distance before exiting.

✦

It was 10 p.m. and pitch dark, and Balram was stumbling through the narrow trails of the bonta his father had warned him to stay away from during his childhood. He had been chased by a pack of dogs and had gone deep inside the ridge to shake them off. But now he couldn't find his way back. The ridge had gone pitch black by the time he got rid of the curs. In the dimness, he couldn't tell where he had reached.

Exhausted, he came to a stop near a boulder and sat down, trying to understand the direction he should take. But he wasn't able to figure out where he had come from, let alone where to go.

A sudden rustle from the bushes sent him clambering away. Without realising it, he ran further inside the ridge, more lost than he already was. Stopping next to a tall tree, he tried to gain composure and think. But his heart was pounding loudly in his chest and an unnameable fear gripped him. He tried to reason with himself: it was not as if there were wild animals around—it was said that there were crocodiles in the ridge at one point but there weren't any left now. Human civilisation had taken over. It was turning into a leisure park. He had nothing to be afraid of.

So why did he have this awful sense of trepidation? He looked around as he sank on a rock, trying to even his breathing. Maybe if he sat still and listened to the sounds, he would hear the traffic and figure out the way. He just needed to calm down and gain a sense of direction.

He got up and began walking slowly. He could hear nothing other than the soft rustling of the trees and periodic hooting of owls. Bats whizzed above him—brazenly close to his head. Bushes rustled occasionally as he passed by. Mongoose? Porcupines? Maybe just squirrels. His heart was racing despite himself.

Suddenly, he felt eyes upon him. A shiver ran through his body, making him go cold even in the summer heat. The nape of his neck bristled. Afraid of making a sound, he turned around slowly, trying to sense the gaze, and toppled over a tree root. Then suddenly, the branches above shuddered loudly.

He looked up and his mouth opened in a scream.

There, nestled against slender branches and drying leaves, were monkeys, perhaps hundreds of them, all staring down at him silently, their teeth revealed in the most twisted grins he had ever seen.

✦

It was mid-afternoon when he regained consciousness. The ridge was dipped in a sepia tinge and all the sounds seemed muted. He stirred, terribly disoriented for a moment. Then the image of the wild faces came back to him.

He froze in horror at the memory. Then he realised he was stark naked. He scrambled up in alarm and looked around wildly. What was happening? Where were his clothes? His body was covered in marks and scratches, and his back hurt. Making as little noise as he could, he looked around to see if his clothes were flung behind the rocks and trees. But they weren't there.

A sudden snapping of a twig made his head jerk in the direction of the sound. It was just a wild rat. It skippered away.

His chest was heaving with fear. He looked around, trying to judge where he was. Was he where he had collapsed the night before? What had happened to him? He walked around trying to recognise the place, but the leaves under him crunched, too loudly, he thought. The ridge was unusually quiet. Every sound echoed.

A sudden weakness seized him, and he wobbled and fell on all fours. He was still disoriented. He tried to take another step, but fell down again. Dread settled over his heart. Had he been drugged? How was he going to escape? Desperate, he bounded forward, still on all fours. He would get away from the spot and find his way out somehow.

He came out of the clearing, and instinctively, turned around.

He was surrounded by monkeys again.

His mouth opened in a blood-curdling scream. And then he fainted.

✦

Loud chattering rising in crescendo. Balram opened his eyes. A large tawny monkey's face was inches away from his. He could smell his foul breath. Whimpering, he tried to move back but his head was pressed against a tree.

The chattering became louder as the monkeys realised he was conscious. He tried to rise, despite the bared teeth and menacing looks of the moneys, but fell down again. There was a dull ache in his backside. He could barely move his hips

Suddenly, the monkey who was closest to him clutched him and shoved him sideways. Then it grabbed his shoulder and flipped him over. Balram lay face down, too scared to resist. He could hear it chatter aggressively, stamping on the dried leaves and clutching his back with his leathery hands…as if straightening him into position. Balram allowed himself to be moved around, realising what was going to happen. There was no escape.

The chattering grew louder as he screamed in pain. They were cheering, excited, triumphant.

Balram tried to free himself but the monkey grabbed him roughly by the hair, twisting his neck back. He closed his eyes in pain and fear, tears running down his face, as the monkey shoved his hand roughly inside his asshole. 'Nahi!…Nahi!' he howled like an animal.

Suddenly, the chattering cleared to give way to human voices. There were men around. Balram froze, listening to screeching mingled with words.

'Ab meri baari.'

'Nahi, meri.'

'Nahi, meri.'

'Nahi, meri.'

They were quarrelling, repeating the same thing over and over again, sometimes chattering, sometimes talking. Balram tried to turn around to see where the men had come from but could only see monkeys. They were of all sizes, leaping from one place to another, some of them sporting huge erections as they gathered around.

'Ab meri baari.'

'Ab meri baari.'

'Ab meri baari.'

'Aah, aah, ooh, ooh!'

'Aah, aah, ooh, ooh!'

'Aah, aah, ooh, ooh!'

The monkey that was raping him was still thrusting into him, heaving and grunting, his black hairy hands clutching his waist tightly and hurting him. The other monkeys were watching impatiently, jumping up and down, their chattering getting more aggressive, somehow lewd. They wanted their turn. Some came closer to inspect, greedily eyeing his ass.

The monkey raping him suddenly stopped. Balram felt him convulse, shuddering uncontrollably as warm liquid spilled on his ass and trickled down. Its hairy body slumped against him for a brief moment before drawing away.

The other monkeys were in a frenzy. Two or three got hold of him and began fighting with each other. One monkey tried to drag him by the leg.

'Ab meri baari,' they were screeching.

'Aah, aah, ooh, ooh!'

'Ab meri baari.'

Balram felt nauseated. He screamed and stumbled over, the semen of monkeys smeared over his buttocks, and vomited, even as laughter rose around him.

'Jaldi. Woh bhagne ki koshish kar raha hai!'

'Pakad usse!'

'Aah, aah, ooh, eeh eeh!'

'Jaldi.'

'Jaldi.'

'Jaldi.'

He opened his mouth to scream again. But his voice had changed.

He was screeching like a monkey, bounding from one corner of the clearing to the other, trying to dodge the monkeys who were trying to corner him and rape him again.

✦

When Balram came to his senses, he found himself in a hospital. His wife and children were standing next to his bed, looking down at him with tears in their eyes. Sushma started wailing when he looked up at her and grunted. He was still in pain and could barely move his hips. She began sobbing noisily and flung herself at his feet.

'Haye bhagwan, kya ho gaya mere aadmi ko.' She clutched his feet and kept wailing.

'Chup kar' he snapped at her as he squirmed, trying to rise. His anus hurt sharply.

Apparently he had been sedated because he kept crying in his semi-conscious state. The doctor that came in after some time, grimly told him that he had been sodomised brutally, multiple times, or by multiple people, so that there were tears in his butt hole that they had to begin treating. The police had come by but they were unable to lodge an FIR due to the unusual circumstances. His wife too had refused to believe that he had been raped, and did not consent to filing a case for that. She kept saying that men could not be raped—only women could be, despite being counseled by the nurses.

The doctor was kind but helpless and advised Balram to rest. He said they will test him for possible STDs and give him painkillers. He also recommended going to the police since it was a case of gang rape, and the culprits were operating in an area close to a university campus.

Balram listened in silence, barely processing the words, his jaw clenched as he felt a wave of nausea again. Sushma continued sobbing in the corner and he would have slapped her if he had the energy. He was feeling increasingly sick and his head felt like it would explode.

'Doctor…' he began slowly.

'Yes?'

'Bandar…bandar.'

'What?'

'It was…it was monkeys.'

'What?'

'It was monkeys. At least thirty…fifty of them…Maybe a hundred. They raped me.'

There was stunned silence. The nurses and ward boys seemed to freeze around him.

'What are you saying?' the doctor asked uncertainly.

'Doctor sahab,' he said, trying to keep an even tone. 'There are monkeys in the ridge. They raped me. Not men.'

'Balram, you are in shock.' The doctor said, sounding somewhat uncertain and uneasy. But he was trained to treat these cases with clinical rationality. 'Please rest,' he told him gaining more confidence. 'Perhaps we will get you in touch with an organisation that deals with such… incidents. I know the lady who runs one. Don't you worry!'

But Balram did not care for NGOs.

'Sahab, believe me. It was monkeys. I know it sounds absurd. But it is true.'

The doctor hesitated. 'Fine, Balram. I will take note of that…and I will take up this matter with the police if you want.'

'But what would the police do? No…tell my wife to come here.'

But Sushma did not understand. In fact, her wails grew louder when she heard him narrate the bizarre story. She thought he was going mad, apart from having been emasculated. She had not even understood sodomy, believing it to be castration.

'Toh kya wo napunsak ban chuka hai?' she had wept before the nurses.

Balram hadn't expected anything more from his dim-witted wife. He did not know whom to discuss the incident with.

✦

Balram did not know what to make of what had happened to him in the ridge that night. Had he just imagined that monkeys had raped him, not men? He could no longer tell how much of it was hallucination and how much of it was reality. Had his mind somehow skewered up the memory due to the horrible brutalisation of his body? Was he losing his mind? Was it trauma?

He couldn't make up his mind even after days of reliving the incident. It kept coming back to him in flashes…stumbling around, being unable to balance on his legs, his anus hurting unbearably because of so much thrusting…

And the monkey faces—the oddly human-like monkey faces with wicked grins and lascivious stares. He remembered vividly how they bounded around, jumping from one place to another, watching him lecherously as he was raped by the larger monkeys.

Balram tried to shake off the images. Now that he knew he had escaped, the panic and fear had receded somewhat. He had come to terms with the incident—he had to, or he would lose his mind. And he knew he was hanging by a gossamer thread. If he allowed himself to slip, he would fall into a hysterical state that he might never recover from.

But the chattering haunted him at all times. At night, the sea of monkey faces came back in his dreams, and he woke up drenched in sweat. The screeches mixed with human voices echoed in his ears.

✦

A month passed.

Balram recovered slowly from the physical injuries, and the trauma also abated somewhat.

Out of an urgent financial need, and because he seemed fine now, his wife began pestering him to resume work. She had pushed the whole mishap into the peripheries of her memory and no longer believed her husband was 'raped'. She explained to herself that Balram had tried to do something experimental in sex—he was always telling her to do new things—with some other woman and it had gone wrong. Or perhaps he had merely been unfaithful to her and the mistress had attacked him after some argument—maybe he had tried to break up with her.

It was a comforting explanation. She was upset thinking he might have had an extra-marital affair, but felt better knowing that her husband hadn't been raped by men and emasculated. That she could not live with.

And so Balram began work, slowly at first, gaining momentum as the days passed. The men around him did not have the slightest inkling of what had really transpired in the ridge, and neither was the police informed. He knew there was no point. People would just call him psychologically disturbed, or worse—chhakka.

And so he kept shut, carrying around the secret, like he carried around the continual dull, throbbing pain in his anus which he did not tell anyone about.

✦

One day, about six weeks after the incident, Balram was ferrying some passengers through the campus when suddenly, a sting of pain shot up his backside. He yelped with the sudden shock of pain, and collapsed sideways, groaning.

The students sitting in his rickshaw did not know what to do. They tried to talk to him but he was groaning in pain and could hardly open his eyes. They scurried away, scared.

An hour later, when the pain subsided, Balram realised his pant was wet and sticky. He reached down and saw his fingers were covered in blood.

Pain was shooting though him still. He reached down and felt the spot. There was a slight protrusion there. The pain was excruciating.

✦

Another month passed. Balram was unable to ply his rickshaw now. The spot between his butt was growing steadily and was now nearly six inches long.

His wife had left him and gone to the village with their children. She was horrified to see the strange growth on her husband, and suspected a contagious disease. She would go to Vaishno Devi to offer prayers. All this could have been the doings of a malignant spirit or someone's curse. She would try to get rid of the evil eye somehow.

Balram, horrified at first, became calm despite the grotesque and strange appendage on his ass. But as it grew longer over the next few weeks, he came to terms with his tail.

✦

A year passed. There had been strange tales in the city about a series of bizarre attacks by a mysterious 'Monkey Man'. This man was described variously as shaggy black, hairy, and terrible looking. He struck only after midnight, scratching and gouging people he happened to encounter. Sometimes he stole into people's houses and broke things, or just marauded through dark alleys, attacking anyone who was alone and unguarded.

The police was unsure of what to do. Rumours floated around. Some said the creature could leap from buildings and some said he could become invisible.

The city was in the grip of the mass terror unleashed by the 'Kala Bandar'.

SUBTERRANEAN LOVE

Hamza Omar lived in a barsaati, on a double-storied house that belonged to his distant uncle, in the inner sections of Noor Nagar, Jamia. Although he lived alone and did not have too many needs, he had begun to grow tired of the small and slovenly room. The building belonged to his uncle on the maternal side, and he built this room for him when he moved to the city as a favour to his mother. It was a dingy and ugly room with exposed walls. There were perennial wet patches of a sickly white and green shade on the walls as fungus had formed.It got worse during the monsoons. A fuzzy layer of fungus formed on the ceiling as well and the room got unbearably musty. In summer, the room heated up like an oven, baking him as he sat under the slowly rotating ceiling fan that churned hot air. In winter, cold winds crept in through the nooks and crevices, making it impossible to stay warm at night.

The toilet was even worse. It was a tiny enclosed space in one corner of the room with a dark, gaping hole in the floor and two bricks fixed on either side for squatting. The hole was connected to a pipe that ran down into the main sewers of the street and the excreta directly fell into the main pit through it. There was no way of ensuring everything washed away without sticking to the walls of the pipe since there was no flushing mechanism. Hamza would usually have to throw down mugs of water to clean it out, but sometimes avoided it because clean water was too dear. And so the noxious fumes rose up from the depths of it and made him dizzy while he sat over it every morning to do his business. Sometimes he had the heady feeling of falling into the deep dark tunnel, into piles of his own shit that rolled into an endless river of the city's sludge. It looked like an ominous void in the dim light, and greatly disconcerted him if he happened to look down. Monsoons made things worse. As drainage systems malfunctioned all over the city, feculent waters flowed up the drain. Very often, murky sewage reached the brim with solid turd and dead insects floating in it. Sometimes, rodents swam up and infested the room. One morning, he discovered a baby snake floating in the water, dangerously close to the surface of the hole over which dangled his precious parts. He jumped away with a yell and pushed the stone slab he used to cover the hole with back on.

After many long years had passed, Hamza decided that he would move out of the barsaati once and for all. He had been planning to move for a long time but never had the resources. His uncle let him live there on half the rent but now that he had a steady job as a rickshawwalla, he could think about taking up a better establishment. The barsaati was an absolute shit hole. And just because he was single didn't mean that he should live in such insalubrious conditions. He was becoming a man and could no longer live like he used to as a teenage boy, not caring where he slept at night as long as he had a roof above his head. He had lived in squalor for long enough, and could not make this a way of life. Besides, he could never ask his mother to visit him because she couldn't climb up the flight of stairs.

More importantly, what if a lady was to come into his life? He was in love, after all. What if he was to ask her to be with him and she said yes? How could he possibly have her live with him in this dirty matchbox of a house? Of course, he couldn't afford a proper quarters yet. He was still too young and poor, and entirely on his own. But perhaps a small room in the decent looking building in Abu Fazal, shared with a couple of boys of his own age, wasn't too unrealistic even with his paltry savings. Then some years later when he had more savings, he would take a flat of his own and make a family.

In the meantime, he would figure out a way to win over Nadia Siddiqui of Zakir Nagar, the beautiful girl he wanted to make his wife.

✦

Nadia was a student of English Literature. She went to the university library often, and came home laden with books. Hamza knew she was a bookworm and often spotted her walking on the pavement with her nose deep into a book, her black glasses hanging on the tip of her sharp nose. At such times he would be tempted to ride up and offer to ferry her, but it was much more enjoyable watching her dodge potholes on the way without looking up from the book. She lived in a big house in Zakir Nagar, and he sometimes sat in the neighbourhood so that he could have a view of her balcony where she liked to sit and read.

Hamza had seen Nadia for the first time when she was hailing a rickshaw on a hot day in May outside the campus gate, about a year ago. He was some way off and had been too struck by her beauty to respond to her calls and had simply remained transfixed to his seat, his mouth agape with a, 'Ya Allah…'

The next few days he kept spotting her, either outside her house or near campus. But he did not manage to give her a ride for at least three months of consistent trying. Finally one day, she came to him on her own.

He was sitting outside the university gate when without warning, two girls climbed onto his rickshaw, and instructed him to take them to the NFC market. He was half asleep so he turned to make a snide comment and refuse, but stopped mid-sentence seeing that it was her.

She was looking at him with impatience and said, 'Chaliye!'

With his heart pounding in his chest, he pedaled them to their destination. When she got off, he wistfully looked after her. She wasn't just beautiful. She was alluring in the most strange and spellbinding way. Hamza was besotted. After that day, he didn't know how he would live without her.

✦

Since the day Hamza first gave Nadia a ride, he began to keep a lookout for her. He knew her timings and was present wherever he knew she would be. If he spotted her from a distance, he skidded towards her before she got to any other rickshaw—but only if the area happened to be crowded and she wouldn't notice his eagerness. He had to be discreet. He did not want her or anyone else to see how he vied for her. And he didn't want her to realise that he ferried her regularly. To be on the safer side, he kept a cloth over his face so she wouldn't recognise him. But he knew that even if he didn't cover up, she would not remember him, unremarkable and ordinary looking as he was.

This continued for the rest of the year—a whole semester in the university. Gradually, he relaxed his precautionary measures and began to ferry her around more often than before. From once a week it became twice a week, then thrice, then four times, and soon, it was only he who took her around. His friends, the other rickshawwallas in the campus area, soon figured out what was going on and agreed on his insistence to never take her around even if she came to them. She was fixed as only his, and it became a rule they could not flout. If someone happened to ferry her despite his warning, Hamza confronted them. They were amused at this and pulled his leg to no end. If on occasion Nadia happened to walk by his rickshaw, or stood anywhere in the vicinity, they hooted loudly, teasing him for his edginess and calling him 'Majnu' and 'Joru ka ghulam'.

Hamza wasn't really bothered by any of this. He even rejoiced in the titles and accepted them as if it was an honour to be known as Nadia's lover and slave.

It had been nearly eight months of his growing obsession with Nadia, when one day while he was pedalling towards the university with her sitting in the rickshaw, one of the rear tyres got punctured.

He did not stop immediately. He slowed down somewhat, but kept going. She had appeared to be in a rush and he did not want her to be inconvenienced because of him. He certainly did not want her to get off mid-way and take another rickshaw. And so he laboured on for several minutes and finally reached the campus.

She paid him as usual and dismounted, then almost as if she hadn't, gave him a smile and walked away. Hamza felt as if his heart had swelled up in his chest.

✦

The week after that incident, Hamza had the strange feeling that Nadia's eyes were on him as she sat on the passenger seat behind him while he took her around. He also began feeling that she had noticed it was he who ferried her every day.

Damn, he thought. He would have to give it a break for a while. If she realised he was stalking her like some sort of a maniacal lover, she would probably report him to the police.

But giving a break did not help. He had not ferried her for over a week when one day, while standing in a cluster of rickshaws waiting for passengers, she appeared out of nowhere and ignoring those immediately around her, called out to him, 'Hey you, come here!'

He hesitated, completely taken aback. What should

he do? He looked at his friends and they were grinning gleefully. The idiots! Their faces were sure to give him away.

'Hey, you!' she called out again. 'You there!'

He looked towards her finally, feigning a confused expression as though asking, 'Who, me?'

'You in the red shirt. What are you waiting for? Hurry!'

Petrified, he pedaled towards her and mumbled, 'Ji, huzoor.'

'What is your name?'

'H...Hamza.'

'Take me home, Hamza,' she instructed. Then her voice softened and she said almost coyly: 'I'm sure you know where I live.'

✦

Hamza, in his growing fixation with Nadia, began neglecting his friends. He had stopped meeting them, and in fact did not even wait with them at their usual stop as he earlier used to every evening. Instead, he began hanging around Nadia's house in the mornings, and around the campus during evenings.

He had also stopped worrying about his finances, and usually refused passengers if he knew Nadia would be leaving from campus and he might get a chance to ferry her home. At first, he thought he deserved the break because he had been driving himself very hard in the past few years. But it became his habit to while away time, day-dreaming about his precious beloved, and hoping to get a glimpse of her as many times as possible during the day.

Very soon, his three close friends, Ali, Mohammad, and

Mihir, began to grow worried by his careless behaviour. When it all started, they had humoured him, and even encouraged him as he mooned over the female. But now they could see it was getting out of hand. They chided him for being an idler, and berated him almost as often as they managed to get hold of him.

'Hamza, you cannot be so callous, brother,' Ali told him one evening while they were sitting on his terrace, drinking Bhingree. 'You must not neglect work.'

'Yes, Hamza. Ali is right. You should not forsake your work in this manner. Who will earn for your family?'

'Hamza, we think you should get back to work with us. We know how you feel about the girl but it is in your interest to prioritise your work over all this,' said Mihir.

'I understand what you say, brothers. And I know you want the best for me. But don't ask me to stop what I am doing,' Hamza told them frankly. 'I have to see Nadia as often as possible. If I don't, I begin to feel miserable. And then I cannot do anything at all the whole day…but you won't understand. You have never been in love, have you? All you do is chase after those silly girls you want to sleep with! What do you know of real passion?'

'Brother, be sensible,' Ali tried to reason.

'Ali, truly, I cannot sleep at night if I don't get to ferry her,' he said calmly. 'I feel like the light of my life has left me.'

'Hamza, this is not love. This is junoon.'

'Perhaps it is, brother,' he confessed. 'But I am helpless before her beauty.'

✦

That year it seemed like monsoon came in winter. The city was soaking, and there was water everywhere.

Hamza continued to ply his rickshaw despite the rains, unable to afford a break from work. The university was closed so work was hard to come by anyway. To add to his misery, Nadia had not stepped out of her house in days. His eyes felt parched for a glimpse of her. And he went by her house several times during the day, ignoring the gusts of cold wind and rain, soaked completely, his teeth chattering as he tried to keep a hold on the rickshaw despite his trembling shoulders.

Within a week of this, he fell sick. He tried to continue work as before, but got so weak that he was forced to stay in eventually. One night he lay shivering in his cot, murmuring Nadia's name in delirium.

When Ali, Mohammad and Mihir came to know he was sick, they came over and berated him again for his recklessness. Then they brought him medicine, rotis and dal, and forbade him to step out of his house until he had recovered.

But Hamza felt he was suffering from a different kind of sickness. It was a sickness of the heart that could be cured only by seeing Nadia.

That evening when his friends left, he got up and walked out of his building with the single-minded thought of seeing Nadia before nightfall no matter what it took.

Outside, it was still raining, although the thunder storm had ceased and there was no wind. The streets were crowded as people tried to get their work done before the weather worsened again. Hamza quickened his pace. Vehicles whirled around him, whizzing dangerously close to his feet. People pushed past, yelling angrily as he walked, almost as if in a dream-like state. He was so lost in his resolve to see her that he did not realise he was barefooted until he had walked straight into a pool of clogged drain water that had risen to well above his knees. He waded through it unflinchingly, and finally reached her neighbourhood.

He didn't know if his inner voice had called out to her, or if it was divine intervention, or if it was merely a coincidence, but the moment he stepped into the street that led up to her house, he saw her pacing in her balcony, her nose buried in a book.

He stopped dead in his tracks. His heart felt like it would give way. He was seeing her after nearly a month.

She was still very far—the street was at least a kilometre long and he could only make out her silhouette from where he had stopped. But he could even recognise her shadow in a moon-less night when the only source of light was the stars above.

He began walking towards her again, and then slowed down. Should he go any closer? What if she saw him? But seeing her after so long, he felt a strange thrill run through him. Desire emboldened him. So what if she saw him? He couldn't care less.

He came to a stop directly beneath her balcony, and stood staring up at her with absolute abandon. After what seemed like a whole hour, she titled her head, ever so slightly, and looked down to meet his eyes.

Just then, a matronly voice called out her name from

somewhere inside the house. She turned and left, without so much as a blink.

✦

'Take me to Purana Qila.'

Hamza looked up and was startled to see Nadia standing before him in a jet burkha, her hair covered entirely by a headscarf, and only the round of her face, flushed with excitement, showing against the black.

His mouth fell open in bewilderment. Had he heard her right?

'Hurry!'

Spurred by the urgency in her voice, he swung into action. Puranas Qila was easily fifteen kilometres away. He was half tempted to point that out, but kept shut. Who was he to say anything? If she asked to be taken to Taj Mahal on his rickshaw, he would bloody well take her.

But why was she in a burkha and why did she want to go the qila? And why in heaven's name did she want to go on his rickshaw when she could have easily taken an auto or a taxi? Not that he was in a position to complain. Without uttering a single word, he began pedalling. Behind him, she was talking to herself as they pulled out of Zakir Nagar. He heard her clearly: 'I don't get to step out of the house at all. It is so rare that I have the privacy to go anyplace I like by myself, let alone travel to different places. And oh, do I long to travel and see the world…I want to see the pyramids in Egypt and Macchu Picchu in Peru…I want to go to the Louvre and see the paintings and then go inside the Buckingham Palace in England. And oh, how I long to see Italy! The Colosseum looks so grand in the pictures...and France! I want to see the Eiffel tower and the catacombs and the small cafes along the cobblestone streets...Oh, I wish to see the whole world! But Ammi won't ever let me. She won't even let me go to the mall alone! Urgh, what am I going to do? I hate her!'

He listened to the exotic names without knowing what they were. And he dared not make any indication that he was listening. He didn't want to break her reverie. Besides, he was afraid of being snubbed if he spoke.

He continued to pedal, his eyes fixed on the road ahead, and his ears straining to catch anything else she might say. As they moved, the weather changed above their heads. Clouds gathered and began rumbling. It became dark, and the winds grew fierce. The traffic on the main road thinned as he reached it, and as though people around didn't see the lone rickshaw crawling along the wide roads, they went on, towards Pragati Maidan, and finally reached the Old Fort.

'Now wait here,' Nadia ordered as she dismounted. Then, without any explanation, she walked inside the fort. He saw her walk towards the boating section, hire a pedal boat, and row to the middle of the lake.

Hamza kept watching her, breathing heavily, his heart beating heavily from the long ride. But something told him it was not because of the exertion. She had looked him in the eyes a moment longer than was needed. And he had seen something different in them this time.

✦

'Come back at midnight.'

They were right underneath her house. Nadia was looking at him and had barely whispered these words as she handed him the fare. The cool coins had jingled in her palm and fell into his, and he had stared unbelievingly into her deep brown eyes framed with voluptuous lashes. It was twilight, and in the cool blue-tinted evening, it did not seem like her lips had moved, or her eyes had twinkled to give away anything at all. She had said it simply, and there was no attempt to gauge his reaction or response.

Hamza was dumbstruck. Without another word, she turned and walked away, through the tall gates of her house, and did not look back as she disappeared inside.

Hamza stood frozen for several minutes, still processing what had happened. Then a light went on, on the upper floor and he came back to his senses. He realised the house was empty. Where was the rest of the family?

He stood there for several minutes and then cycled away. Why had she asked him to come to her at midnight? What was on her mind?

Night fell around him as he entered the congested area of Batla House. His mind was so saturated by the invitation that he forgot all about the ride to the qila. Had it even happened? Had he really pedaled nearly thirty kilometres with her in his rickshaw? And had she actually asked him to come to her at night? What did she want? He was suspicious. It couldn't be possible that she wanted his company. Why would a girl like her invite him just for the heck of it, and that too at night?

His mind was racing. Could she be in love with him? As much as his heart strained, he did not want to be so presumptuous. Trying to contain his excitement, he wondered if she simply needed another ride. Or perhaps her family members were returning at midnight…It dawned on him then. Of course her family was returning at night and they needed help with the luggage. She wanted a coolie to carry their suitcases!

He shook his head in wryness. How could he even for a moment imagine he would be invited to her house after midnight as a lover? It was an absurd idea.

And yet, he couldn't shake off the feeling that she hadn't asked him to come at night to help with luggage. Still, his rational mind was too afraid to cherish hope.

✦

Time passed sluggishly. Everything seemed decelerated. Hamza felt as though he was in a dream and time had slowed down, stretching languidly just to torment him. Never had hours seemed so lengthened, nor evening so prolonged. By 8 p.m., he was certain time had stopped altogether and the hour to meet Nadia would never arrive.

As he sipped tea at a small teashop, he wondered what he would say to her when he would meet her that night. So far, only she had talked, and he had merely done ji-huzoori. This time perhaps, he would get to say something to her. Did she know how he felt towards her? She probably did. Did it mean that he should now propose to her? No, he couldn't do that. It would scare her off. And what if she did not reciprocate? She might try to get rid of him. He was just a poor rickshawwalla after all.

He resumed work with those doubts buzzing in his head. Then at 9 p.m., he took a break again and the same thoughts came back to him. But newer concerns came to him too. He hadn't thought about the most important bit: his clothes. In the dark, he looked down at his patched up sweater and frayed pants that was a tad bit loose on his frame. Raising his arms, he sniffed his armpits. The scent of winter sweat made him shudder. He would go to the barber after work. He would have him soap his hair.

Right after dinner, he went home and took a long bath. Luckily there were two buckets of water stored for emergencies, and he used both, generously lathering himself with Lifebuoy, and scrubbing his face and neck with vigour.

He reached her house long before it struck midnight. He had been waiting for nearly an hour when exactly at midnight, she opened her window and called out his name.

'Hamza...'

Her voice traveled down to him from the window and played on his ears as though she was right next to him.

'Climb up the tree.'

And he did. Swinging from one branch to another, he went higher and higher, right up to her window. Then balancing himself on one branch, walked right up to her balcony and jumped down before her.

His heart was pounding. She was standing before him in a moonlit square, her face glowing with the excitement of her transgression. She wore a loose white robe, translucent even in the dimness.

'I know you are in love with me,' she said evenly. Her long, jet hair flowed behind her in an abundant mass, dancing coquettishly in the wind as she came forward.

There was a sudden heavy gust and he felt it press

against him, pushing him towards her. The trees around began to whoosh loudly, swaying in the cool drafts that had started up. Rain clouds rumbled some way off.

As they stood there looking at each other, the trees seemed to sway faster and faster, and the lightening began to sound again and again, almost as if trying to mute them—her, as she stood before him and uttered the most beautiful words he had ever head:

'You made me wait for four hundred and seventy three days. But you are here now. Won't you come inside?'

✦

Their clandestine meetings, nocturnal at first, gradually became diurnal too, as love gave them a kind of recklessness that is common to new lovers. Fuelled by the audacity of their actions, they became more thoughtless and impulsive, meeting whenever they wanted, going around the city on his rickshaw despite the surveilling—and now suspicious—eyes of society, utterly unthinking about the consequences of their indiscretions.

Hamza was floating in the rosy haze of what he had always imagined but never experienced: romance. Their meetings at Nadia's house were filled with what seemed like the nectar of all the flowers in Shalimar Bagh back home. Her face had the beauty of the Dal Lake in winter when shikaras glided over the cold waters with sobriety. And her eyes, he felt, contained all the playful mischief that Allah had dared to put in one woman. He was completely besotted by her charms.

Most of all, he was spellbound by her body. She seemed

to have been crafted meticulously just to drive a man crazy. Every day when he climbed the tree to her room, she lay in wait for him on her narrow, feminine bed that cradled her soft, naked form that was ready to receive him. The very sight of her fair suppleness drove him to his wit's end.

And so, every day they made love until daybreak after which he climbed down the tree and went home. They had built a wall around themselves, shutting out social constraints, and their own voices that told them it could never work out between them.

But every day when Hamza climbed down the tree and walked back to Noor Nagar, his home, his legs felt like lead and his heart seemed heavier, as he went back to his reality of poverty and penury—a world which had no access to Nadia's, and certainly not a world fit for her to be brought into.

✦

A year had passed since they had confessed their love for each other, and now Nadia, twenty-one years of age, a graduate of the university, famed for her beauty and intelligence in the rich circles of her Nawabi family, began to be seriously pursued by a string of impressive suitors. The men were confused at first by the girl's reluctance, then sensing competition, became more insistent. They were confident about their power and fine breeding. If materialistic gifts didn't please the girl, then some poetry, some romance might. They were awed by her beauty and wit, and tickled by her steadfast evasiveness. Her unattainability made them more aggressive in their attempts to win her hand in marriage, and they lavished her family with extravagant gifts, sent formally through the elders in order to to increase the pressure.

Her parents who had not given her marriage a thought before this, were baffled at their luck. It was clear that the time was ripe because the proposals that were flowing in were too tempting. They could see the men's keenness, and were flattered by the generosity that the politically-influential and aristocratic families showered upon them, who were fairly modest in comparison. Besides, they had two more daughters to marry off after Nadia. And so, they blessed their fortunate daughter and delightedly discussed the offers.

After two months of receiving expensive gifts of various kinds, they decided to finalise the best match for her. Soon, the Siddiqui house became host to different families, from Lucknow, Kanpur and Allahabad, showing off their worthy scions. But Nadia, to everybody's disappointment, was completely unmoved. She remained utterly stolid in the face of offers of extravagant mehers, and the promise of a life of luxury.

Nadia's mother, Shabeena, a staid middle-aged woman who had never known passionate love and who had lived twenty-five years of a dull and utilitarian marriage, told her in a matter of fact way one day that she had reached the age when she must marry before she became an old maid. When Nadia dismissed her advice, she chided her and told her to make up her mind quickly and select a groom before the suitors, fine as they were, lost interest and moved on. After all, how many girls could boast of receiving such good proposals? She could not afford to miss this opportunity of marrying well. She might not be left with too many options later.

After one hundred days of maintaining silence in the face of forceful and audacious wooing, Nadia rejected all the men one by one. Shabana threw a fit the night she refused the last one. She slapped Nadia across the face and left a gash under her right eye. Then despairing for her daughter's disfigured face, plunged her hand into a pot of boiling tea in grief.

Early next morning, Nadia walked into her bedroom and told her in a soft voice that although the suitors were all accomplished and would have made good husbands to any woman, she had rejected them because of a vision she had had some months ago. In the vision she had been told by a Pir that she should only marry a man with grey eyes. He had warned her that if she married a man whose eyes were not grey, they would not be able to conceive a child.

Shabeena was horrified at this, but skeptical. She tried to reason with Nadia, but she was adamant. Finally, out of superstitious fear, she conceded to postponing the marriage until such a man with grey eyes came along. What if the vision truly was a divine warning? There was no match that merited such a risk. Nadia was just twenty-one after all. They could wait a couple of more years. Perhaps she could do a Masters in the meantime. Besides, she was guilty for inflicting violence upon her first-born. Nadia was her 'dil ka tukda', and she had struck her so heartlessly. The scar would stay on her cheek forever.

✦

After two years the time came again to begin looking for matches. By then Shabeena suspected that Nadia was lying about the vision—out of virginal fears against marriage perhaps. She tried to counsel her about the conjugal duty that all women have to fulfil to keep their husbands. But Nadia rubbished her mother's concerns and stuck to her narrative saying that her husband has to be a man with grey eyes. Finally, Shabeena summoned a Pir to allay her fears.

But strangely, the Pir affirmed Nadia's vision.

The family was thrown into a fix now. Where would they find a suitable bachelor with grey eyes?

The hunt began. Advertisements went out in matrimonial papers, messages were sent to distant relatives (even the ones living abroad), about the strange requisite in a groom for Nadia.

Little did they know that Nadia already belonged to such a man. Hamza's eyes were the beautiful shade of moonstone in morning sunlight.

✦

It was late autumn, and the wind had begun to feel cooler on the skin. Some trees had begun shedding, covering roadsides with heaps of stiffened dried leaves, while others seemed to blossom despite the season, as though they were indifferent to time.

Hamza and Nadia had discussed their strategy to elope. They knew that her family would never agree to their relationship, and would probably threaten to have him jailed. They might even hasten Nadia's marriage process for fear that she would run away. Her mother had already begun to suspect that she was having an affair. She had grown vigilant since, and rarely allowed her to step out unchaperoned. She was sure to coerce Nadia into marrying the first bachelor with grey eyes that came along without considering anything else.

One day when Hamza was leaving Nadia's room at the crack of dawn, Shabeena was awakened by the sound of a crow cawing from the tree Hamza had swung down. Irritated because her sleep had been disrupted, she got up to shoo the bird away. She was about to draw the curtains back when her eyes fell on a man's retreating form. Hamza, unaware of having roused Shabeena, turned to look up at Nadia's window to smile before jumping over the fence.

Shabeena's heart gave an unpleasant thud as she realised what was going on. Without raising an alarm, she ran towards the stairs leading to her daughter's room. Her husband must not know or he would not spare Nadia's life. She was hers alone to punish.

When she burst through the door, her chest heaving with fear and anger both, she found Nadia sitting by the window feeding the birds. There was nothing suspicious about her appearance. Her room looked like how it was the night before, her eyes full of sleep, and her skin nude as always. But a woman, especially a mother, can recognise the signs of impurity on her daughter's countenance, that too in the unguarded state that Nadia was in.

The unselfconscious flush on her cheeks from the early morning lovemaking had given her away.

Shabeena saw it and gave an animal-like cry for grief of her daughter's indiscretions.

'What have you done!' she screamed lunging forward and grabbing her hair. With the strength she had never revealed before, she dragged her and flung her on the bed. Then she ripped open her nightgown and saw in the glare of the uncompromising sun that had leapt up from the horizon as if just for this, the bruises her lover had wrought upon her body by night.

She staggered in fear of the Almighty.

'Nadia Hussein, did you let him take your virginity?'

Without waiting for an answer, grabbing both her legs she parted them roughly, praying that her maidenhood was still intact.

'Yes, Ammi,' came the simple answer of a woman in love. 'We are one.'

✦

Just as even sweetened milk curdles in heat, Hamza and Nadia's love began to sour when summer arrived next year. Nadia was despairing for she could no longer find any pretext to delay her marriage. And Hamza, knowing their future, and frustrated due to his helplessness, became aggressive and short towards her. He knew there were no chances of his prospects improving. And when Nadia begged him to elope with her, it only stung him because it was proof of how he could never win her hand in marriage in an honourable way.

But the situation was tense at the Siddique household. After the discovery of their affair, Shabeena was determined to have Nadia marry before summer ended. She had found a good match, and this time without bothering about the

Pir's warnings, threatened Nadia that she would tell her father everything if she did not agree to marry this time.

After weeks of nearly starving herself in misery, Nadia relented. Hamza had disappeared, and she was weak without him.

The niqah was held in July, and Nadia was packed off to Defence Colony. Her shauhar owned a law firm there and his two storeyed kothi became her home now.

But suddenly after a year, Hamza returned. He was now the owner of a hundred and fifty rickshaws, and the building in which he was earlier a tenant. His uncle, who was heirless at the time of his death, had named everything that belonged to him, in his name.

Hamza had only one thought when he inherited the money: to claim Nadia.

And with this, Nadia became an adulteress, making love to two men at night—her husband before midnight, and her lover who had always been in her dreams after that.

✦

Nadia couldn't deceive her husband for long. Abbas Abdal Khan was a shrewd advocate, and could recognise the signs of deceit on people's faces. He found out about her infidelity very soon, but instead of divorcing her, blackmailed her into staying faithful to him or face the wrath of their community, as well as a legal case of adultery which would strip her family of respect in their community.

Nadia did not care for the money, but she knew that if her affair was discovered, her family would be ridiculed. Her husband's family was influential and would ensure it.

After a week of resisting, she acquiesced to being locked up inside the house.

✦

Nadia had spent ten months as the advocate's prisoner. In these ten months, Hamza had taken to drinking, and had wasted a lot of time doing nothing. Money flowed in through the rickshaws he rented out, but he spent most of it on liquor.

Then one day, he quit abruptly and took to staying in Nizamuddin's dargah. He was looking for relief from the pain of being separated from Nadia. He thought that perhaps the holy place would provide some respite. But there was none to be found anywhere.

A year had passed this way and he did not get a chance to meet Nadia. He felt he was withering away. The house she had moved into was a fortress, and she was kept like a prisoner by her husband. He had proposed going to the police and filing a case, but Nadia would not hear of it.

'I am a willing captive,' she had told him through the window of her room one evening. 'I cannot bring shame upon my family. It would be catastrophic to divorce the advocate and then try to marry you. He will destroy me and my family. Please go away, Hamza. We can never be together…I have come to terms with it.'

In this way, Hamza pined for her once more in his life.

✦

It was a damp, wintry night. Hamza was on the first floor of his house when he felt a drop of water splash on his face as he lay on the settee under the fan. He opened his eyes to see where the water had come from and to his astonishment, saw that the ceiling was wet and dripping. There were puddles of water on the floor near the edges and much of the furniture was already soaked.

At first, he didn't register what was happening and sat confused, still dazed from the nap. Then it dawned on him. He sprang up and dashed to the door and pulled it open. Immediately, water that had collected outside spilled into the room. More water was cascading down the stairs, and slowly flowing out into the street through the main exit. Hamza ran upstairs, his feet splashing in the murky water that he knew had flowed out from the toilet hole in the barsaati that he kept covered with the stone slab.

When he reached the terrace, it seemed like it had turned into a pool. Quickly, he unlocked the large antique lock that he kept on the door and barged inside. The door of the toilet was shut, but water was flowing out from the gap under the door. He strode towards it, and yanked it open. There he saw the gaping dark hole overflowing with sewage. His stomach turned at the sight. Just then he became aware of the terrible stink and holding his breath desperately, went to retrieve the stone slab to cover it. He could feel solid waste squish under his feet as he moved.

Then just before he could drag the slab over the hole, there was a loud whoosh—the sound of suction when water flows out of a clogged basin. He felt the water changing direction around his ankles, and in the dim light, saw a vortex form as the sewage began to flow back into the hole. Bewildered, Hamza stepped back as the force of the water increased and it flowed in from the rest of the room. The water that was flowing down into the rest of the house had also changed direction and was travelling back towards the hole. He backed out of the barsaati, into the terrace, even as the water was getting sucked towards it.

Within minutes, the water was gone. Hamza ran towards the toilet and saw that the hole had emptied. Stunned, he stood staring into it for several minutes. And then he heard her.

'Hamza, come to me...'

It was Nadia's voice, drifting towards him through the subterranean passages under the city, beckoning him towards her.

'Nadia...?' he murmured, walking towards it. The hole was dark and pit-less. He jumped in without another thought.

✦

Hamza walked every second of the next twenty-two and a half hours through the narrow, blackened sewers of the city. He had travelled back and forth in the city from Nadia's house several times and knew the directions he had to take. His compass was leading him to her.

The rats, the stench, the dirty and contaminated water did not seem to touch him as he walked. He was seeking the south where his beloved was.

✦

The advocate had no idea that underneath the very bed he lay every night, was a hole that his wife's lover had dug, through which she escaped every night to meet him and make love to him, just hours after making love to him.

✦

Another year passed. Nadia had not borne a child till now and the advocate was beginning to grow angry with her. But knowing it wasn't her fault, he let her be. He did not know that Nadia had been on daily contraceptives since her marriage, determined to not bear his child.

But Nadia was beginning to feel maternal stirrings herself now. She longed for a child. And yet, it was not possible for her to conceive—she did not want Hamza's child to grow up believing another man was its father.

Another year passed. And with each passing year, her body filled out a little more, her curves softened further, and her hips became wider. Her womb was crying with the emptiness of an offspring, and her breasts longed to suckle a child. She knew that the void within her couldn't be filled unless she became pregnant.

Hamza listened to all this in silence. But how would it be possible for him to give her a child unless they moved somewhere else? He was willing to start work somewhere far, but how could they evade all the social constraints binding them while they were still within the city? And then what would happen to Nadia's family?

He did not have to think too much. One night when Nadia went down the hole under the bed to meet him, she carried with her money, food, and a suitcase containing her clothes and documents.

But the sound of her tinkling bangles awoke the

advocate. Realising what was happening, he erupted in a loud howl and upturned the bed—only to see his wife disappear in the darkness of the hole he had never known about.

He leapt down and chased after her. But the passage was poorly lit and slippery, and Nadia too fast. He kept pursuit for several metres but seeing she had gone a great distance already, turned back.

That night, nobody believed his story. The hole had disappeared, and the advocate sounded like a lunatic raving about underground tunnels. A manhunt for Nadia soon began. Several days later, when she wasn't found, it came out that he had kept her captive inside the house. The advocate was eventually booked for murder.

✦

After running several miles in the sewer, Nadia and Hamza fell into a hole and catapulted into the wide drains of Delhi which, as if knowing they were escaping the world around them, swept them along.

✦

The subterranean drains under the cities were unending. Nadia and Hamza swirled and swirled in the dark nothingness, not knowing where they would be swept to, gripping each other lest they be separated.

For days, they drifted, carried along by the currents, sometimes slowly sometimes flowing swiftly. They knew they had travelled miles. They knew they had come to other lands. But there was no light, only darkness and night.

The murky waters soon took them into a river. The frothy waters churned and churned around them, terrible and unrelenting, refusing to release them. And they submitted to the will of nature.

Nadia only prayed that wherever they landed, they would be happy.

✦

Several days passed. Weeks went by. The sun came up and went down, the skies changed, the stars shifted their alignments. The lands around the river kept changing, like a montage of landscapes. And Nadia and Hamza flowed along, propelled by their destinies, buoyed by the force of their love and desire to be with one another.

After many more days, they could see the horizon in the distance, marked by half the sun which was being swallowed by the ocean that lay ahead.

✦

After floating in the waters for a month, they reached the neutral grounds of Sri Lanka. It was a colourful country, and they were no longer perceived as ill-matched or separate from one another. They looked alike, and spoke alike, and were immediately understood as belonging together.

The strange lands provided them many new opportunities, although it took away much too. But they knew they had reached there for a reason, and after great labour. They believed their love had the strength to move divinity and were not afraid when they had to begin life anew.

Nadia had salvaged her papers—she was a graduate from Delhi in India. Hamza, although illiterate, would pursue his passion and make music. It was not too difficult to claim the status of immigrants, and after some minor hiccups, a straight path to happiness rolled out before them.

Several years later when Nadia had become a greying old lady, and Hamza, a wiry old man, they were sitting in a house by the ocean, watching their eleven grandchildren play in the sand as the sun set beyond the waters.

'If you pester me again with your soppy old songs, I will leave right now and go home to my mother,' she threatened, turning away.

'But my dear,' he chuckled as he looked at her, his grey eyes dancing in mirth like they did when they were young. 'Where will you go? All the currents lead you back to me.'

DREAMING IN DELHI

The stench was around Raja as he pedaled through uneven mounds of garbage in the Ghazipur landfill, straining on the seat to keep balance as the tyres skidded on the carpet of semi-solid waste. His polio-ridden leg made it harder to keep steady. He had to swing sideways to push the pedal down on that side.

The tallest mound of garbage loomed ahead of him. Above him, eagles and vultures spiralled in a slowly dimming sky. He spat out the gutka that had been in his mouth, and pulled out the gamcha he kept tucked under the handle to wipe his face. It was a particularly sultry day. It had rained sporadically until noon, and iridescent puddles of dirty water gradually reduced under the monsoon sun, causing more humidity. It seemed like the muck was brewing in the heat, emitting more rancid odours, more toxins into the city.

Swarms of flies hovered over the mounds, flying into his face as he laboured forward. He slowed to unwrap the gamcha that he had wrapped around his face. The stench was not overwhelming—the kind which usually comes from garbage that has been dumped freshly and is still decomposing—it was a dull, constant smell of accumulated filth, strong but not intolerable. It was all-pervasive; an omniscient scent of rot sitting over a narrative of deterioration so great that it seemed larger than life, like a miasma of some eternal putrefaction—the gargantuan stink of a Rabelaisian decay.

As he cycled, he blanched occasionally, whenever his eyes landed on something distinctive, like a dead cat or a dog in the piles of otherwise nondescript waste. Even after years of working in the landfill some sights could really turn his stomach. Once he had had come across a severed human hand and the image of the decayed flesh had haunted him for days. But those were his younger days. Scavenging had hardened him now. Still, Ghazipur never failed to surprise him.

Raja turned sharply at a clearing and pedaled eastwards. Above him, hundreds of hungry eagles flew around in the sky, hovering low enough in case a rodent dared emerge out in the open. An occasional eagle could be seen diving sharply to catch its prey. Raja wiped his brow again. Up ahead, a large flock of crows and vultures were hopping around, scavenging in the mass of rubbish. They had probably found a dead animal. A shudder ran through him. What if he died out here someday and his body was left rotting under the unrelenting sun? His flesh would be pecked clean, and his skeleton would get buried under the city's waste. The landfill would be his tomb.

He diverted his route hastily, not wanting to disturb the congress. A tick-infested mongrel that had been sniffing around, gamboled up to him just then and began trotting alongside, barking amicably. Raja grabbed a plank of wood and brandished it angrily, and the cur scuttled away.

He had reached his usual unloading spot and climbed down to dump the garbage he had collected that morning. When he was done, he pedaled deeper, between the rising mounds of filth that rose up further into the grey sky, his rickshaw moving easily without the load. Then when he could no longer manoeuvre through the jagged surface, he parked the rickshaw and dismounted, and galloped up the nearest slope, his bad leg banging against any piece of junk that was jutting out from the ground, his rubber chappals flapping against all sorts of debris and detritus.

When he reached the summit, he pulled out his gunny sack and a stick with a magnet on one end, and began walking around, stooped slightly over, his myopic eyes narrowed to spot metal and valuables in the rubbish. If he was lucky, the magnet would fish out coins.

✦

Raja reached his jhuggi late that evening. He had got into a scuffle at the scrap metal shop and the owner had slapped him. The issue was quite simple: Raja had found a queer-looking piece of metal in the landfill that day and the dealer had wanted it with the rest of the metal he had hauled in. Raja had refused. He was certain the metal was not scrap material—it looked odd and significant—a smooth cubicle chunk of metal, considerably heavy. He wanted to show it to someone reliable to determine its true value. But the dealer, in a fit of rage, had called him a lunatic and struck him. They had parried for a while until the neighbouring shop-owners intervened and began shouting at Raja. He had then got on his rickshaw and pedaled away, hurling abuses:

'Dekh lunga tujhe madarchod! Kutte ki maut marega, saale bhosdi ke.'

On his way home, he thought of going to the next scrap metal dealer. But he knew he would try to swindle him too. They were the same after all. And they mistreated him more than usual because he was lame. He knew that the sight of his twisted, misshapen leg repulsed them. They did business with him only because he was the best collector there was.

With a grunt, he stripped off his clothes and collapsed on the tattered mattress in his tent. It was wet because of the showers but he didn't care. His eyes were beginning to close.

And then he remembered he had to meet Pinky that night otherwise she would throw a tantrum. He hadn't seen her in a week and she was already quite upset that morning when she had barged into his shanty. Besides he had no food. He would have to go to her.

With another grunt, he hauled himself up. His leg was hurting suddenly so he had to bend completely sideways to be able to walk. When he neared her jhuggi on the other end of the slum, he tried to straighten so that the limp didn't look so bad. But it hardly made a difference. He was a cripple and Pinky knew it very well. It was good that she was a dwarf. She wouldn't have started a relationship with a lame man otherwise. A current of anger ran through his body at the thought. After all the hard work he had done, all he got was a dwarf woman's pussy to fuck. The bitch! After eating, he would have her massage his leg. Otherwise he wouldn't even fuck her.

✦

The next morning Raja went to the landfill with a heavy heart. The previous day's haul was still with him and he wasn't sure if today's haul would fetch him an income, considering the fallout with his usual buyer.

He braced himself and pedaled all the way to the first shop and unloaded the items.

'You're here again, haraam ke pille. I knew you would come begging,' the dealer guffawed.

Raja took one look at the twisted grin on the man's face, and heaved the pile back onto the rickshaw. Then without turning to see the reaction on the man's face, he pedaled away. He would find a better dealer. He was the best one in his trade after all.

✦

It was twilight by the time Raja reached the landfill. He was tired and hungry, and wanted to be done quickly so he could return home and cook a good meal for himself. Perhaps he would even buy a bottle and drink with his mates, Ganpath and Dharam. He had been working very hard lately and deserved some self-indulgence. Besides, he couldn't remember the last time he was intoxicated. One bottle that night would really ease his mind. And then maybe if he was in the mood at the end of the night, he would go to meet Pinky.

He had cycled a good way inside the landfill but continued pedalling, lost in thoughts. Ganpath and Dharam had come with him, but had fallen behind as he had pedaled deeper and deeper. He could no longer hear their voices as they quarrelled about some whore both of them had been fucking.

Just then, the acrid smell of something burning reached him. He braked hastily and looked around. Towards his right, clouds of smoke were rising into the sky from the ground below. 'Bhenchod…' he murmured. He hollered to Ganpath and Dharam and pedaled closer to investigate. An enormous heap of garbage had been set fire to, and it seemed like the whole section would be reduced to ashes.

The flames were spreading outward quickly. He pedaled closer, craning his neck to see if there was anyone in the rising firing below. A dog in one corner was barking at the fire, then as the fire came licking at it, scampered away yelping.

Raja was about to turn back when suddenly, a piece of wood under his back tyre shifted and the rickshaw tilted to one side. He let out a surprised howl and swung his weight to the other side to keep his balance. But his bad leg banged against a metal hook protruding from the ground, and in the shock of pain, he let go of the rickshaw handles. He seemed to hang in balance for a split second. Then the rickshaw tilted all the way, hanging precariously at the curving edge of the hill. Before he could react, it began to slide backwards. The ground had turned to sludge because of the showers that week and there was no way the tyres could form a grip.

'Ganpath! Dharam!' he yelled with all his might. 'Bachao!' He dug his feet deep into the muck, pushing the handles forward with all his force to keep from sliding off. If he let go, he would catapult straight down into the fire along with the rickshaw.

After some straining, he managed to straighten the rickshaw enough to push it back up on even surface. Panting, he collapsed on the ground, drenched completely in sweat. The rickshaw was safe. And so was he. But there was a sharp, stinging pain in his ankle. He was bleeding. In the twilight, his weak eyes had not spotted the rusted piece of junk, camouflaged as it was in the debris.

✦

Within a week of the incident, the scratch that seemed to have dried up, began oozing blood mingled with some yellowish fluid. He squeezed out the pus, and the cut dried up briefly, but by the end of the day, it swelled up with pus again. It was extremely painful to walk, and the whole foot had distended and become reddish purple.

Raja continued to go to work, pedalling his rickshaw with great effort. But every time he put pressure on the injured foot, mind-numbing pain seared through his body and the cut leaked with foul-looking fluids. One night, he lay in bed, writhing in agony. His neighbour, Chote Singh, upon finding him delirious with fever, took him to a nearby clinic.

Two days later, Raja found himself in the general ward of a hospital. The hall was in turmoil as nurses rushed here and there, helping patients in different stages of sickness. Some were diseased while some were injured. A few lay still in their beds, unconscious or semi-conscious. One or two were hobbling around, supported by family members or a nurse or two.

It seemed like the commotion around him had roused him. A nurse told him he was knocked out for two whole days.

Raja was suddenly aware that there was someone next to him. He was sharing the bed with another patient. Almost immediately he became aware of wetness under him. He scrambled up realising what it was. The man had pissed in the sheets.

'Bhenchod!' he yelled, edging away from the wet spot. 'Nurse…' he tried to stop a nurse as she rushed past. 'This man has pissed on the bed…'

But the doctors and nurses went by without bothering. He tried to call out for water, but again, nobody paid attention. There was too much disease and sickness around for anyone to bother with him.

Trying to muster energy, he sat up. His left arm was attached to a pipe which was dripping solution from a bottle above his head and it rankled as he moved. Was he so sick that they had to stick pipes into him? He lifted his leg to examine the gash. It had dried up again now and the swelling had subsided. But his foot had acquired a sickly blue-black hue now. He could hardly move or feel his fingers.

Just then a nurse came up with a tray of medicines. She handed him some tablets and asked him to swallow them. Then she pulled out some gauze and cotton, and smearing some brownish ointment on the wound, began dressing it.

'Why is it looking like this?' he asked her over the din.

'Because it is rotting,' she said flatly in a Malayali accent.

Raja lay back against the headrest. The man next to him was twitching in his subconscious state, and he felt a sudden impulse to push him off the bed. Instead, he shut his eyes and fell asleep.

✦

Raja's condition worsened over the next day. The wound seemed to be drying, but his foot looked worse than ever. The doctor was unable to determine the cause of his fever and after some cursory tests, put him on medication for Hepatitis A. Raja dreaded staying in the hospital for longer. Pinky had come to tell him that she could not pay for his treatment anymore, and he did not have enough to cover the expenditure. He cursed the piece of metal that had caused all this.

That night, the fever rose again. He hardly remembered anything when he gained consciousness the next day. The nurse told him that he had bled heavily from the nose, and his eyes had become bloodshot from the high temperature. To make things worse, his foot had begun to swell up again.

That afternoon when he went to the toilet, he discovered he was getting bloody diarrhoea. The rest of the day, a jet of excreta mingled with blood issued from between his buttocks onto the already soiled bed, almost every hour. He felt faint and exhausted, and let the shit gather without stirring. When the doctor came in the evening he saw that Raja's skin was covered in rashes and sloughing, in diaphanous layers, one patch after the other.

The next day, without intimating him, he was transported to a smaller ward in the hospital. Outside, the doctor assembled some junior doctors and medical students to discuss what could be the next step. They suspected radiation poisoning after finding out he scavenged metal in landfills. The only solution was to clean him up and put him on treatment.

The next thing Raja remembered was seeing at least ten nurses gathered around him, wearing masks and gloves, and holding up brushes and cloths. Almost faint with a pounding headache, he was made to lie down on the floor. Then he was given a scrubbing for what seemed like many hours.

Two days later, after having briefly slipped into coma, he recovered consciousness, quite unexpectedly, and found that the pain in his leg was gone.

Then he saw why. Instead of the twisted, Polio-ridden leg, lay an impotent stump bandaged heavily with gauze. The Malayali nurse told him in the same flat tone that all the symptoms were of septic shock, not radiation exposure as the doctors had earlier suspected. His foot had gone gangrene because of the gash. They had to amputate it to prevent the infection from spreading further.

✦

Raja was discharged from the hospital for lack of funds. Ganpath took him home and lay him on his mattress. Then after bringing him some food and helping him eat, left.

Ganpath did this for the next few days, but after a week or so, his wife refused to let him take food for him because it was adding to their household expenses. They had four children to take care of and feeding another individual was too much of a financial burden on them. So when Ganpath stopped bringing him food, Raja turned to Dharam for help. But Dharam who was already reluctant to keep in touch with him now that he no longer was the useful scrap metal collector he once was, declined blatantly, and disappeared from his life. Pinky had already broken up with him and had sent her new lover to ask for her money. The man had punched him in the jaw and threatened to kill him if he didn't return the money in a month.

Raja accepted this as his fate. He lay in bed for a few days, unable to move out to work. His neighbours brought him food sometimes, but mostly stayed away. At night, his moans and screams rented the still air. He flailed and cried in his dreams, reliving the accident in the landfill over and over again. Each time in his dream, a large piece of sharp metal pierced him in the leg. The image of his body rotting into a mass of grey and green haunted him. He often woke up, drenched in sweat, his chest heaving and his heart pumping violently.

The people around thought Raja was losing his sanity. They sympathised with him at first, but then the nightly screams became too disturbing. Nobody liked to have their sleep interrupted by his blood-curdling howls. Soon they gathered in his house and told him to shut the fuck up or they would have him thrown out. Raja knew it was not an empty threat. People had such superstitious fear towards disability or any sort of malformation that it wouldn't take them long to exile him.

And it happened in the next few days. Raja had not yet gone back to plying his rickshaw and barely had any money left when the Lalaji came around to collect rent for the jhopri. Raja tried to beg and plead with him, even lay down on the floor at his feet, but to no avail. The man was a shark and was not ready to forgo the rent. Raja then asked for another day and somehow crawled up to Pinky's blue and pink house to ask for a loan.

But he had reached Pinky's house at the wrong hour. She was with a customer then—her regular—and was in no mood to interrupt the session for his sake.

'What do you want now, Raja? Haven't you leeched off me enough?' she stood at the door looking haughtily at him, with her blouse open and her saree half undone. He felt very small. Even though she was at least two feet shorter than him, it felt like she was looking down at him from the height of contemptuousness and indifference.

'Pinky, I want one last favour. Just another loan. I will pay you back within a month. Please, I really need money right now. Look at my condition…'

'Haye bhagwan!' she cried in exaggerated despair. 'Is this why I loved you? So that you could keep looting me? Get out! Get out you freak!'

And she cried out to her customer who was lying in bed waiting for her to return. The man, naked except for a translucent gamcha that hardly concealed his organs, kicked him in the groin and told him to fuck off.

'Nikal yaha se madarchod! Nazar mat aiyo yaha. Dusra

taang todke gaand mein ghusa dunga. Saala haramkhor. Nikal!'

By next evening, Lalaji's men came and dragged Raja outside. They threw out his stuff, meagre as it was, after him. And left him cowering in the dark, in full glare of the disgusted neighbourhood.

✦

The skies rumbled in the distance and a clap of thunder sounded menacingly from above. Raja was lying face down in the sludge on the main road near Nizamuddin. The thundering had roused him, and he stirred painfully, looking around to see where he was. Then he saw cars and the roads. How did he get there? His mind was absolutely befuddled. Then he grew aware of a throbbing pain at the back of his head. It seemed like someone had clubbed him and he had lost consciousness. And sure enough, he felt a protrusion right above the nape of his neck. There was some crusted blood in his matted hair too and it crackled when he touched it.

Even without looking to see, he knew he did not have his possessions. They had been stolen, obviously. The city would not have left anything on his back if he had lain unconscious for another day.

He clambered on his elbows and looked around. Some feet away at the traffic signal, a few ragamuffin children were begging. The drivers in the cars occasionally passed some coins into the children's palms and rolled up their windows again. He watched as the children ran to a nearby bhelpuri wala when the signal changed. His stomach rumbled loudly at the sight of the spices being tossed into the fluffy murmuras. How he would love some bhelpuri and a cup of chai. Maybe…maybe he could beg that day, eat with that money, and then think about what he would do after that.

Thinking quickly, he lifted the stump and dragged himself to the middle of the road. He had no time to lose. This was the peak hour and he had to utilise the opportunity. A cripple like him was sure to draw pity. He would easily get enough money for a full meal by evening.

But just when he was about to extend his arm to ask for money from a woman in an auto, the traffic signal changed.

Hundreds of horns seemed to blare at the same time. The cacophony rose in a crescendo, and he ducked in fear, away from the angry glares and shouting. But his stump had twisted in an odd angle so that he could hardly pull himself into a position where he could drag himself off the road. The cars around him were revving their engines threateningly. The Maruti directly in front of him shuddered and honked, nudging him away with its fender.

Then out of nowhere it seemed, a pair of strong arms raised him clean off the road and carried him to the footpath. He turned to see who it was. A eunuch, her face painted pink and features darkened with kohl, was scowling and berating him over the honking.

'Have you lost your mind, cripple?' she screamed, gesticulating passionately as she put him down. 'Do you want to die?'

Raja could barely respond. His stomach heaved, as if he was going to vomit. But he had nothing in his stomach that he could throw up. After lurching a few times, he passed out.

✦

The tinkling laughter of a woman coquetting with a man roused him some hours later. He was lying in the partition between the two large pillars of the flyover above, and the shadows cast by the orange street lights cast dark shadows on his frame. Without saying anything, he looked warily at the people clustered around in the plastic tents. Some women were cooking rotis in an open flame, and he watched hungrily as the naked children swamped around to get their share.

With some difficulty, he sat up and looked around. The eunuch who had saved him was nowhere to be seen. Instead, there were small groups of people huddled around at the edge of the pavement. It seemed like a makeshift settlement. Would they let him be there with them? He knew the answer before the question even formed in his head. He was sure to be thrown away from there as well.

He suddenly felt scared. There was no one to help him. He lay back again in the dark. The shadows gave him anonymity. Maybe he would lie there until daybreak and try to beg again when the office hours began. Then with the money he would buy a meal and somehow go to Ganpath. He would sympathise with him after seeing his condition. He was sure of that.

Just when he was about to drift into sleep, he heard footsteps coming up towards the corner where he lay. His heartbeat quickened. What if someone saw him and threw him out? Where would he go in the dark? He opened his eyes nervously and saw a woman walking up. She yelped when she spotted him in the dark and came and stood before him with her hands on her hips, her face twisted into a leering grin as she stared down.

'New here?' she asked, as she beckoned to her mates some way off. When he didn't respond she said, 'Do you want a fuck?'

Raja watched as she wiggled her melon-sized breasts and then slapped them so that they almost popped out of her blouse. The orange light highlighted the gaping curves, and he felt a stir of lust in his loins. Just then another prostitute appeared and stood by her side. They stood there looking down at him.

'What is it? Why don't you say anything? Wasting our time? Do you want to fuck or not? Tell us quick or we will leave.'

Before he could say anything, the other one exclaimed, 'Oye, look! He is a cripple. Look there!' she pointed at his stump, half concealed in the dark.

'What!' the other one almost jumped back as though his body repulsed her. 'Chee! Aye haye! Oh lord, are such bad days upon me that I will have to take cripples on the street to fill my stomach? Chee chee!'

'Let's leave!' the other one snapped irritably. 'This one doesn't even look like he has any money. Come on now, let's go! I want a client tonight. Last night that man I snapped up at...'

They walked away, talking between themselves. Their whorish paraphernalia glittering and shimmering in the night light as they crossed the street towards the unlit side.

Raja exhaled loudly. He hadn't realised he had been holding his breath all this while. The women's breasts that were so temptingly exposed had aroused him. He looked down at his stump miserably and saw his penis jutting out through the broken zipper of his ragged pants. He hadn't felt so horny in ages. He began to rub his erection. Directly in front of him, the families living in the two tents were growing quiet as the night progressed. He lay back, jerking his penis as he thought of naked women, escaping temporarily from the sordidness of his situation.

Suddenly, he heard the tinkling of bangles again. His eyes flew open and he saw yet another prostitute standing before him, completely blocking his view of the pavement and the roads.

'What is it? What do you want?' he said hoarsely. He hoped she didn't sense the fear in his voice.

'I see you are having fun by yourself. Why not fuck me?' She grinned. 'I can do everything.'

'No...go away. I...I don't have any money.'

The prostitute hesitated. 'You don't have any money?' When he didn't respond, she said, 'Hmmm, alright. Doesn't matter. What is wrong with you?'

'What?'

'Can you work?'

'What do you mean?'

'I mean, are you healthy or do you have a disease?'

'Why do you want to know?' Raja was suspicious.

'I mean, I just wanted to know if you are you fit enough to work. I could get you work.'

'What work?'

'First answer me, you idiot,' she snapped irritably. 'Don't waste my time.'

'I…I used to be a rickshawwalla…until about a month ago.'

Just then a man appeared. The woman turned to say something to him, and he bent forward and raised Raja's shirt.

'What're you doing? Get away!'

The man said something to the prostitute and walked away. She was still there, looking down at him.

'Who was that man?' he asked suspiciously. 'And why are you here? Just leave!'

'I have food here in my purse,' she said ignoring his question. 'I could give you a good fuck, and food too.'

Raja felt a chill run down his spine. What did she actually want from him? 'Why? Why would you?'

'Because I haven't fucked in a long time,' she said simply.

'But why me?' He knew something was up. What had the man said to her?

'I'll fuck you, and suck your hard cock,' she said and unhooked her kameez, lowering it just enough to expose her breasts. 'Want these?' She made them bounce, while wiggling her eyebrows.

Raja's breath was caught in his throat. The magnificent pair of breasts shone in the street light. He felt suddenly weak.

Before he could realise what was happening, the woman bent down and grabbed his arm. He felt a sharp prick.

And then it dawned on him. He opened his mouth to

yell for help but his jaw felt heavy. His whole body was swimming. Then it went black.

✦

It was daytime. The traffic was in full force around the flyovers. Cars whizzed past, and the intermittent blaring of horns rose up around him. He propped himself on his elbows and looked around, disoriented. The place was different. Where was he? He scrambled up to check.

And then he saw the blue board of signs next to the traffic signal. He was in Chhattarpur.

It all came back to him in a rush. The two prostitutes, and then the third one who had injected him with something because of which he had lost consciouness. With a growing sense of dread, he felt his arm where she had pricked him. Sure enough there was the small hardened bump of a drug accumulated underneath his skin.

As if on cue, he grew aware of the stringing pain on his thigh. Hastily, he lowered his pants. He cried out, in shock more than pain. The skin seemed to have melted into the flesh underneath. The mass itself had shrunk slightly, as if it had dissolved and reduced.

First the limb was gone, and then the skin on the stump was burnt with acid.

As a child, his mother had told him that his leg was crooked because it was once too beautiful, and evil spirits had cursed it. He did not know about how beautiful it once was, but she seemed right about one thing. He really was cursed.

Raja felt the day begin to dim suddenly. The scene

around was suddenly sucked into a vortex between his eyes and he fainted.

✦

Raja regained consciousness after what he felt was just a few hours. But he knew it had been longer.

Just then the signal turned red. Automatically, he stumbled forward, slamming against the sides of cars, crying for alms, tears falling down his cheeks. His disfigured body attracted more disgusted looks than ever before.

But they tossed him money more readily now. And he had to pay the trafficker.

✦

Raja was climbing the mound of debris in the landfill he knew so well. He had taken a staff and was almost upright by leaning against it as he walked. He limped slowly, getting used to the appendage, and soon managed to quicken his pace.

He had reached somewhere in the middle of the heaps. The stench was around him as usual. And he didn't mind it. He had come to Ghazipur after very long. It felt like homecoming.

It was still bright, and the sun could be seen setting into the horizon in the distance. Raja paused for a moment to watch it disappear, then resumed walking. A cluster of buffaloes was huddled in one corner, and he came upon a pack of dogs that barked at him rabidly. Some tried to come close, snapping at his ankle, their fangs exposed lethally and the diseased saliva dripping from their mouths. Snarling, he swung his cane around at them and they slunk away, growling, their jaws still bared menacingly.

The pain on his thigh began to increase because of the exertion. The ill-formed skin over the burns was stretching painfully as he moved. He touched the surface and felt the stickiness of pus mingled with blood.

The sky was getting dark quickly. Wincing in pain, he walked onwards, clenching his mouth shut lest he screamed in pain. He was a man on a mission, and there was only one thing on his mind now. He had to find enough scrap metal to make his own rickshaw. Once he had all the metal, he would build the best rickshaw in Delhi. Then with the money he would make, he would go to the Safdarjung Hospital and get his burns treated. Hell, he would even get his stump treated. They could do that now with all the modern technology. They would even give him a prosthetic leg and he would be whole again.

The thought seemed to buoy him. He bounded forwarded frenziedly, infused with new strength. His dreams didn't seem too impossible now. He had been a cripple all his life but had it ever deterred him from aiming big? So what if his leg had been amputated now and he had some burns? He was still functioning. He could do without the leg just fine. Once this rickshaw was built, he would earn money as before and everything would be better. He would even go to the police and lodge an FIR against the prostitute and her pimp who had exploited him. And then he would take his own personal revenge on the randi. God knows how many other men she had trapped in the same manner.

Raja heaved a sigh. A sudden grief had seized him. The city was becoming such a hell-hole. There was no safety for honest men like him. Without any fault of his, he was stripped of everything he ever had. This truly was the Kalyug. There was no space for humanity...but each and every sinful individual would pay dearly for their acts. He knew his tormentors would suffer. The thought gave him some comfort.

He had climbed to the top of the landfill now. In the distance, cars went by on the roads, with their headlights flashing. The lights in the buildings were beginning to light up all around too. He turned around slowly, admiring how the florescent and yellow dots shimmered as nighttime settled over Delhi. How pretty the view was from where he stood. The serenity offered such solace even though he had lost so much.

Not too long ago, his mother had told him that he would be a rich man if only he kept up his hard work. Raja laughed to himself. She was but the wife of a dhobi in Mumbai and had had no idea of the cities up North. All she knew was that if Raja went to Dilli, he would do well in life and earn daulat and shauhrat in due time.

He let a lone tear trickle down his cheek. Never in his life had he thought that it would come to this. When he had come to this city, he was so sure that he would repay his father's debts and establish a good life here. But all those dreams had long perished. Instead, he was left with an amputated leg and perforating wound that was testimony to all that the city had taken away from him when it was supposed to have actually fulfilled his dreams.

Poor, naive woman, he thought, picturing his mother's face, sweet even in times of acute desperation. Did she ever think her Raja would scavenge in people's shit when he grew up? Did she ever think he would be the prince of garbage, the shahenshah of sewage?

Just then he became aware of a deep sense of exhaustion somewhere deep within his soul. It gripped him and spread though his chest, into his whole being as though it was flowing through his veins. He swayed unsteadily, still holding onto the staff, then he allowed his good leg to buckle.

He was sitting now, still at the top of the landfill and with the best view of the city he had ever seen in his life. Suddenly, the awareness of his mortality struck him. How fragile human beings were. They were all helpless to the will of destiny.

It was the night of an eclipse. The round orb of the moon hung low on the eastern sky, and was already beginning to show a sliver of the earth's shadow on its ivory surface.

✦

He was feverish with agony. He knew that the new skin and tissues had ripped, and the end of his stump hurt tortuously as he lay rolling in the muck. He drifted in and out of consciousness, afraid that he would not live to be rescued the next day by the waste-pickers. The pain was excruciating.

When he regained consciousness, the sun was beginning to show slightly through the clouds. It was going to be a rainy day, Raja could tell. Yet, the light was brilliant and shone in his face through the haze until he finally opened his eyes and looked around. The place was deserted. There was only garbage all around. Rotting, moulding, diseased garbage. It was a wonder how he ever eked a living out of it.

He sighed and rolled over to look on the other side. At a distance he could see a pack of dogs sniffing around in the garbage, but otherwise, there was no movement. His eyes landed on a pile of what seemed like bones. Animal bones, he hoped. Suddenly, the landfill that he was so attached to didn't feel like his place of redemption anymore. It seemed alien and hostile. Even the road under the flyover where he rolled around and begged seemed like a better place.

With a groan he lay on his back again. Above him, hundreds of vultures flew around languidly in circles. They seemed like they were waiting for something. But he was still alive. He felt a momentary surge of hope and energy. It wouldn't be long before he was discovered and taken back. Maybe Ganpath would chance upon him.

But the day passed, and no one came around. Initially, he tried to keep a lookout and screamed occasionally for help, straining as much as he could. But he was exhausted and in intense pain. Soon, he drifted into a semi-conscious state in which he was only aware of the shooting pain in his lower body.

In the evening, he mustered enough strength to stand up again. He could see some children playing at a distance, but none of them responded when he yelled out to them. They couldn't hear him over the main road traffic.

He realised that he had forayed not only to the very top of the landfill but also very deep inside. He wasn't accessible to anyone now, and neither could he go back himself. Even the slightest movement made him scream. He knew that it wouldn't be too long before the new skin gave out completely.

Clutching his side, Raja dropped to the ground. Metal and glass debris, mixed in sludge, crunched under him as he fell. He drifted into a fitful sleep.

✦

He woke up to an odd scratching on his leg. It continued for a while, then stopped. After some time, it began again. He extended his arm to scratch the spot and his hand came in contact with something warm and fuzzy. Looking down he saw a huge rodent staring up at him. It sat dully, unbothered by him, and looking absolutely certain that he would not harm him. Raja quickly brushed it away, and it scampered some way off, half-heartedly it seemed, then disappeared after a while.

It happened again some hours later. This time there were two of them. They sprang away when he swung his arm out, but had the gall to return, their black eyes darting mischievously, their whiskers flicking, alert and intelligent.

And then he saw the others. Hundreds of them, peeking at him together, from behind random corners, their beady eyes fixed on him. His eyes widened in terror as he realised he was completely surrounded by them. Instinctively, he clutched his stump and howled menacingly. No! He wasn't going to let the vermin get him.

But the rats scurried around, dashing here and there, some even bounding close enough to be caught in his hands. They were too fast. They ran as if in frenzy, strangely excited, even bounding over his good leg when they had to.

Then they seemed to gather around—a sea of brown and black, breathing, pulsating with energy and hunger—darting back and forth, daring a peck or two.

The feast had only just begun. Seeing his exhausted state, they began nibbling: little sets of yellow rodent's teeth working through his skin and flesh. They began with his stump. It still had the unhealed, new skin. And the parts which had healed where the soft tissue had grown over the cut, were also thin enough to be lacerated with their sharp teeth with ease.

Raja let out a last howl as the rats climbed over him, enveloping him. He rolled over in pain, and the rats stuck to him, rolling with him in the dirt. They had found their meal, and they weren't going to let go now.

At last, Raja gave in to the onslaught, accepting his fate. Even the pain had disappeared somehow.

The last image that he had was that of a giant rat next to his face, sniffing all over before proceeding to cut into his lips.

THE LOVER IN FIROZ SHAH KOTLA

Hussain leaned impatiently against the brick wall of Jami Masjid and sighed to himself. It was 3 p.m., and he had been waiting for Faizal for nearly two hours. He needed to get back to the metro station. He couldn't afford to miss work for the third day in a row.

The sky was overcast, but it was sultry. His shirt, which had got drenched with sweat in the morning while plying his rickshaw, had dried now, but the patches were all too visible. Feeling conscious about his appearance, he hastily loosened the upper buttons. His neck was sticky and grimy and he knew he looked shabby What would Faizal think? He wiped himself with his sleeve and groaned in annoyance. There was still no sign of him.

Feeling thirsty, he took a long draught from the bottle he was carrying. Some of the water dribbled down his chest and dampened his shirt. The wind that had started up cooled his burning skin momentarily. He sank to the ground and began pulling up grass growing around him.

Where was he? Had he decided not to come? He couldn't even call to check as he had no balance on the phone. The least Faizal could do was send him a message to update him.

Clucking his tongue in annoyance he stood up. He would take a walk around the masjid, and maybe even up to the fort to kill time. If Faizal did not reach when he had completed the round, he would leave.

As he began walking, rain clouds gathered and dimmed the evening sun which was glowing dully behind the greyish milkiness, throwing beams of light across the sky. Unlike the past couple of weeks, the air did not feel cool and pleasant, but oppressive. Hussain breathed in the humid air with difficulty. He would walk straight ahead towards the edge of the gardens, before walking along the walls of the masjid. This would give Faizal more time. Hussain really did not want to leave without meeting him.

Enjoying the gentle breeze that had started up unexpectedly, he sauntered further in, watching the good Mussalmans enter and exit the mosque for the evening prayers, their faces somber with devotion. He almost went in himself, but decided against it. He would instead go into the fort. Perhaps he would go have a look at the baoli from above. It had always fascinated him.

He entered through the archway and walked slowly along the dim passage, towards the staircase leading up. The scent of incense was around him. People who had come to pray to djinns passed him by, glancing at him with preoccupied faces then looking away as they hurried off.

He looked around, quietly taking in the air that seemed pregnant with magic. He had come upon the chamber where the major invocations took place on Thursdays. There were signs of weekly exorcisms everywhere. Half-burnt candles lay in corners, and oil from lamps kept in the crevices had dripped down the stone walls. There were folded pieces of paper tucked in little corners that he knew contained the wishes and prayers of worshippers. He was tempted to reach out and open one, but didn't.

He stood there for a few moments then decided to go back, in case Faizal had arrived.

Just as he exited the edifice and went back into the gardens, he saw the familiar figure, short and petite, walking up to the masjid towards him.

✦

Hussain and Faizal met in Firoz Shah Kotla almost every weekend. When they were in the mood for a change, they went down to the Old Fort or, if the weather was pleasant, to the Lodi Gardens. But usually, they met in Firoz Shah because it was closest to the metro station where Hussain plied his rickshaw.

The biggest problem they faced was of lack of privacy. There was no place in Delhi that gave them the space that young lovers like them needed. Because they were both men, it was still possible for them to avoid arousing suspicion if they walked into old buildings, abandoned alleys, or buildings that were under construction. But generally, they felt they were just as conspicuous as heterosexual couples. Sometimes, in fact, it seemed it was worse for them. Although usually nobody bothered to check why two men went into dark corners in gardens or forts, but if the cops and guards, or even street urchins loitering about realised what they were up to, they would start harassing them.

One day, while they were making out behind the bushes in Lodi after dark, three policemen had walked up. Faizal had not been in favour of sneaking into the park after dark, but Hussain was confident about it and had somehow cajoled him into it. Once inside, they had walked along the lit-up pond, towards the tombs that sat soberly against a reddened sky. It was well past nine, and the place was deserted. It seemed like it would rain soon and so the few people they did see around had probably also left.

At first, Faizal was alert, looking over his shoulder constantly to check if there was anybody around. He refused to get frisky, despite Hussain's repeated attempts. But after a while when he saw the place truly was deserted, he agreed to go behind the bushes. Besides, the thrill of doing it despite the risk was too tempting. And they would only just kiss.

It did begin with a kiss. But soon, they began touching and fondling each other. It was the first time they had touched each other inside their pants, and both of them were panting with desire. Hussain's member was rock hard in his jeans. He wanted to fuck then and there. Faizal, conscious of his desire, and aware of the lack of time, immediately slipped to his knees and began sucking him.

Soon they were fucking. Hussain was in the throes of passion. Faizal's asshole was the perfect size for his penis, and he had never felt so good before. It was difficult to keep from gasping aloud. He clutched Faizal's slim butt and penetrated as deep as he could.

Just then, the bushes behind them rustled.

They froze. To their horror, there were loud footsteps directly behind them. Before they could react, three burly men stepped into the small clearing between the trees and bushes where they were entwined with each other, flashing their torches around. The moment the light fell on their naked bodies, they began shouting.

They were policemen. Hussain and Faizal jumped up and tried to cover themselves, shouting apologies. But they were gay men who were caught performing sodomy. The policemen had found the perfect prey. They were shouting louder now, shoving them out into the open.

Hussain's mind was racing. But before he could do anything, Faizal screamed, 'How can you push us like that? Let go!'

And then the blows began. The biggest of the three began slapping Faizal across the face as the other two looked on. Then the short man kicked him to the ground and began laughing. Hussain, pleading and crying, tried to shield Faizal, but the other men yanked him away and punched him in the nose. Dizzy, he clambered away. They were still beating Faizal who had now grown quiet. He stood limply, receiving the slaps without a sound.

Then he collapsed sideways.

Hussain's heart was in his mouth. Faizal was barely moving as he lay spread-eagled on the ground. A streak of blood had run down his chest, soaking into his torn shirt.

Cowering in fear, Hussain folded his hands and crawled to the men. 'Sahab…Sahab…maaf kar do.'

But the policemen were still jeering. They pulled him up.

'Show us how you were fucking,' one of them said.

'Yeah, let us also see how you bastards do it,' said the other.

Hussain was shocked. The policeman kicked Faizal again. 'Get up, get up!'

When neither of them moved, one of them kicked Faizal in the abdomen.

'Have you seen this? he said, waving his lathi. 'I'll shove it right up your ass if you don't do as we say.'

As if in a reverie, Hussain rose and grabbed Faizal, and pushed him gently to get up. Faizal, disoriented and bloodied, but knowing what to do, turned over. His movement was slow and laborious. And his eyes were blank. Hussain mumbled 'sorry' and began performing oral sex on him.

The men cheered and laughed. 'Now fuck!'

Hussain immediately climbed on top of Faizal and began fucking him, mechanically, slowly, at first, then harder when the policemen shouted at him to go faster. He hoped Faizal would forgive him for this.

The three men were laughing when he was done. Then one of them knocked him on the head. By the time he regained consciousness, the tallest policeman was sodomising Faizal. He kept spitting and slapping saliva on his cock, and with heavy grunts, penetrated him roughly, multiple times. Faizal was lying rigidly, emitting weak bleating sounds like a goat that is about to be butchered.

The other men were rubbing their penises as they watched. When they noticed Hussain was conscious, they took turns to fuck him too.

Hussain let them rape him without resistance. He was just thanking god that at least they would not be arrested.

And once it was over, the men hurried away without a back glance.

Hussain, exhausted and in pain, turned to see Faizal. He was whimpering and shaking some feet away from him. Would he ever recover from this? He was still fragile and new. He was young—just twenty-two.

But no matter. He would grow to learn that abuse was part of being a homosexual man of labour class who had no means of fighting against assault and harassment. He would toughen with time.

But in that moment, watching Faizal cower in the dark without being able to comfort him, Hussain knew what absolute helplessness felt like.

✦

It had been about a year to that incident. Faizal and Hussain's relationship had grown stronger since, and they had become extremely attached to each other. Faizal, particularly, was madly in love with him, and regularly swore to die for love if it ever came to that. His innocence touched Hussain deeply, and he knew that even though they could not be together in the socially legitimate sense, their souls belonged with each other.

But life was going to be tough. Neither of their families knew about their relationship. In fact, they did not even know about their sexual orientation yet. Hussain had tried to tell his mother a few times but each time she had ignored his words and turned the subject to something else entirely.

Nobody else seemed like they would listen or understand. Only his closest cousin who lived in Mumbai knew about it. He worked as a waiter in one of the big restaurants there and was comparatively liberal in such matters. He was very concerned when Hussain had confessed to him, but was completely supportive. He had laughed and joked, and had thumped him on the back saying he would stick with him if there was discord in the family because of this. Until he had met Faizal, Hussain had not anticipated any conflict regarding the subject because he had decided to simply not tell them and live his life as a bachelor. But now Faizal was in the equation. He had to try and bring up the matter, as tactfully as possible because he earnestly felt that his love was pure and his family should really not have an objection to true devotion.

Faizal, however, hadn't had the courage to bring it up with his family. He particularly balked at the idea of telling his Abba who was a retired peon from Kendriya Vidyalaya and orthodox in many ways. He got extremely flustered every time Hussain tried to coax him to do it. He simply couldn't accept that homosexuality was something he did not have to be ashamed about. He needed to embrace it. Just because the society was biased against it didn't mean that they had to live in shame all their lives simply for being in love.

Still, Faizal couldn't do it. Hussain did not blame him for this; he was too young to accept his identity. Besides, it had taken a lot of effort just to draw him out of his shell and accept his sexuality. To expect him to go discuss the matter with his parents so soon, especially when he himself hadn't figured out how to tell his own parents even after being aware of his sexuality for more than fifteen years, was asking for too much.

And so, Hussain waited, biding time until they could find some sort of a permanent arrangement. Their clandestine meetings had begun to irk him now, especially because he knew that the simple solution was to move out and rent a place together. It would even be easy to migrate to another city and live together as flatmates. They need not announce their status as lovers. They could simply be flatmates. Nobody would have to know. Even if Faizal decided not to tell his parents at all—which would probably be the case—they could simply go away and live together without revealing their orientation.

✦

It was a sultry afternoon in the middle of May. Hussain was lolling on his rickshaw after having eaten a heavy meal of chicken biryani at the market. He had parked in front of New Friends Colony, and hadn't found a passenger for the past one hour. He would take a quick nap and then go up to Batla House in the evening.

Just as he was about to doze off, his phone rang. It was Faizal.

'Haan, jaanu.'

'Suno…I have to tell you something.'

Hussain sensed what was coming from his tone. Faizal had been acting strangely for weeks. And although he kept denying it to himself, he knew Faizal was having second thoughts about their relationship. They hadn't even been intimate lately, and whenever he initiated anything, Faizal had responded half-heartedly. And now he was going to breakup.

'Yeah, tell me?' he asked, his heart was beginning to thud heavily.

'I can't…I can't be with you anymore…I can't do this to my parents. They want me to marry a girl from our village. And I cannot go on sneaking behind their back… let us never meet again.'

They were going to meet the next day. Hussain had planned to take him boating to Old Fort, and then for lunch at Chandni Chowk.

Without saying anything, Hussain disconnected the phone and switched it off.

✦

Dark clouds had gathered on top of the ruins of the fort of Tughlaq. The rest of the city was covered in dust, but it seemed like it would rain right where Hussain stood, on the roof of the Kotla. He was gazing blankly into the skies, so uncannily mirroring his heart. Faizal's sweet boyish face hovered before his eyes, blocking out everything else.

Moments later, he came to his senses. He did not remember how he had got there. Standing at the edge, he looked around the gardens numbly. This was where he and Faizal had their first proper meeting…

His chest constricted painfully as he fought back a scream. In the privacy, that the rains afforded him, he allowed some tears to roll down his cheeks, into his beard.

After several moments, he looked around again. The

place was entirely deserted. Then he looked down at the baoli, into the churning waters. The inkiness was strangely inviting as the waters swirled in the downpour.

Then suddenly, something rose up, and floated around just under the surface of the water. Through the mist, Hussain could not make out what it was. He squinted, squeezing the rain out of his eyes.

Then he realised what it was.

The body was bobbing face down, turning around as the fish swam around it, frantic because of an alien body they did not recognise.

Vomit rose inside him. He watched in horror as the form drifted stiffly to the edge of the well where it got stuck in the weed and remained in the shadows.

Even in the haze, he could recognise the bright red shirt on the petite figure.

He knew the body would remain afloat until it was discovered after the showers.

✦

Monsoon had arrived after an unusual period of delay, but had finally settled upon Delhi. The buildings looked bathed and the trees found a new lease of life. Hussain too felt the rejuvenating power of the rains. Faizal had receded into the deepest chambers of his heart and there was now space for new love.

In the turmoil of the season when all the rickshawwallas were plying arduously in the water-clogged roads, drenched from head to toe and exhausted with multiple infections that the weather brought with it, Hussain's rickshaw swept through with effortless ease. He was infused with a sudden vigour, and the new-found power allowed him to skim through the flood, over the uneven roads. To people who saw him, it seemed like he was gliding with superhuman power.

When Hussain first felt it, he smiled to himself. It was the knowing smile of a man pleased by the doings of his indulgent partner. If someone had asked him, he might even have declared openly that it was the doing of Sulaiman, the lover of his dreams, the djinn of Firoz Shah Kotla.

✦

Sulaiman had lived in Kotla since the time of the Sultanate. When Hussain saw him for the first time, he had caught him watching him from the shadows as rain lashed around the fort, a few weeks after Faizal was found dead and he had come to the Kotla to relive old memories.

Despite the trauma of his loss, Hussain was drawn to Sulaiman. They had stood facing each other in the dark, and then as if propelled by some deep mystical force, drew closer.

All of a sudden, Faizal's death ceased to matter. Hussain fell in love with Sulaiman and, as if it was destiny, they made love on the roof of the Kotla, their bodies slippery with rain and aflame with desire for each other.

That night, when the rain subsided and their hunger for each other was satiated, Sulaiman told Hussain his life's story.

Many centuries ago, during the reign of Sultans, the

great pillars of the Mauryan ruler, Ashoka, were being transported from Ambala to Firozabad. Sulaiman, known amongst the Sufi saints for his brave feats, was summoned to aid Sultan Firoz Shah for this purpose. He was put in charge of overseeing the two hundred men who were transporting the pillars. One pillar was to be erected on the ridge in northern Delhi, while the other was to be mounted on a pavilion on top of the Kotla.

Sulaiman remembered how difficult the journey was. They had encountered several hurdles on the way and each time he had to ward them off with his magic. Despite the troubles, he was confident that as long as his eyes were on the pillars no damage could be caused to them. Towards the fag end of their journey, when they reached the boats to ferry the pillars across, he knew that the task would be finished successfully. But just when they began unloading the pillars, Sulaiman who was keeping a strict watch on the pillars, was distracted by a brilliantly coloured bird that suddenly flew by his head. In that moment, the silk cloth with which one of the pillars had been wrapped came away. And as the men hoisted it from the carriage onto the boats, it slipped and fell.

Sulaiman saw the pillar crash and rushed to save it. But the damage was done. Despairing, he raised the pillar in the air and turned it over to see where the chink was. He could fix it easily. But he saw nothing. No matter how he checked, he could not find the spot. And yet, there was a slice of stone from the pillar lying on the ground next to it.

Fear gathered in his heart and formed a thick and painful lump. He examined the pillar over and over again, by daylight and by moonlight. But he was not able to spot the damaged point. The two hundred men who were there also took turns to examine the pillar, but they could not find it either.

After a fortnight of tracing each and every crevice and curve, they gave up. They took the pillars to the Sultan, and after presenting them before him, Sulaiman confessed to his blunder and begged for mercy. But the Sultan was a hard master. Angered upon knowing that a monumental pillar was damaged because of his carelessness, he ordered the Sufi saints to lock him up in the baoli as a punishment.

'You shall remain locked here until you find the damage you have wrought upon this obelisk,' he had thundered. 'When you find it, you will fix it. But until you do, you will be kept captive, even if it is for eternity.'

Since then, Sulaiman had remained inside the baoli, without a friend or foe, wasting away in loneliness.

And then one day, a beautiful man came and stood near the pavilion, and gazed down at him in the waters. He knew that this man could not see him, but somehow he felt his gaze, and for the first time in about six hundred years, he experienced a deep longing within.

✦

Hussain had felt Sulaiman's presence even on the day when he had seen Faizal's body in the baoli. But he had dismissed it thinking since there was no one around.

Then the following night he had a dream from which he woke up feeling strangely excited. His heart was racing, not in fear but with a strange kind of exhilaration. He did not remember what he saw, but he could recall a deep echoing voice that had called out his name from afar, as though from within a long tunnel. Upon waking, he had felt a queer feeling of anticipation. But he couldn't quite understand why.

The next day he was at Faizal's house drinking sherbet after introducing himself as his close friend. Faizal's mother had answered the door and he knew that Faizal wouldn't be home until evening. His father who lived in the village happened to be in town that week, and was asleep in the next room. It was good for Hussain because the moment he was done impaling the mother, he had walked in, and it became imperative for Hussain to kill him as well. Then when both of them had oozed enough blood, he bludgeoned their bodies so that the bones crumbled and he could stuff them in small packets. Then he wrapped the packets in black polythene and carried them to his rickshaw standing downstairs. After stowing them under the seat, he pedaled towards the river.

It was a bright, hot day, but clouds were gathering near the horizon. They seemed to be approaching closer as Hussain pedaled, faster and faster, towards the bridge over Yamuna.

The traffic had slowed near the main road. But the cars were realigning. They seemed to be moving into position to allow Hussain to pass by on his rickshaw. The policemen on the red lights did not notice him as he pedaled by. They did not see the glint in his eyes, or the frenzied look on his face, or even the streak of red blood that followed him up to the river where he dumped the bodies in broad daylight without anybody stopping him. Then, as if on cue, the clouds lingering on the horizon gathered above in a long chain from Faizal's house to the river where he stood, washing away the trail of blood that he had left on the road.

Hussain heaved a sigh of relief. All he had to do now was go back and wait for Faizal. He would take him to Kotla one final time...after all, what he truly wanted was to unite with the one he truly loved.

✦

Sulaiman proved to be the lover that Hussain had always wanted. Upon being freed, he took the shape of a beautiful man of exactly twenty-five, and submitted to Hussain in a way Faizal never had. He was an obliging lover, and knew everything that Hussain liked to do and be done to in bed: he knew how to make him feel pleasure in ways he had never imagined...he knew how to elongate ecstasy, how to unlock different parts of his body to feel sensual, how to hold off orgasms for hours, and how to have multiple orgasms. He had cast a spell over his body.

Hussain suddenly seemed to have everything he had ever desired. The only problem now, was his own family. He could not explain who Sulaiman was. He could not even mention him because they would never understand. This again was a huge obstruction in his way of love and fulfilment, and Sulaiman too felt saddened on this account. But what were they to do? Hussain desperately wished all these obstacles would just disappear.

Then one day, when he returned home from work, he saw his mother and two sisters lying in a pool of coagulated blood. Sulaiman had killed them. Hussain felt revolted at the sight. But good riddance. As if under some trance, he disposed of their bodies like he had disposed of the bodies of Faizal's parents.

✦

After many years of a passionate affair, one night, Sulaiman did not return home.

The next day there was no sign of him either. Hussain remained in the same position in bed, waiting for him to return. But several nights passed, then weeks, and then months, and he did not come back. Sulaiman seemed to had left him forever.

Heartbroken and lost, Hussain felt the lowest that he ever had. What was he to do now? After so much time, he had brought changes in his appearance for Sulaiman's sake. His hair had grown till his waist and his facial features had softened to a great extent as he'd gained weight. He dressed entirely like a woman now and even wore padded bras and an elastic around his waist to give it an hour-glass curve. Except for his penis, everything about him was feminine. He could not ply the rickshaw after changing his gender, so he had forayed into sex work.

Somehow, he became popular very quickly. Several years later, as his fortunes increased, he completed his transformation after a series of expensive surgeries. He had changed his name to Sulaima and was now an exclusive trans escort, well known amongst an elite clientele of South Delhi and Gurgaon.

Then one day, while escorting a businessman from

Dubai at a party in Le Meridian, he was given an offer to make a pornographic movie. Offers flowed in after that and within a year, he became a fashionable transsexual figure in the porn industry. Sulaima was now famous. The days of rickshaw pedalling were long gone and seemed like another lifetime to her. The Kotla became a small blip in her memories as she settled into an expensive flat in Begumpur and led a comfortable and exciting life. Men came and went, and Sulaiman, her djinn, the lover of her dreams, only seemed like a dream—a figment of her imagination.

KABOOTARBAZI

It was the year of ceaseless rain. Thunder showers came day after day and the temperatures dropped drastically. Bhishan Singh was in a foul mood because that morning one of his prized pigeons was found dead inside the coop. It was difficult to maintain cleanliness inside the straw-filled cages, and the perennial wetness and lack of sunlight had taken its toll that season. The birds had fallen sick, and some of them had died within a couple of days. Just the other day, two white pigeons had died, and another handsome Magpie, got so sick that they had to bring him indoors and keep him in a cardboard box, away from the rest of the pigeons. This particular Magpie was one of Bhishan Singh's favourites. Its failing health had put him in a strange mood. He sat with it the whole time, nursing it, trying to feed it diluted milk through a syringe. But the bird died within a week despite all efforts.

Days passed in this manner. The skies remained grey and heavy, and several other Magpies died. With each death,

Bhishan Singh's heart became more and more laden with guilt at not being able to save them. Then one day, a dove died during one of the nights when there was thunder and lightning, and Bhishan Singh felt that he would lose all his birds one after the other. What scared him the most was that the Magpies, Shirazis and Basras had become unusually quiet, and the usual activity inside the coops had stopped completely. The birds sat around listlessly, barely emitting any sounds, and hardly willing to fly around even when he coaxed them. He tried his best to stir them into action with songs and tasty meals, but no amount of expensive bajra managed to induce excitement.

And then, on the hundredth day of continuous rain, when the water in the streets had risen to the waist and shopkeepers on the ground floor had to wrap up their work and carry off their stocks to the first floor, Bhishan Singh decided to take matters into his own hands. He could not bear to watch his beloved birds fall sick and die off for being kept in captivity. They were bored and in want of a race. He would have to do something fast.

✦

Amongst the pigeon whisperers of Chandni Chowk, Bhishan Singh was known as the Badshah of kabootarbazi. He had originally owned seven hundred and fifty pigeons—the largest flock to be owned by an individual in the past five decades.

Before him, his great grandfather, Gambhir Singh, had owned five thousand pigeons. He was famed throughout the city for his pigeon racing skills, and people came from other cities to apprentice under him. But he was selective in choosing his pupils and did not mentor just anybody. Only if he saw the spark in the candidate did he take him under his tutelage.

There was a family legend that once the prince of Kalapur had come to apprentice under him. Summers in the palace were proving to be too dull and this prince needed a new hobby. But Gambhir Singh did not care for the status of his candidate. One look at the prince, resplendent in his white sherwani with a blood red rose tucked inside his button, and he knew the he was up to no good. He refused outright. The prince, offended at first, tried to win him over, but no amount of smooth talk or gold could convince him. Gambhir Singh was a man of staunch principles.

Many years later, the prince returned and stood before Gambhir Singh once again.

'Do you remember me?'

'I do very well,' Gambhir Singh replied.

'I am here to make you an offer.'

'Is that so?'

'Your birds…they say they are the best. I want to buy all of them. And I am prepared to pay any price.'

'My birds are not for sale.'

The prince was flummoxed. 'Do you not know who you are refusing?'

'I did not care ten years ago when you came to me first, and I do not care now.'

'And do you not care for riches? Even after what happened to your trade?' he laughed. 'You are not a wealthy man anymore. But I can make you wealthy again. Quote your price.'

'I will never sell my birds. Leave my house now,' Gambhir Singh replied, his jaw stiffened. There was no space for negotiation.

'Remember your words, Gambhir Singh,' the prince said. 'It is for this that you will lose your title to me someday.'

And with that, the prince left without getting what he wanted.

But his heart was set on the birds. He vowed to defeat Gambhir Singh no matter how long it took.

✦

There were all sorts of stories about how Gambhir Singh had acquired his five thousand pigeons. The most common tale was that it was given to him as a reward by a prince of Afghanistan. The story was that the prince had been visiting India, and while passing through the forest he and his retinue was captured by bandits. They would have been killed had Gambhir Singh, who was passing through with four of his fellow soldiers, not saved him. He had shown good planning and technique, and even though they were greatly outnumbered, had killed off the thugs one by one as they dozed after their drunken revelries at night. The prince, indebted to the five young men for saving his life, had then offered them valuables as reward. Khan chose the prince's ruby ring, Pataudi chose his consort (whom he later married), Chowdhury chose his gold pocket watch, and Hussain chose his emerald-studded dagger. When it was Gambhir Singh's turn to ask for something, he remained quiet for a long time, pondering over what he really wanted. Then to everyone's surprise, he pointed at the prince's flock of pigeons.

The prince was surprised. 'Birds? Of all the riches I offer you, you want the pigeons?'

'I know your pigeons are valuable, Lord.'

The prince hesitated. The birds were indeed valuable. They had been transported to him from Persia and were enchanted. 'How about this emerald necklace instead? You will be a rich man with this.'

'I would like the pigeons, your majesty,' he said with a slight bow.

'I could give you rubies, emeralds, sapphires…' the prince offered. 'I could give you land—even my favourite concubine, Yasmine. She is exquisite. See for yourself.'

Gambhir Singh maintained polite silence. His mind was set on the birds.

'What would you do with my birds, young man?' the prince asked finally. A promise was a promise after all. He would have to relent.

'I will train them to race.'

After a month, Gambhir Singh returned home with the five thousand pigeons inside one large cage that was pulled by the prince's horses. He went on to become a legendary pigeon racer and was often written about in national newspapers and magazines. There were stories around him and it began to be said that he could talk to pigeons and make them do as he pleased. Some even said that his birds weren't ordinary birds. They were immortal.

All of this came to an abrupt end one day and Gambhir Singh gave up his title as the badshah, and retired permanently from pigeon-keeping. It was the year 1919, and the country was in a turmoil. Screams of 'Inquilab Zindabad' reverberated in people's hearts and desire for azadi bubbled in people's consciousness. General Dyer, having banned all meetings for fear of an insurrection, opened fire on a gathering at Jallianwala Bagh, on April 13th.

When the news of the massacre reached Gambhir Singh in Delhi, he sat in shock for many hours. His dear old friend and his whole family had been trapped inside the bagh, and all seven of them had died. The pain of learning about their gruesome deaths had immobilised him completely. His wife and children tried to coax him out of shock but it did not work. Then in the evening when everybody retired downstairs, he finally stirred. Without saying anything to anyone, he went to the roof where his beloved birds were kept, and with an animal howl that rolled over the housetops of the city, released the birds from the coop.

The next morning, the birds were seen perched over the nearby houses, fluttering around sedately, not realising that they had been freed to mark their master's grief. Some of them flew back, not wanting freedom from their master.

As a child, Bhishan Singh had often pictured his grandfather, a young man then, kind of like his own self, releasing five thousand pigeons in a rusty sky. The mental image always sent chills down his spine. People said that the sight of him releasing the birds in the twilight of spring was the most spectacular mourning that the city had ever seen.

As Bhishan Singh grew up, love for kabootarbazi slowly kindled in his heart. By the time he turned twenty, he was already apprenticing, and about a decade later, took over the seven hundred sabaz parey that had flown back into the coop after being released by his grandfather. His mother said that he reminded her of her father-in-law, and encouraged him to develop his skills. By the time Bhishan Singh turned fifty, he was the badshah of kabootarbazi in Purani Dilli, just like his grandfather was so many decades ago.

But Bhishan Singh knew this title was not going to stick forever. He was over a century old now, and his reputation as the most immaculate pigeon-keeper was beginning to fade as younger ones climbed the hierarchy and matched him with their newer, stronger flocks. Besides, his days were numbered now, and who knew if he would be able to race the next year?

And so, Bhishan Singh, in his last bid to retain his title, invested all his energies into training his flocks, knowing well that the exertion was taking a toll on his health. His family protested with him constantly, but he was adamant. He was going to win the race on 26th January, even if it was the last thing he did.

As summer passed, clouds swirled over the rooftop of the Singh house, and before they could brace themselves for monsoon, it began pouring determinedly.

✦

Over the next few months, Bhishan Singh focused all his energies, and a considerable fortune, on the care and maintenance of the birds. His wife and sons tried to keep him from putting in so much money into the sport, but he was not to be swayed. Determined to win the game which he thought would be his last, he refused to think of anything else. His old silver shop in Dariba Kalan suffered because his sons refused to leave their jobs and help out when their father wanted to be at home to care for the pigeons. After a rather heated argument one night, the eldest son decided to move out. He could not go on being in the same house as a lunatic, he said.

For a while, it really seemed like Bhishan Singh had turned into a senile old man. In the beginning it just seemed like he was bothered about his pets, but as the days passed, it became more and more evident that the attachment was 'abnormal', as the neighbours said. He could be found crouching inside the coop for hours, and soon, the only time he came out was when he had to take meals. He had even begun sleeping inside, and no amount of coaxing and cajoling could bring him out.

But despite Bhishan Singh's efforts, a hundred, out of the seven hundred pigeons that were left, died over the course of three months. He was plunged into depression. His wife and the other three sons tried their best to revive him but to no avail. Even offers of buying new birds did not entice him. Soon, he became hysterical with grief. His cries of despair shot across the city in the wee hours of the morning when he began counting his birds and found that one or the other bird had died the night before.

Then one day, Bhishan Singh's wife saw a lone pigeon

flying from the terrace, into the house, and through it, until it was out of the window on the farthest end. The sight was strange and she, a superstitious woman, knew something was amiss.

That night, a fire broke out in the house. Bhishan Singh's wife, their sons and their wives perished in it. The birds had managed to get out. Only the pigeons and Bhishan Singh remained in the burning embers of a house that had stood in the middle of the old city for over one hundred years.

✦

Bhishan Singh's eldest son who had walked out on them, confessed to starting the fire the following week. He was booked for arsenal and murder of seven individuals, along with attempted murder of another. Apparently, he had tried setting fire to the pigeon coop, but because the coop was damp from the day's shower, it did not catch fire. What however caught fire were the wires that were protruding from the window just next to the coop. These wires were directly connected to the television set in the house downstairs, and the flames carried through them in an instant, setting the TV aflame in no time. The fire swiftly spread through the rest of the house and before daybreak, everything was in cinders.

Bhishan Singh, who had slept next to the coop on a cot, woke up to the screams of the neighbours in the wee hours of the morning. It was then that he realised what had happened as he slept. As if in a daze, he climbed downstairs, wading through the smoke, coughing and wheezing the names of his wife and children whose charred remains lay on the beds.

He passed out in shock.

✦

Amongst the dead bodies, there was a man lying at the top of the stairs, just near the door of the terrace. He was covered in soot, lying right behind the accumulated possessions of the family that had grown redundant over the years. When Bhishan Singh had hurtled down the stairs into the burnt chaos, he hadn't noticed the intruder. Later when the neighbours came in to help them, and the police arrived to conduct investigations, the man was discovered, unconscious, and in need of immediate resuscitation and first aid. He was a local rickshawwalla who had apparently tried to enter the house and help the family. They hailed him as a saviour who had risked his life to rescue the Singh family. The family had not survived and Bhishan Singh had suffered burns, but the rickshawwalla was declared as a local hero. People began to recognise him in the streets, and stories of his bravery soon reached the international media. The BBC World reported a week later:

> Muslim rickshawwalla's heroic attempt at saving a Hindu jeweller's family from a fire that broke out in their house has become a symbol of communal brotherhood. Nawab, 28, will receive cash money from the community as reward for his courage and selflessness. He says that he will use the money to fix his rickshaw, and the roof of his house in Old Delhi…

✦

Although Bhishan Singh was a romantic, he was not a fool in money matters. Apart from his silver shop, he had a knack for stocks. He earned substantially from dalali, and had invested in several shares, periodically profiting from them. The gold, bonds, and other shares that he owned were safely stashed inside the lockers in different banks. His house, although incredibly old, was insured against fire and theft and natural calamities. He had remained in a state of shock for several weeks, but when he regained his sanity, he bounced back to his original self and soon began reconstructing the house.

People were not surprised at Bhishan Singh's resilience. He was known as a consummate businessman, shrewd and manipulative, and utterly obsessed with making money. What they however did not realise was that he was incredibly sentimental about his possessions. What was seen as materialistic tendencies, was actually a deep rooted attachment with his family legacy.

'My family is dead and all my possessions are lost. The house that had stood here for over a century—the house that saw many generations of the Singh family—has been reduced to ashes. I am a lost man…but I will not leave this world after bringing down my family legacy to rubble. I cannot leave this behind: a burnt memory of the past, and a son who is a murderer and criminal…this is not how I will be remembered.' Bhishan Singh was determined to find redemption before death. And only his beloved pigeons could help him.

✦

December finally arrived. The pigeon keepers of old Delhi were in a flurry to begin training before the annual racing on Republic Day. The men could be seen on their terraces, clucking to their flocks that flew up and around and returned to their positions upon instruction. Because of the rains, the men had fallen behind on training and were keen to make the birds practice as much as possible before the day arrived.

Bhishan Singh was amongst these men, although now he had a considerably smaller flock to train. The number of birds had reduced to five hundred and seventy-five, and he felt extremely disadvantaged because of that. Nonetheless, he decided to go ahead and train them as hard as possible.

The people in the neighbourhood talked amongst themselves when they saw him training his birds. They said he was still in delirium because of the death of his family. They gossiped about his odd obsession with the birds, and how despite everything, he went on about the sport like a madman.

Some people were however more compassionate. Old friends and distant relatives sympathised with him and his apparent existential crisis, knowing how he always associated victory in the sport as his own personal victory in life. They felt he deserved to fight and win the upcoming race because only that could recompense for his loss.

But whether people understood or not, Bhishan Singh single-mindedly trained his birds to win the contest. He was the badshah after all, like his grandfather. And he was going to be remembered as that.

✦

The birds were getting tired of the incessant practice. More than a hundred had perished over the past one year and many of them were still recuperating. The weather did not help. It hardly ever stopped raining, and the cold was unbearable. Still their master refused to be careful. What would he do if they died off altogether? How would he win the wretched race?

The birds contemplated revolting. They were the only ones who had not deserted his grandfather when he had released all five thousand of them. They had returned to the coop out of sheer loyalty. And they had served Bhishan Singh after his death with the same kind of loyalty. They were veterans. They did not deserve such harsh treatment so many years later.

But Bhishan Singh was possessed with the idea of winning the race, and the birds couldn't possibly disobey him. Where would they go, after all? They were fine, domestic birds, living in the family for more than a hundred years. They were unused to the harshness of the outside world. How would they ever survive amongst the crows and eagles and vultures? And how would they find food? They would have to hunt for it every single day. It was better to stay in the coop as Bhishan Singh's flock. At least the meals were guaranteed and there was no need to build nests or compete with the other birds. It was a compromise, but it would have to do.

✦

The fall of Bhishan Singh's fortune was the talk of the town for the next few months. When it began to die down, another mishap happened and it seemed that there would be no end to his misfortunes. In the last week of December, there was an attempted burglary at Bhishan Singh's house. People said that the evil eye was upon him.

What nobody knew however was that the thief was not interested in Bhishan Singh's wealth. He only wanted one thing—Bhishan Singh's most prized possessions: his pigeons. And it was the same man who was found in the house the day after the fire.

✦

The rickshawwalla who had been proclaimed the hero of Chandni Chowk, had disappeared from public attention within a few weeks. After the hullaballoo created by the media also died down, nobody really bothered about him. People forgot his face and 'heroism', and his pathway to prosperity seemed to have been cut off midway. A few weeks later, the last article appeared on him in a rather obscure youth news journal. It was full of youthful angst:

> Nawab went back to rickshaw-pulling soon after the fire accident where he risked his life to save a family living in Chandni Chowk. While seven members of the family perished in the fire, Bhishan Singh, 96, survived. Nawab received ten thousand rupees as prize money from a local MLA as a token of appreciation for service to the community.
>
> But where is Nawab now? How long will it be before he is reduced to a life of poverty and penury? The local rickshawwallas who made him into an icon have reportedly said that Nawab went back to the

neighbourhood for more financial help, but they had scoffed at him saying that he had exhausted his due and didn't deserve more. It was alleged that the MLA said that Nawab had been given the money only because of the media attention.

Ibrahim, 26, a rickshaw-puller in the same area said, 'The two months of easy living when Nawab no longer had to ply his rickshaw must have been a sweet experience for him. And after having that, how could he not want more? How could he give up that comfortable life?' Abul, 21, said, 'After the sudden coming into wealth it did not seem fitting that Nawab should return to his earlier existence. Rickshaw pulling did not seem to be his destiny. He was meant for higher things. Why else should he have survived the fire, and after surviving the fire, get a reward and become famous? Why else should he have been declared a hero? A messiah of Hindu–Muslim unity? All of these things could not have been a mere coincidence? There was a greater design—god's own hand in this…'

How foolish could people be, Nawab thought as he read the article with growing amusement, while sitting on the velvet settee next to the balcony in the mansion that belonged to the old prince—Gambhir Singh's old rival.

✦

Bhishan Singh was beginning to despair. His flock was reduced in numbers, and his competitors confident that he stood no chance. In fact, they had begun to treat him with pity, like they would an ageing man, and their condescension drove him crazy. He began to drive his birds harder. There was only one way to win the race—he had to make sure his birds were the swiftest and the most elegant. There was no room for even small errors. They would have to be trained so well that there would be only one clear winner. His competitors would know then who the true master was.

But the birds were ancient, and Bhishan Singh knew that winning the race was going to be difficult. He wasn't as good as his grandfather, and much older now.

He was driven to despair, unable to think of any way.

And then one evening, when he had just closed the coop and climbed down to his bedroom to retire for the night, there was a knock on the door. He opened it, and found a young man standing before him.

'What do you want, son?'

'My name is Nawab, Singh sahab. Do you not remember me?'

The face was absolutely unfamiliar, but the name rang a bell. He was the same boy who had tried to save him and his family during the fire.

'Why, yes. I remember you very well…but why are you here so late in the night? What do you want?'

'I have come to make you an offer,' he said stepping inside. He knew the offer was good and Bhishan Singh would relent easily. After all, he was going to give him what his old heart desired the most: first position in the annual pigeon race.

The scheme was all very simple, and Bhishan Singh would have no part to play in it except that he would teach him the language of the magical birds that he alone knew, and bequeath his entire flock to his master, the prince. Nawab stated this clause with absolute confidence, knowing it wasn't too much to ask for. After all, Bhishan Singh was practically heirless, and so old that he would not live to play in the next Republic Day. The upcoming race was his last opportunity to live up to his own reputation and win the title he coveted so much.

Bhishan Singh, all too aware of his impending death, agreed. It was his last shot.

✦

The grand plan proposed by Nawab was to make sure that Bhishan Singh's flock was the best amongst all the competing flocks. And since many of his birds had died, there was only one way to guarantee their win: by making sure that the competing flocks were disadvantaged in some way.

It was eventually decided that the best way was to eliminate competition altogether. The main targets were Bholanath Chaudhury, Abdul Ali Khan, Mirza Pataudi, and Shahid Hussain, sons of former pigeon racing champions, Bhishan Singh's old friends from the army, whom he had given a hundred birds each from his prized flock as gifts of friendship. But the young men were ungrateful and displayed an utter lack of reverence for their father's old friend. Thwarting them at the game was Bhishan Singh's only way of re-establishing who the alpha was.

'Amateur fools!' he called them to their faces whenever he came across them. 'Money cannot buy skill or talent. That comes only with time. You boys are new to this and stand no chance because it is only I who has invested years into the sport. You haven't! Bloody newbies...no respect at all. I have been playing this for sixty years! That is commitment. Not this superficial fascination that you have...pigeon racing is NOT just a hobby, do you understand? It is a communion. It is a communion!'

Sometimes when he saw them practicing on their terrace, he hollered abuses at them. The neighbourhood ladies covered the ears of their children and shrieked at him, but to no avail. The residents of Ghalib Street in Chandni Chowk heard, ignored, and sometimes humoured the rather frequent outbursts of Bhishan Singh, knowing the poor old man's days were numbered.

✦

Abdul Ali Khan's flock was the first to disappear. One morning he woke up before the usual time with a strange intuition. Then as if in a trance, he climbed up the steps to the terrace where he had built the coop for his one hundred pigeons passed on to him by his grandfather. Wordlessly, he walked through the early morning winter fog and came and stood before the empty coop. The door was hanging open, swaying slightly in the breeze.

Throwing back his head he let out a howl and sank to his knees. Through the tears he was scanning the murky skies for his beloved birds.

✦

The mystery deepened as Chaudhury, Mirza Pataudi, and Shahid Hussain lost their flocks too in the following week.

A meeting was called. It was concluded that it might have been an accident, or a case of negligence. But it was too much of a coincidence that three other men had 'forgotten' to lock up the coops and lost their entire flocks right before the race. Surely, some mischief was afoot. It would be foolish to not look into the matter closely.

The police was called. There was some confusion. Nobody really knew how to treat the case, and the goons were reluctant to do anything. But the four men were rich and influential. The local MLA was contacted, and eventually, an FIR was lodged. Finally, investigations began. The policemen climbed from one terrace to another, asking questions, chatting with the locals, often stopping for tea and samosas, and lounging on the cots on people's terraces when they took a break.

Nothing came out of the week-long search. It did seem like the men had simply forgotten to secure the cages. The senior policemen, bored of the case and relieved that nothing much was found, consoled the men by invoking god's will and the strange ways of destiny.

Soon, the file was closed, and the case dismissed.

Amidst the chaos, Nawab rested peacefully. He knew his plans were going how he wanted them to, and it wouldn't be long before Bhishan Singh's flock would be handed over to him.

Little did anyone know that the birds that were stolen from Chaudhury, Khan, Pataudi and Hussain, had been tied up together and transported all the way to Lucknow on Nawab's rickshaw. It had taken him thirteen days to cycle all the way there, but at last, the deed was done. The birds were now locked up in the estate of Mohammad Qasim, son of the prince of Kalapur who had once sought to apprentice under Bhishan Singh's grandfather. Now, many years later, he had decided it was time to fulfil his promise to his father and seek revenge for the perjury done unto him by Gambhir Singh. He was bored with life and needed something exciting.

The truth was that Mohammad Qasim was not a very bright prince. He had never strategised in his life and when the brilliant idea to sabotage Bhishan Singh struck him, he was blown away by his own cleverness. He knew that this idea would take him places. Who knew, he might even manage to acquire a great fortune out of it. If his mother was alive, she would have been proud of her son's shrewdness and ingenuity. He was indeed very clever.

It was the first time Qasim had an aim in life. The thrill of it was not only a novel experience, but also incredibly arousing. That night he made love to Nawab, his manservant and secret lover, with renewed passion. After pleasuring him for the third time, he told him about his new-found ambition. He needed his help, clever as he was.

After some hesitation, Nawab had agreed to help. After all, the ex-prince was his only source of livelihood. And then, he was particularly good at fellatio, despite being old and fat…

✦

Seizing Bhishan Singh's flock wasn't the original plan. Nawab had spent many weeks contemplating his options. He thought and thought and thought, and spent nights talking to his other lovers about all possibilities. Finally, he figured that it was not enough to thwart Bhishan Singh to avenge Qasim's father. Losing his birds would be his greatest defeat.

The following week he went to Chandni Chowk to live there for the next six months. In his heart he carried a genius conspiracy—the key to luxury and comfort. How had he not thought of this before?

✦

A few days before the race, Bhishan Singh woke up at dawn and as usual, went to the terrace to see his beloved birds. He had kept his part of the deal and taught Nawab the language of the birds. Now the main contenders were not participating that year and only seven pigeon keepers were against him. Bhishan Singh knew that none of them stood a chance.

There was however a new participant. Who was it? He did not know. He was something of an enigma. The other day someone had mentioned Lucknow...

It was then that he realised that his birds were gone.

Before he could react, there was some commotion on the terrace to his immediate right. He turned to see what was happening. A portly man wearing a bright checkered suit with a red tie, appeared, smiling dazzlingly. He was wearing dark sunglasses in the dimness of dawn, and held a cigar in one hand.

'Bhishan Singh, I hope you are well today,' he called out to him while making a slight bow. Bhishan Singh couldn't respond. His birds had disappeared. What was happening?

'Greetings from my late father, the prince of Kalapur!' he said, tipping his fedora.

Prince of Kalapur? Bhishan Singh couldn't place it. Was it the same prince who...?

The man laughed. 'What happened, Bhishan Singh? Cat got your tongue?' Then in a rather cocky manner he turned and opened a cage. Nine hundred birds flew up and circled the sky, then landed back in perfect synchrony. He did it again, and again, and again.

Bhishan Singh stood frozen in his spot. He watched as the man made a flourish, and the birds formed a chain in mid-air, and then circled around in a perfect oval, flying swiftly, gracefully, sliding over the wind as though they were swans in a lake.

He knew in that instant that this man would win the race.

But the birds seemed familiar...They were his own... and the birds of Khan, Pataudi, Hussain, Chaudhury!

Shocked at first, a slow smile appeared on Bhishan Singh's face as he watched the birds swoop down—the birds that originally belonged to the prince from Afghanistan, and then his grandfather. He knew that he wouldn't have to worry. They were his, after all, and trained for decades to listen to the sons of the Singh household.

That night the ancient pigeon whisperer rose to his terrace by moonlight, and held a communion with the entire flock of nine hundred birds, united after a long time. The birds knew what their master was asking of them. They began clucking and moving around, eager to carry out his instructions. Suddenly, the birds did not seem to mind the challenge. It was an important task, and it was important they performed it well.

✦

On the day of the race, the skies were alive with pigeons and different flocks rose up and swirled around, and then swooped down towards their masters, settling back into position. The crowds were looking forward to a good spectacle. The suited-booted gentleman from Lucknow had created quite a stir in the past few days and people knew that he would win. They gathered on their rooftops, knowing that they would be witnessing the race of the decade—maybe even century—as mad old Bhishan Singh was defeated, and his family name in pigeon racing destroyed. They were there to witness his downfall. They laughed together at the thought, and scanned the skies for the best and most promising flocks that would seal the case.

Just before the race, there was a commotion. The ex-prince had driven up to the house in a yellow Beetle, with him was another man they couldn't recognise. Then suddenly, they realised who it was. The rickshawwalla who had once become the hero of town!

There was a sudden hush, then an abrupt outbreak of buzz as people began talking loudly, confusedly. What was the rickshawwalla doing with the sahib from Lucknow? What could it mean?

Before anyone could make sense of what was happening, the race began. The man from Lucknow came forward and made a flourish. But nothing happened. The birds remained where they were. The crowds looked on, puzzled. Mohammad Qasim turned to look at Nawab and Nawab looked back in confusion.

Just then Bhishan Singh rose up, and raised his arms in the air. The people turned to look at what he was doing, wondering what he would do without his birds. Some men discussed whether they should go over and make him go inside his house so that people did not humiliate him. Khan, Pataudi, Chaudhury and Hussain were drinking tea on Khan's terrace when they saw Bhishan Singh stand on his terrace with his arms wide open, his head thrown up, as if in a silent embrace with the almighty. Khan, pitying the state of the old delusional man, kept his cup down and made to go, when suddenly, there were loud gasps all around.

A dark whirlpool of birds was expanding above Bhishan Singh's head. The nine hundred black and white pigeons swirled in a neat whirlpool just over Bhishan Singh's head as he raised his arms directly above. Then, as though he was Zeus orchestrating winds, he moved one arm in an elaborate flourish and the birds twirled around like a wave rolling over the coast.

Mohammad Qasim watched in horror as the birds he had stolen flew around the ancient pigeon whisperer as though they were possessed by him. He seemed to be in a trance and rose on his toes, and swung his arms around, moving his hands in circles and spinning, like a ballet dancer, as the birds obediently followed the movement of his hands. Then, almost magically, the birds spread out and came together, and flew out and in again, arranging and rearranging themselves in perfect synchrony as though they were patterns in a kaleidoscope that kept changing into different designs.

The crowd watched in rapture as the birds danced in the winds, even as their master danced, his own ancient dance that his grandfather had taught him when he made the pigeons fly during nights when no one was looking.

✦

The early risers of Old Delhi probably did not see the pigeons of Bhishan Singh fly over their houses towards Lodi Road where Mohammad Qasim and his lover were lodging.

At about 5 a.m., Nawab, roused by a low crash, got up to investigate what the ruckus was about. Mohammad Qasim was dozing next to him, naked except for a pair of woolen socks. He prodded him sharply, then when he didn't respond, got up and went into the living room of their suite.

Just then he heard gurgling sounds. The sun wasn't out yet and he couldn't see anything in the haze as he looked outside through the glass doors of the balcony.

But the gurgling was getting louder…and there was the unmistakable sound of wings flapping…

And then the first rays of the rising sun hit the building. Nawab's mouth opened in a silent gasp as he saw the entire balcony covered in pigeons. There was a loud bang. He let out a scream as a pigeon flew up against the glass window and crashed against it.

Mohammad Qasim, hearing the commotion, waddled up, his modest manhood slapping against his spindly legs. Nawab was frozen by the window.

'What happened, Nawab? What happened?'

Before he could reply, a cluster of birds flew into the glass doors again. There was a loud cracking noise as a zigzag appeared on the glass. The birds flew back and crashed against the doors one more time. Within moments the glass shattered.

Nawab and the Mohammad Qasim screamed as the birds flew in, hitting their faces with their wings and beaks.

There was a moment of confusion. The two stood fixed to their spots, terrified as the pigeons flew around, whizzing by their heads, pecking at their eyes. Pigeons—grey, black, and white—on chairs, sofas, tables, the floor, the clock, the rugs. They were everywhere.

Before Nawab and Qasim could run towards the door, the birds flew at them.

✦

The morning joggers in Lodi Road heard the faraway screams of Mohammad Qasim and Nawab as the birds carried them higher and higher, into the misty clouds, until they were right above the Yamuna.

Only the cows grazing by the river saw the two bodies being dropped into the waters. Their screams were drowned by the regular office-hour traffic of New Delhi.

PYGMALION

It was a night of loneliness as Pezhman, shut out from the outside world, dipped his fingers into the mound of clay, and began fashioning a face. There was load-shedding in the area, and dark clouds that had formed a wall across the full moon sky, had plunged the neighbourhood in darkness. Inside the house, Pezhman's only source of light as he sat stooped over his work, was the flickering candle on the window sill, that made the wet clay glisten in his hands. He sat in the circle of light in the room, still, except for an expert finger moulding the clay, like a man lost in prayer.

As the eyes appeared, large and almond-shaped, there was a low rumble outside. Cracks of thunder sliced through the inkiness, and the clouds in the distance lit up momentarily. There was loud thunderclap and it began raining heavily. The sleet crashed against the window, and the sound grew steadily until it was all that Pezhman could hear.

Darkness seemed to be closing in around him. All he

could now see in the dim light was the earth that was taking shape under his fingers and taking on the likeness of a woman's nose and lips. As the whole face emerged from the lump, he grew excited. His hands moved faster, expertly shaping the eyebrows and countering the cheeks.

He was breathing heavily now. His hands seemed to glide over the surface as though he was caressing the sculpted head. Surrendering to his creation, he closed his eyes and leaned over the face in pleasure.

The scent of wet earth drying in summer seemed to permeate him completely.

He had created his mate. His Gazhbiya.

✦

Pezhman plied his rickshaw in the main market of Paharganj. He sometimes went up to the railway station, but never beyond. He had been living in the area for eight years, and after moving from one job to another in the first year, had settled into the work of a rickshawwalla. Since then, every morning, he took his rickshaw to the metro station where the rest of his mates gathered to begin the day's labour, and stood in wait for passengers. He did not take a single day's rest and did his daily business with dedication. He never hesitated to put in more hours of work if it was necessary.

There was no doubt that Pezhman was a hard-working fellow. His friends and the neighbourhood residents said the same. And for this reason, he was the centre of attention in the street where he lived. Everybody—especially the matrons—were deeply impressed by him because he was a quiet and decent fellow who kept to himself. They liked his mannerisms, and appreciated the way he kept away from alcohol and all forms of intoxication, unlike their sons or husbands. Most importantly, he worked diligently and seemed to be a fine bachelor—a suitable boy for their daughters who had come of age.

But Pezhman had no interest in marriage. He did not feel the urge to settle down yet, even though he was already nearing the age of thirty. Instead, he nursed his true passion: that of making forms with clay. Whatever free time he got, he put it in sculpting little statues that he kept around the house. The money that was spared after feeding and clothing himself, he invested in paints with which he coloured these statues. All Pezhman wanted was to someday have enough money to set aside full days from rickshaw-pulling for sculpting. Perhaps when he had the time and money, he could take sculpting classes to gain that perfection in his craft that he knew came only through proper apprenticeship. And maybe someday, he could make it his source of income, like it had been for his ancestors for so many years.

Pezhman's family had migrated from Bikrampur in East Pakistan, and settled in Kumartuli in Bengal during the Partition. They were a family of potters, and during the months leading up to Durga Puja, worked as idol-makers as well. In fact, Pezhman's grandfather, Abul Aleem, had been a famed artisan in his time, and was approached by the richest aristocratic families for sculpting the idols for their barir pujo every year. His fame had grown so much over the many decades of his career that he had worked as the idol-maker for hundreds of pujas, and was revered amongst the elite circles of Calcutta. By the time he had sculpted his five hundredth idol at the age of ninety, people had begun saying that the divine spirit entered the idol fashioned by his hands.

But a curse was upon Abul Aleem. He had got into a spat with the head tawaif from whose backyard he took the sacred earth with which he made the idols, and in a fit of rage she cursed him that his fame would die out with his son. They had been lovers and Abul Aleem, a philanderer back in the day, had slept with another tawaif. Besotted with his new courtesan, he was completely unfazed by the curses and forgot about it completely.

Some years later when Abul Aleem's son, Hamid Aleem, came of age and took on the craft, he saw to his dismay that his son was not a natural like he was. On the contrary, he could hardly handle clay and whatever he made became disproportionate or simply looked distorted.

It soon became evident that Hamid Aleem was not talented or skilled enough to keep his father's legacy alive. He could hardly make ends meet while working as an idol-maker, and as a result, the family gradually slipped into poverty. It was then that Abul Aleem recalled the curse. Some years later when he passed away after turning ninety-two, his name as an idol-maker attenuated quickly in the absence of a capable successor.

Hamid Aleem was in despair at his own incompetence. After some years of struggle, when his son, Pezhman was just about ten years of age, he decided to move to Parvatipur where he took up the work of hair-loom. He now weaved the hair meant for the idols of Durga and other goddesses. And somehow at this, he was as good as his father was at idol-making.

Some years later, when it was Pezhman's turn to take up the occupation of hair-loom like his father and carry on the new legacy, he realised he had no desire or inclination towards it. Alas, the talent of moulding clay had skipped a generation. Instead of inheriting his father's talent in spinning hair, he had inherited his grandfather's talent in idol-making, and even as he agreed to working with his father when the time came, he knew that his true calling actually lay in sculpting.

For some years, Pezhman laboured at the craft of hair-spinning out of respect for his father. Then when he could not suppress his passion for sculpting anymore, he gathered the courage to confess to him about his true ambition, expecting him to be appreciative of his honesty at least.

But Hamid Aleem was a conservative and superstitious man. Under no condition did he want the accursed work of idol-making that had ultimately spelt doom for him, to begin in his family again. He flatly instructed Pezhman to continue the same line of work as him or be disowned. Pezhman and his mother tried to reason with him for several months after this. But it was either his ego or his fear that made him absolutely rigid on the matter, and he forbade Pezhman from ever taking up the occupation that he himself had long forsaken.

Thus, Pezhman worked with his father for many years. After his demise, he moved to New Delhi with his mother, who died within the same year. Unable to fulfil his dreams of becoming a sculptor in the city, he eventually fell into the labour of rickshaw pulling which ensured a steady inflow of cash, if nothing else.

But the unfulfilled desire to sculpt stayed in him, fermenting slowly in his heart. And even though he went around pulling his rickshaw all day, behaving like any other rickshawwalla and doing everything that was characteristic of one, in his heart he knew he was more than that. He was no riffraff, like the other men—the lawless labourers whom you couldn't distinguish between because they were all alike and faceless. He was different. He was a sculptor. He had 'kala'. After all, it was in his blood.

Pezhman struggled for some time to somehow practice his art after he got done with work every day. But rickshaw pulling was no mean task. It drained him so completely that despite having a deep yearning for sculpting, he rarely had the energy to make anything. Besides, the labour was such that it could suck out all creativity from a man. It was so gruelling, so utterly mechanical, that it took enormous will power to stay inspired and retain the zest for life that an artist must have to be able to create any kind of art.

There was hardly any inspiration around anyway. Every day the streets came alive with the droll locals, or lower middle class tourists who were staying in the cheap run down motels there. Junky college kids in their commie outfits came to photograph the market with their large, expensive-looking phones and cameras. Hippy foreigners with their dreadlocks and frayed clothes could be found sitting in the roadside tea shops and chatting with the locals, their pale mouths twisted in fascination at the poverty, dirt, and backwardness. Their western minds were fixated on the idea of the still savage orient, and their supposedly sublime 'Hare Rama, Hare Krishna' that could supposedly bring them inner peace which was not there in the sinful West. Although they were cheerful and friendly, Pezhman regarded them with absolute disdain and rarely ever obliged them if they tried to talk to him or hail his rickshaw.

After work every evening, when his mates retired to their homes where their wives and children lay waiting for them, he simply went home, to a gaping mattress and a gaping window that overlooked nothing in particular. He usually collapsed in exhaustion and drifted into fitful dreams. But sometimes he stayed awake staring outside the window for hours, shutting out his present reality, and trying to recall flashes of his earlier existence when his grandfather was alive and carved goddesses from nothing but lumpen clay.

He remembered that as a child, he used to lie awake watching his grandfather sculpt at night. He wasn't allowed to get up and go near him, but he watched intently from his cot for as long as sleep evaded him. In the distance, the calls of jackals could be heard. Jheejhee poka chirped all around them. Sometimes, a frog came hopping up to where he lay and he would grab it and squish it, and release it just before it pissed in his hands. The last image of his grandfather working frenziedly against a starlit sky, by the light of a hurricane lantern, even as the rest of the family slept in the house, stayed in his mind as he drifted into slumber every night.

One particular night was etched vividly in his mind.

That night he was feeling particularly sleepless as he watched his grandfather work. The grey-blue curtain of Eastern skies formed the backdrop against which Durga rose as her sculptor, although from another faith, moulded her with absolute reverence.

That day Pezhman understood that there was no greater worship than an artist's creation of art. His father was having trouble carrying on the work of sculpting, but if he could ever match his grandfather's passion when he grew up, the name of the Aleems of Kumartuli would not go in vain.

✦

Just when Pezhman decided that he would actually never marry, he came across a woman named Cherry.

Cherry was an escort who had recently moved into the building across from his on the inner interstices of Paharganj. Her window was right opposite his, and sometimes when she was in the room and there was enough light, he could see her moving around the house doing chores in a manner that was utterly removed from her trade. He liked watching her like that, engaged in domestic affairs. At such times, he felt she was living a role that women were best at fulfilling. And he felt that it suited her very much.

But at night when he returned late and she was still up, he had a completely different view of her. She would be in various stages of toilette, transforming under the layers of make-up she caked on herself to cover her dusky complexion. During such nights, he saw her lounging on her bed, half undressed, tired after a night of labour, as affected by insomnia as him and falling asleep only when the sun came up.

Sometimes, if he was unfortunate, he saw her with men—her regulars, who barged into the room and fucked her, and then lay on her bed, exhausted, naked. His blood boiled when he saw such scenes unfold before him. He could do nothing but watch her naked form please the foreign bodies. Somehow, he comforted himself by thinking that it was only her trade—her labour—and she did it as mechanically as he pulled his rickshaw during the day. And it eased his pain somewhat.

And so on such nights when he saw her naked, he did not see her as an object of his sexual desires. Her bare breasts were beautiful, her deep navel was sensuous, and the cut between her thighs would have aroused any man. But her body, while it was at work, did not affect him… it was only when she was alone and unselfconscious that he could actually want her as a lover wants his beloved.

It was not long before he managed to have an exchange with her. One day when he had ferried her from the main market and dropped her at the building, he dared a glance at her as she rummaged in her purse for change. Suddenly he got the feeling that her name had to be something else. 'Cherry' didn't quite go with her aura, now that he had seen her up close.

'What is your name?' he blurted out.

'Cherry,' she said, almost as if she too had blurted it out without intending to, then after narrowing her eyes at him suspiciously, she turned to go.

It was only after she had disappeared into her building and Pezhman had turned his rickshaw around to go back into the bustling streets of the marketplace, that he heard her sweet voice drifting back towards him with her real name.

'Gazhbiya…'

It was the whisper of sweet spring after a spell of winter.

Pezhman knew in that moment that he was in love with her.

✦

Pezhman's love for Gazhbiya was that of a shayar for his muse. She was his inspiration, his only desire for art. Her beauty made him create remarkable forms from clay.

Very soon, Pezhman's room became a sepulchre filled with replicas of Gazhbiya in all shapes, sizes, and poses. Sometimes, he sculpted busts, sometimes he sculpted her full body, and according to his mood, he decided the style of representation. Some sculptures were perfectly proportioned and were her exact replicas, while some acquired different, and often odd proportions, according to the way in which he perceived her in that particular mood. In fact, Pezhman enjoyed deviating from her real shape, distorting her features or accentuating them as he wanted. Sometimes he enlarged her bust or reduced them, rounded her buttocks and sometimes flattened them. He once rounded her nose, and then, sharpened it slightly more than it really was. Then once, he altered her chin, and she looked absolutely different.

He thus played around with her form as he pleased. It

gave him a sense of power, a feeling of control over her. He felt like he was her maker, her creator, and there were no limits to his hold over her. He could practically shape her as he wanted. And it pleased him immensely to be able to do this.

On nights when she was with her clients, he immersed himself in this work to distract himself from the mad, ballooning jealousy that threatened to explode in his chest.

Since the day she had told him her name, he had only one desire: to create her life-size mould. He wanted to replicate every sinew of her body. He wanted to recreate Gazhbiya, in clay, to touch, to hold, and keep for himself, for he could not do so in real life.

✦

Months passed. Gazhbiya, conspicuous because of her beauty and youth, as well as the nature of her work, soon became infamous in the neighbourhood. People began to gossip about her and openly cat-called whenever she passed by. Pezhman knew that the matter was building up and the tolerance of people towards her was bound to snap soon. He suspected something untoward would happen to her, but he could do nothing because nothing had actually happened so far. Still, the apprehension never left him.

Then one day his fears were confirmed. He had come home late from work and feeling too tired to cook anything for himself, walked down to the nearby dhaba to get dinner. The street had emptied of the outsiders and the dhaba only had locals at the hour. After talking to some men he was acquainted with, he sat down and ordered food. He had just sat back in his chair when he heard loud voices coming from the end of the lane where he lived. Two men seemed to be shouting at each other. Pezhman froze for a moment, intuiting the worst. Everybody else at the dhaba, including the boy who was slapping chapatis into the tandoor, also seemed to freeze, their heads turned in the direction of the voices, alert in case there was a need to intervene. Who could be fighting at this hour?

Then it struck him. Without a thought, he scrambled up and ran towards the voices. He came into view of the two men who were holding each other by their collars. They were standing in the middle of the street, and behind them, with the whole crowd's eyes on her illumined face, was Gazhbiya trying to pull them apart. The neighbours had already spilled into the street from their houses and were looking on, without showing any signs of wanting to break up the scuffle. As Pezhman drew closer to the scene, he felt the wave of hostility coursing through the mob, which he knew was actually directed towards Gazhbiya.

The men were clearly her lovers. For a split second, he felt a rush of pleasure seeing her distressed over them. How convenient it would be for him if they mauled each other. But something had to be done before there was blood, or Gazhbiya would become the centre of attention of the whole controversy.

He strode forward, pushing aside the onlookers, and with some difficulty, pulled the men apart. The taller of the two fell away, but continued shouting at the other. The other one shrugged him off violently and strode away, yelling incoherently.

'Fucking whore!' he yelled at Gazhbiya. 'I will see to it that you pay for this!'

Shocked, Pezhman turned to look at her. She stood looking away expressionlessly, her shoulders stiffened at the audacity of the man, but strong against the moral righteousness and disapproving stares of the people around. Then without meeting his eyes, she turned and walked back into the building as though nothing had happened.

Pezhman watched her retreating figure. A sense of dread dropped in on him. He knew that she was in trouble now. So far the neighbourhood had tolerated her presence, out of curiosity, even fear. But now they would not spare her. Already, the buzz of censure was rising around him. He heard snippets as he looked around.

'She is a whore. What else did you expect?...'

'These kinds of things can't happen right under our noses...'

'We can't allow this kind of debauchery to take place in our neighbourhood...'

'What will the children learn...?'

Pezhman walked into his building and climbed up the stairs to his room. He went to bed and looked out towards her bedroom which remained darkened throughout the night. He wanted to reach out to her, but he knew she would not have it. Her eyes were forbidding.

✦

The next day when Pezhman stepped out, he could see clusters of people talking amongst themselves. They were talking excitedly, their faces scrunched up in disapprobation like the night before.

It was inevitable. He had always known that Gazhbiya's transgressions would not be tolerated for too long. These people were not just self-righteous, they were also regressive, with little understanding of a single woman as beautiful and independent as her. He was angry at them suddenly. So what if she traded in sex? So what if she let her body out in exchange for money? She was fierce and self-sufficient. The people who gossiped about her, and so brazenly condemned her as though they were the custodians of women's chastity and morality, were actually people with little work and preoccupation. Most of them were, in fact, hypocrites and fucked whores at every opportunity they found. Some of the men, he knew, had even tried to make advances at Gazhbiya on various occasions. A few of them regularly misbehaved with her. The married ones were somewhat discreet, but the younger ones openly harassed her, under the nose of the same neighbourhood that claimed such moral superiority. His blood boiled with anger thinking about the filthy bastards. He himself had to intervene a few times in the past when he found someone harassing her. But Gazhbiya did not seem to like it so he watched from a distance as she tackled the men herself.

But this time, he wasn't sure whether she would be able to fend off those hounds. The dull sense of trepidation returned and settled into his heart, spreading slowly through the rest of his being.

✦

Pezhman had thought that now that Gazhbiya had come into public scrutiny, she would curb her wayward ways and avoid getting into any further scandal. But that was not to be. Just a couple of days later, while the murmurs about her immorality were still high, Pezhman was woken up in the middle of the night by a familiar voice shouting at the top of his lungs. It was the same tall man who had abused Gazhbiya and threatened her before. This time, he was inside her house and was confronting her directly. He could hear the abuses as clearly as though someone was screaming them from the next room. Nervous for Gazhbiya, he went and stood at the window watching intently in case she needed help. All of a sudden, the man came forward and ripped off her clothes after pushing her against the wall. She disappeared under the man's bulky, panting frame while he entered her. Pezhman, horrified, almost shouted out, then bit his tongue and stood rooted to the spot, staring at their naked bodies as they writhed and panted in unison.

The day after that, the same thing happened. The man was back in her room and was fucking her violently. Pezhman stood at his window, watching helplessly, his teeth gritted as the scene of animalistic sex unfolded before him.

The next day, he saw them fighting. Gazhbiya was throwing things around while the man kept hurling abuses at her. Although the manner in which they fought scared Pezhman and he feared for Gazhbiya's safety, he preferred it to them having sex.

He was beginning to think that this would become a daily routine and he would unfortunately have to be privy to their affair. But one day, about a month after the first incident, it stopped abruptly. Gazhbiya was found dead in her house by her neighbours.

It was mid-afternoon when he heard the news. At first he thought it was a rumour. Then realisation set in. Leaving his rickshaw in the middle of the street, he ran up the alley to her building. It was flooded with people. He pushed past everybody and bounded up the stairs, to the room which he knew belonged to her. The horde of police officers and neighbours seemed to slide away as he moved forward to see the bloody scene.

He opened his mouth to scream but his voice was stuck in his throat. It seemed like a bad dream.

The body lay on the floor next to a window, spread-eagled, naked, in a pool of blood which had oozed from her neck. Her head had been lopped off and it lay about a foot away from her body. Her hair was matted with the blood and was sticking to her face. Her arm was twisted at an odd angle.

He would never forget the death in those large staring eyes that he had once loved so much.

✦

They took the body for a postmortem while the police combed the area for any possible clues or witnesses. Eventually, they came to Pezhman and asked him multiple questions for his clear view of Gazhbiya's house from his window. He answered all the questions honestly and in detail, and became a witness for the case, later testifying in court about the man with whom Gazhbiya had spent her last days. He wanted to do everything he could to punish her killer.

But he was breaking apart from inside. It was extremely

hard for him to keep himself from collapsing in grief while all the investigations were going on. He could barely answer while he was grilled about her sex life and other personal details, but knew he could not let any of the pain show. If the police knew he was shattered by Gazhbiya's death, they would immediately suspect that he had been involved with her and might have had something to do with the murder. And so he kept his tears and screams bottled inside, and faced the police with a straight face and even voice.

Somehow, during the whole interrogation process, Pezhman found out where they had kept Gazhbiya's body. After the postmortem, they had shifted her to a morgue where all the unclaimed dead bodies were kept temporarily before being disposed.

✦

The city was under the spell of a harsh winter. Fog encased the streets at night when it was bathed in a feeble moonlight. The orange lighting from the lamp posts spilled here and there but did not permeate the dark corners.

Pezhman had been cycling around the same road outside the morgue for an hour, trying to find a way to enter without drawing attention to himself. Gazhbiya's body had been brought in that afternoon, and it would be cremated soon since the autopsy was already done. He had to rescue it before such a travesty was committed.

Dogs howled at a distance. The gates were locked so he parked his rickshaw right next to it and swiftly swung up. Then he climbed down and landed with a heavy thud. Seeing there was no one around he made a beeline for the building. Some guards were sitting in a huddle around a dying bonfire in the other corner of the premises, but they seemed to be dozing.

He looked around for a way to get inside the building without entering from the main gate. There was no way he could get past the receptionist. The only way was to climb up to a window and get inside.

An old kikar tree stood next to the building towards the back. He ran to it and quickly climbed up, to the topmost window, and found himself staring into a room full of corpses covered with white sheets. The sight unnerved him. He would have to browse through the bodies to find her.

He tapped the glass window with a stone a few times until it cracked, then slowly dismantled the broken glass and unlatched the window.

There were thirty-three unclaimed dead bodies—found in the city on that day alone perhaps. He knew how Gazhbiya was lost. How had the city claimed the rest of them?

Some rats scampered by his feet, breaking his reverie. Cautiously, he went up to the first body and tore open the white cloth covering it. It was a man.

He went up to the next. It wasn't Gazhbiya either.

The thirty-third body, at the very end of the room, was Gazhbiya's. Her head had been stitched on. But whoever did it had done a rather shoddy job. Besides, her face was lost forever. There were too many cuts and marks, and her eyes had frozen in the last of moment of shock as life left her body. He was repulsed.

As quietly as he could, he tore away the rest of the

cloth that was binding her, and pushed her into the sack he had brought with him. Then he dragged her back to the window.

But her limbs were sticking out clumsily through the holes in the sack, and her arm kept swinging away from her body. Unable to balance the sack properly, he finally twisted her arm back, and shoved it in. There was a loud crack of bones breaking that set his teeth on edge, but he had to do it. It was for her good. Once he rescued her, she would be fine.

After climbing down the tree, he half ran towards the gate dragging the sack with him, terrified of being discovered. Then with a loud grunt, he swung the sack up and threw it over the gate. It made a loud thump as it hit the concrete. He cringed in fear, looking around towards the gatekeepers. But they did not stir. Quickly, he climbed up and landed next to the body. Then he lifted her in his arms and took her to his rickshaw where he placed her as well as he could under the seat. Without another thought, he pedaled back home.

✦

Gazhbiya was granted a new lease of life. The clay head he had sculpted was a replica of her face—smooth and untarnished, and in fact, even more attractive than before. He had never seen her look as beautiful as she did now.

And now she did not look forbiddingly at him.

On the first night, Pezhman brought her a beautiful red salwar kameez. He dressed her up and lay her on his bed. Then he made love to her, his bride, his art, his creation.

A miracle then happened. She came to life in his arms.

He was shocked when she stirred under him for the first time. Then seeing how she had come alive with his touch, he went mad with desire. He began stroking her vagina and kissing her breasts, and to his delight, she held his organ and touched it to her wetness. He was startled by her boldness. But her act meant she was opening up to him and he didn't want her to be ashamed of her desires. He wanted her to ask him to do what she wanted. He wanted her to express her needs. He had no use for a shy woman. He had created Gazhbiya to be his mate—his equal. And he wanted her to reciprocate to his moves with equal fervour.

Soon, Gazhbiya began to respond more actively, holding him to herself as he entered her, and clinging on until he was spent after desperate lovemaking. He was beginning to enjoy it. He had never imagined Gazhbiya could be so adventurous in bed. No wonder she had many clients when she was alive.

It wasn't many days before Gazhbiya found a voice. She began with moaning and sighing as he thrust inside her. And soon, she began saying words.

The first thing she uttered was his name. He was jubilant. He could tell that it was his passion that had infused her with life and brought her back to the mortal world. Each time she seemed more alive than before. Nothing but true love could do that. His love was divine.

Pezhman felt that god was finally listening to his prayers.

✦

Gazhbiya's body seemed like it was meant for him. It was soft and malleable, as if it shaped itself to fit him and his every mood.

Each time he made love to her, he discovered something new about it. He had never noticed these details before—when he would spy on her for hours from his window. It was extremely exciting.

What was more thrilling was that Gazhbiya was now able to remain alive for longer—even after their lovemaking had ended. They would lie together in the dark, sweaty and panting, inhaling each other's scents. And it was only in the wee hours of the morning that she would slip away.

Things were beautiful and idyllic. Their situation seemed very domestic to him. Pezhman was a happy man for the first time in many years.

Then one night, while making love, Gazhbiya turned Pezhman over, and clutching his hands with superhuman strength, got on top.

Pezhman was surprised at this sudden display of exuberance. Then he gave in to her moves and began enjoying the act. The fact that she not only initiated sex but led him through it, guiding him from one position to another, turned him on. The naked desire in her eyes stimulated him. And soon he began looking forward to her uninhibited experimentation in bed. There was nothing she didn't want to do. He felt he was lucky to have a woman who had no sexual scruples.

But Gazhbiya began to get too rough. Her acts in sex were still arousing, but there was now a streak of meanness in her lovemaking. When she seduced him, her face did not merely show desire as it did before—it revealed a strange hunger that he now discovered was absolutely insatiable. She did not want to stop at all. As soon as he was spent, she would immediately try to get him erect again so she could climb on top and they could fuck again.

What really surprised him was that Gazhbiya refused to obey him. Earlier, she used to do as he directed. But now, she blatantly disregarded his wishes. There was a time when she was all about pleasuring him and serving him in bed. Now she had become absolutely selfish; it was all about *her* body, and *her* pleasure. Even when he was on top of her it was only because she wanted it that way and not because he was the dominant one. Pezhman felt that even her submissiveness was domination now, and he got the feeling that he was there only to serve her and fulfil her desires. He tried to ignore the feeling by telling himself that it was just her new-found sexual energy that led to this. But he felt more and more emasculated by her as the days passed. Still, he was glad that she wanted him all the time. It was a sign of his virility and high libido that she was so lascivious.

But days passed and her sex drive grew steadily. Eventually, Pezhman began to lose interest in sex because of her ways; it was no longer enjoyable and always felt forced. Her insatiable lust had sucked out his energy completely. And he was aware that she was no longer in his control. Because of this, he began to grow suspicious of her. A libidinous woman as Gazhbiya was sure to take more lovers if he did not satisfy her.

Then one night after work when he was walking

up towards his building, he saw a man exit the gate and slink away into the shadows. Immediately alert, he strode forward. Who would leave the building at this hour? He ran up the steps to his room and burst in.

Nothing seemed amiss however. Gazhbiya lay in the same spot where he left her in the morning. Maybe the man had come from someone else's house. He relaxed at the thought and immediately felt guilty. Why did he even suspect his beloved Gazhbiya? It was not good to mistrust her.

But the same thing happened again the following week. And then it became more frequent. He would regularly see men emerge from his building and escape into the night before he could chase them. When he would rush upstairs to check on Gazhbiya, he could sense that someone had been there with her before him. But, of course, he had no proof.

It wasn't too long before his suspicions inflated. And he realised she had not one but many lovers.

Mad, hot, frothing jealousy bubbled in his chest. He fought with himself. Should he confront her? Was she really betraying him? He decided he would reign in the fury. He would wait and watch. It wouldn't be too difficult to find out who these lovers were. And then he would finish them off, one by one.

Before he could lay a plan to catch Gazhbiya red-handed, he walked in on her one night locked in embrace with a man. They were naked, and fornicating roughly. He stood frozen in shock. In their haste, they had not even bothered to lock the door. When he entered, they stayed entwined, panting like dogs in heat, unable to disengage.

Finding his voice, Pezhman uttered a howl and flung himself on them. The man jumped up and began tackling him. But Pezhman had a tight grip on his throat. He clutched hard and tightened his hold further. The man's eyes began to pop and his face went purple. The vein in his forehead was bulging.

Just then something hit him on the head. Almost blinded with pain, he let go, tottering on the mattress, his hand clutching the back of his head as a thick, warm liquid oozed through his fingers onto his neck. Dazed, he turned to see Gazhbiya, still naked, standing over him. The hair that he had spun for her with so much love and tenderness was wild and tangled over her shoulders. She looked possessed. She was holding up the hurricane lantern with which she had struck him. It was dripping with his blood.

Drip, drip, drip.

Then he blanked out.

✦

Pezhman regained consciousness some hours later. Gazhbiya's lifeless form lay on the bed some feet from him. He scrambled up to see if she was alright. The wounds of the night before were etched on her skin. There were bruises and scratches. Her nipples were cut and raw.

He recoiled in disgust. The sight of her mangled, decaying body by daylight turned his stomach. He wanted to back away from it but didn't. The dark, matted hair was sticking to her face, and slowly, he removed it.

The painted white face with unseeing eyes seemed to leer at him. The mouth was red but the lips were misshapen now, and the smile grotesque. Pezhman scrambled up, staring down at the twisted face in horror. What by night had seemed beautiful was ugly by daylight. How had he been so blind? His hands began shaking. What had he done? She was rotting away right there in his room.

He would get rid of her that night, he decided.

✦

It was 3 a.m. in the morning. Not a soul was in sight. Pezhman dragged the body down the steps, through the street, towards his rickshaw that he had parked in the shadows in the nearest alley. Then he stowed it under the seat and pedaled towards the morgue he had brought her from.

It didn't take him long to climb through the same broken window and drag the body in with him. Once inside, he took it to the same corner at the end of the room, and laid it straight, perfectly aligned with the other bodies there.

With one last kiss on her hardened, lifeless lips, he turned to leave.

✦

The newspapers tried to solve the mystery of the dead body that had appeared mysteriously in the morgue after six months had passed since its disappearance. The staff could not explain how it had happened. What they found most disturbing about the case was that the body that had a severed head, now had a clay head in its place, and which had an uncanny likeness with the woman's face. Who had stolen the body, and why did they return it? And why was there a clay head on the corpse's neck? Who had taken pains to replicate the woman's face and attach it to her neck?

These questions died out in a week. Public memory is transient—it jumps from one subject to another. And there are always plenty of strange things happening in the city. Nobody talked about the prostitute named 'Cherry' anymore.

THE ATTARWALA OF GULABI GALI

'Strange scents used to hang around Abdul Ali Baccus's rickshaw.'

These are not my words—I was told so by a local in Ballimaran. According to the man, people who rode in Abdul Ali's rickshaw always said that there was a distinct scent around them at all times. It was different for everyone. It smelt of 'freshly mowed grass bleeding dew in monsoon' to some, to some it smelt like the 'raat ki rani blooming in late September'. It was a rather odd phenomenon and no one quite understood it.

Which was okay by me, and did not bother me at all. What I didn't understand was why these people became so soppy with their descriptions and ejaculated mellifluous poetry at the drop of a hat. To my South Delhi mind it was really quite distracting, apart from being pointless. There was absolutely no utility for such florid detailing, especially to a reporter such as myself who just wanted to write a little filler on the damned rickshawwalla for his magazine.

But I suppose these people in Old Delhi couldn't entirely be blamed for their roundabout ways. What a middle-aged woman told me in an interview was true: this part of the city was filled with too many things to pay attention to one. And so no one really thought too much about the scents, or Abdul Ali, until much later.

Still, I wonder how these people were so slow to catch on. How had no one even had one small, sneaking suspicion when all the strange things began happening? One would think that in such a close-knit space, anything abnormal would immediately be linked to Baccus who was known for having a mysterious past. But none of the foggies I talked to had bothered to conduct any investigations. And funnily, no one even speculated about Abdul Ali Baccus and his scented rickshaw even though it struck them as strange and uncanny may times.

But of course, no one did anything constructive around here. That was why there was perpetual pandemonium in this place. If people had just been a little vigilant—which they clearly are about the most insignificant and utterly random issues—I wouldn't have been removed from the story I was working on to work on this absurd and irrelevant piece of urban legend. No, not legend. Scuttlebutt. Urban scuttlebutt. All so I could write a cock and bull story about a crazy old perfumer-turned-rickshawwalla. After all, as my half-witted editor told me in the most solemn tone, it was my business to 'unravel the curious tale of the Baccus family', or I could lose favour with the committee that was going to decide my promotion. The latter sentence he didn't have to say aloud. I deduced it from his nasty condescension. Obviously then, I had to swallow my pride, hold in my sarcasm, and whip up a juicy and sinister story, with the appropriate amounts of suspense to qualify it as a third grade thriller, because *that* was what the pompous fools in my office liked.

After much whining and moping, I began making rounds of the formerly glorious (but now odious) Walled City, trying to find a scoop on the blasted attar shop in question. Unfortunately, the archives had no records on it, and I had to plunge directly into the despicable, superstitious, and disgustingly prejudiced masses that populated the area, interviewing them, which meant jogging their godawful memories to make sense of their warped accounts which were far too tainted with speculation and imagination for my liking.

Not that I was complaining because of the work. But doing research on rumours and hearsay was simply not to my taste and in fact, turned my stomach. I would have liked to believe that I was meant for higher things—like covering the present situation in Palestine. But all my youthful ideals were being systematically dashed to the ground, and so mercilessly at that, that even though I had always known they were misplaced, I was left feeling rather Sisyphean. When the case had come up in my office, I was already knee deep in another story, but the editor had pulled me out (by the balls I would say) and shoved me into this.

Sometimes I feel that a reporter's work is the worst form of labour in the modern capitalist society. There is hardly any appreciation, and then there is a whole lot of nonsense to deal with. For instance today, I was told in sombre tones by the locals, after roaming the streets in the damned heat of July for hours, that when they rode in Baccus's rickshaw, they had an odd feeling that they were being made to 'feel something deep within them'—something they had not thought about for very long—and that the scent around them titillated repressed feelings just enough to startle them with some old memory—though not enough for them to trace or understand it, but enough to befuddle them with hazy images of the past.

My ears bled listening to such preposterous hogwash. Still, I went home and began working on the story, enslaved as I was by the magazine that paid me a salary (meagre as it was).

After much struggle, I wrote:

> The people of Chandni Chowk say that Abdul Ali Baccus was a man who had suffered much. He was a benign old man and there was a serene dignity about him which people respected. Every day when he went and stationed his rickshaw at a spot near the metro station, the other men made way for him and let him take his spot as usual. The locals did not trouble him or quarrel with him, and the police left him alone. It was a small locality after all, and people were empathetic. They remembered the tragedy of the Baccus family, and Abdul who had once been the famous attarwala of Purani Dilli…

✦

Several years ago, there was a perfume shop at the corner of Gulabi Gali which was known by the name of 'Nazreen'.

It belonged to Abdul's grandfather, Mir Baccus, who had acquired fame over the years as the most consummate perfume-maker in Delhi. The shop was small, dimly lit, with just enough space for someone to sit across from the maker and tell him what they wanted. The shelves lining the walls had rows and rows of small, differently shaped vials containing scents of varying shades. Light reflected on the crystal bottles, coruscating across the faces of the eager customers waiting for their mix of perfume to be prepared, and giving the shop a remarkable kind of iridescence despite the lack of lighting.

Basheer, Abdul's father, had taken over the family business of perfume-making in the year 1920. He was born in Hyderabad, and had moved to Delhi when his father decided to open an attar shop in Chandni Chowk after learning that business was good in the city. Earlier, they had a shop near Charminar. But competition was stiff there. The perfumeries around their shop had been established decades before his and had earned a reputation amongst the best patrons. Mir Mohammad found it difficult to keep up with the quality and fame of their mass manufactured perfumes that were made with raw materials brought in from France at that time. In 1899, after the holy month of Ramzan when they suffered grave losses, Mir Mohammad unstoppered each and every vial of attar in his shop and poured them in the drain outside. Then he told his wife that they were leaving for Shahajahanabad the next day. They were a family of seven then. They packed up their house and moved to a small house near Khari Baoli. A year later, Mir Mohammad had set up his shop in Gulabi Gali.

Yet, he did not earn the kind of money he had expected. Gulabi Gali was located in the inner interstices of Chandni Chowk, too far from the main market where big, flashy attar shops had already established their monopoly. There was little he could do to bring customers to his shop although he knew that the attar he sold was the best in the market—much more refined than the blends that the other shops produced. Still, he was new in the locality and had to struggle to create a clientele amongst the dispassionate crowds who remained unmoved by his rigorous touting.

That year, Mir Mohammad tried everything. He began peddling his wares on the street, went up to the main market where the everyday commerce took place, and finally, up to people's homes. Nothing worked though, and gradually, he was pushed to the brink of poverty.

Then tragedy struck. In the year, 1904, when the thirst for Swaraj was crashing over the nation, his wife Bilkis, and the youngest three of his five children, succumbed to Malaria.

But the worst was yet to come. In 1905, when news of the partition of Bengal hit them in shock waves, Mir Mohammad was counting the last annas before he would be driven to the local moneylender to feed his two surviving children. Basheer and Noor were teenagers then and aware of their father's sufferings. They tried to help him revive the business, but to no avail. Finally, they left everything up to Allah.

Then one day their moneylender came around to tell them they had to repay the debt immediately or lose the shop due to the mortgage.

Mir Mohammad stayed out very late that night. Basheer, in his mid-teens, got worried and was about to step out to search for him despite the protestations of his sister, when suddenly, he appeared at the door and without saying a word to them, went to sleep. Basheer was half-angry at him, but did not have the courage to say anything to his father.

The next day, there was a sudden change in him. What was it? Noor and Basheer were curious, but afraid of his temper, dared not say a word. Basheer was itching to ask him where he had been the night before, but didn't have the guts knowing his father could flare up at the slightest.

And then suddenly, there were buyers at their shop. Like bees to blooming flowers during the season of pollination, they kept coming, seeking the scents that their father mixed for them. Noor and Basheer were baffled but ecstatic. Within a month the customers grew to such a number that when they closed the shop to go home, they came to their house making requests. Theirs was a small house at the end of the street. Suddenly, the secluded area where only residents ventured, began to be visited by outsiders from all parts of Purani Dilli. Gradually, as Mir Mohammad's reputation grew, people from other parts of Delhi began arriving as well. Basheer and Noor, welcomed the sudden spurt in business and caught on beautifully, helping their father with ease and expertise.

And so, in the midst of political turmoil, the bottles of attar in their shop that had earlier begun to gather dust, were emptied and refilled with steady alacrity.

Mir Mohammad soon became the most sought-after perfumer in town. It was common knowledge that no other attarwala had the talent of Mir Mohammad Baccus. He created perfumes according to the need of each individual, different for everyone, while the other perfume traders, old and established as they were, brought in raw materials from different parts of the country, and manufactured barrels and barrels of perfume of the same kind. But in Mir's entire career, no two perfumes he had made had ever been alike. Each had distinctiveness like their possessors did. And it was impossible for anyone but him to replicate the scent. Requests for specially blended perfumes flowed in, in letters addressed to the 'Attarwala of Gulabi Gali'. The demands were often very strange. But Mir Mohammad never disappointed a soul. He was gifted with the perceptiveness of a clairvoyant and the sagacity of a savant. He was known to mingle scents with the precision of an apothecary. He could give you scented concoctions that would bring you what you coveted. People said that he could make a scent out of anything, and for anything.

Soon Nazreen's distillations became so well known that people came from as far as Bombay and Calcutta to ask for his scents. Sometimes, in the wee hours of the morning when the locals were asleep in their houses and there were no prying eyes, sahibs and memsahibs came on rickshaws, veiled under large hats and parasols, to meet Mir Mohammad, and purchase his special attar. Late after midnight when no one was likely to be roused by the low whirring of Royce engines, Maharajas and their ranis came in their sterling Silver Ghosts, parking discreetly in the dark gullies, and vanishing in the quarters of Mir Mohammad, who now took in royal visitors at all times of the day out of security concerns. He hadn't relinquished the old house despite having earned enough riches to buy an entire lane in the main market. But his visitors, royalty or politically connected, were humble in the face of his artistry. After all, the rich and the powerful always had unfulfilled desires. And Mir Mohammad's perfumes gave them what they wanted.

For many years, Nazreen thrived on the dreams and desires of such perfume-seekers. It had become known amongst people as the key to fulfilment.

When it was time for Basheer to take over, he rose to the moment with confidence. But times were different. One night, when he was returning home after spending the day with his friends, he saw a group of men passing by on the street with banners and placards, chanting slogans at the bystanders. The Muslim League had been formed.

Basheer sensed change in the air. He went straight home to find his sister alone, trying to adjust the radio channel for news. They did not know what to expect now that such a thing had happened. 'What would Abbu say?' he wondered out loud, his heart thumping with a strange sense of anticipation.

That night Mir Mohammad returned home late for the second time in his life. This time he did not go straight to his room without speaking to them. Standing before them in his crisp white kurta and chooridar that stretched over his still taut chest, he declared in a full voice that he was going to join the party.

✦

Delhi was now the capital of India. Mir Mohammad's involvement in politics grew quickly, and it became imperative for him to devote time to his party rather than handle his trade. Soon, he began staying away for extended periods of time. Trips to Karachi and Lucknow became an ordinary affair. Due to this, the attar-making business slackened considerably.

The first World War brought further losses as it meant an end to Mir Mohammad's exports to Europe. But Basheer, now a strapping young man of twenty-four, stepped up and asked for the reins of the business. His sister was now married and settled in Lahore. And he was the lone heir to the shop in Gulabi Gali.

Mir Mohammad, now completely taken up with his dealings with political leaders, was glad to see his son take charge. Basheer sold the attar sensibly, and displayed keen business acumen. Mir Mohammad was proud and satisfied. But when one April morning, news of a massacre at Jallianwala reached them, he knew it was finally time to pass on his knowledge of attar-making to his son. Faint voices demanding a separate nation for Muslims could also be heard and he wanted his son to become financially independent and secure.

✦

Amongst the many clandestine activities of Mir Mohammad, the most enduring one was his love for Begum Nazreen Farhat of Katra Neel. One December night, long before he had held any affiliations with the Muslim League and was merely an attarwala, a burkha-clad woman had stepped into his shop to purchase his perfume. She was clearly a wealthy woman and had come with a train of attendants. Since the shop was extremely small, she had told her maids to wait outside, and had herself sat on the cushion before him, tinkling with bangles and anklets. She was wearing a niqab over her eyes, and all Mir Mohammad could see through the mesh was that her eyes were lighter than brown—almost golden—kind of like the quartz ring on his finger.

Once behind the voluminous screens that he kept in his shop to give his customers privacy as they made their demands, she lifted her veil over her head and told him plainly and clearly that she wanted an attar to increase sexual desire in her husband towards her.

Mir Mohammad would have prepared the scent for her. But the small shop was already filled with a scent: of Begum Nazreen's porcelain white skin. For several moments, he sat mesmerised by it, unable to speak or move. Finally recovering, he got up and went into the storeroom to make the blend of attar as she desired.

Since then, Begum Nazreen began coming to him every fortnight for refilling her vial of attar. Both of them knew it was possible for him to give her a bigger vial, but neither pointed it out. It seemed like both enjoyed their brief encounters, strictly commercial as they were.

Before this, Mir Mohammad had never judged his customers. But for once he couldn't understand why a beautiful woman as her needed anything other than herself to arouse a man. Her face was round as the moon and lips small and full. Her eyes were lined with soorma and seemed most alluring. Her cheeks were flushed, perhaps from the embarrassment of asking for the kind of attar she needed, or perhaps because Mir Mohammad's eyes were always fixed upon her with open appreciation. But it quickly became evident that the attar that he gave her had no effect on her husband, because each time she came, she requested him to make it stronger.

After several months of Begum Nazreen trying inexhaustibly to seduce her husband, she stepped into his shop one evening, just before sunset, and raised her niqab once again. The strong scent of his own kama attar, mingled with the delicious scent of her skin, permeated his senses, and Mir Mohammad realised at that moment what she truly wanted.

He later told her that it wasn't the attar that had made him possess her, but her own raw scent.

Mir Mohammad kept his association with Begum Nazreen a secret from the world, and his own family, for several years. He was mindful of her reputation and did not want to jeopardise her position in society. Besides, he did not desire her in the ordinary sense. Neither did he expect her to reciprocate in the conventional manner. He was merely in love with the scent of her skin. And all he wanted was to be able to have it around him always.

✦

As political unrest grew around them, debts began piling up. Basheer had begun to despair about the business as his father became more disinterested in the shop due to his party commitments. It reached a point where he felt compelled to ask him for permission to sell the shop. It was then that Mir Mohammad told him about the pir he used to visit outside Sunehri Masjid every Sunday, who had given him the secret to making magical perfumes.

The pir was a blind old man who had once come to his shop to ask for money many years ago. Mir Mohammad had been kind to him and had given him a full meal apart from money. The pir, sick and exhausted, and on the brink of death, promised to reward his generosity someday. Mir Mohammad remembered this and went to him when he began suffering losses. The pir, indebted to him for his life, granted him the wish. And since then he could trap the scent of anything he wanted and bottle it up in a phial.

Jubilant, he began by trapping the scent of his wife, and called it 'Aruba'. Then he captured the scent of earth, the street on which he lived, and his house. Finally, he began trapping the scents of people around him. Soon, women began coming to him to trap their dying husband's scent. Young men came to ask for the scent of their mistresses. Young women, who were getting married, came to ask for the scent of the homes they were leaving behind. Some came seeking the scents of the lovers who had jilted them, and some came to get scents that would make them love the partner they never wanted.

Slowly, Mir Mohammad learned the art of making scents for other purposes too—to attract luck, to trap love, to seduce, to repel, to hypnotise, to remember, to forget. He knew how to mix a perfume for everything.

Basheer, astounded by his father's fantastic tale, soaked

in the knowledge like skin soaked in attar. Already, the image of himself as the best perfumer in the world flashed before his eyes. He would do his father proud.

But that was not to be. Mir Mohammad was martyred in the Non-Cooperation Movement soon after Basheer took charge of the business. But he did not despair this time. He renamed the shop 'Nazreen ke Attar'—according to his father's will—and permanently took the place behind the counter in their shop in Gulabi Gali.

Basheer had a long and fulfilling career. His only failure was his son, Abdul Ali Baccus.

Abdul Baccus gained the knowledge of distilling perfumes from his father when he was merely fifteen. He showed great promise in the beginning, but it soon became clear that he could do nothing without Basheer. As years went by and the market changed, he found it difficult to keep business up in the face of globalisation when locally blended perfumes went steadily out of fashion and international brands became accessible. The shops in the main market were selling exotic sounding perfumes in stylish bottles. They were called 'Titanic Love', 'Mussoorie's Memsahib', 'Retro Rani', 'Princess' and so on.

As more time passed, Nazreen attars lost their charm. Abdul's afeem consumption worsened the situation. After several years of addiction, he began to forget the wisdom of his forefathers. He could no longer remember which plant had to be mixed with which flower to produce what effect. His shaking hands, reddened eyes, and perennially intoxicated state turned many of his remaining customers away, until finally one winter after the death of his father, he was forced to shut down the shop that had not closed for a single day in the past one hundred years.

✦

After losing all his fortunes to crack, Abdul Ali had moved ahead in life and taken up rickshaw pulling to make a living and survive in the city. The glorious days of attar-making had ended a long time ago, and he had realised that there was no use being tormented about the lost glories of the Baccus family. He was a man of little needs and all he needed was his usual ganja and the occasional crack when he had the money.

The only string to the past that he held onto was the family house. After nearly a hundred years, when it didn't seem like time would ever ravage it, the house was beginning to disintegrate. Mossy patches and long-running cracks held testimony to the era gone by. The broken down furniture inside gave indications of once abundant resources that had now perished, disallowing maintenance or refurbishment.

And yet, Abdul did not sell it. The other rickshawwallas gossiped behind his back about the apparent luxury he lived in, and often made snide remarks about his misplaced nostalgia, because he was a rickshawwalla living in a rich man's house. His poverty to them seemed comical. It was unlike theirs which had the depth of poignancy.

Then one day, because of all the construction around the old house, due to the opening of a cafeteria in a haveli next door, one of the walls at the back crumpled causing one side of the house to tilt in above his head like an ark in the ocean. It was quite a miracle that the rest of the house did not give way because of the sudden shift in weight when all the pillars on one side collapsed. None of the people around heard the crash and it seemed like the walls had powdered soundlessly. When Abdul Baccus woke up in the morning, he was in full view of the rising sun behind monsoon clouds.

But he was flowing in cocaine-induced dreams. Through half-opened eyes, he saw the sky glowing divinely, and believing he was dreaming of jannat, fell asleep again.

But he could not escape reality for too long. There was a march of MCD officers following the mishap. They came with their notebooks and pens and cameras, and endless measuring tapes. They flashed their torches around, shouted orders at each other, and crunched the debris under their tireless rubber boots. Their helmets gleamed in the light, escaping through the gaping hole in the roof. In the part light, their eyes looked glazed, as though they were devoid of humanity. And under their work jackets and protective gears, their hearts were steeled, like the equipment they brandished at the century old possessions of the Baccus household.

The house was declared a 'dangerous property'.

One of the kindlier officers came and spoke to Abdul Baccus sympathetically: 'Abdul Miya, I regret this. But these walls would have collapsed over you next.'

Helplessly, Abdul Baccus watched the ancient house, already falling to pieces, being slowly and meticulously taken apart. Goaded by this injustice, and guilty of forfeiting his forefather's business as well as the house, he at that moment vowed to unleash misery upon the people around him who had brought this about.

But there was only one thing he knew and could do, old and wizened as he was—make an attar for his revenge.

✦

There was bedlam in the neighbourhood.

It began slowly: a man returned home to find his wife on top of another man. He strangled the naked man, even as his wife pleaded with him on her knees in front of the all-seeing neighbourhood.

Then a woman found her husband fornicating with their neighbour's wife. She pulled the woman off by the hair, and after a brief tussle, flung her over the balcony onto the street below, killing her instantly.

Next, two couples were caught exchanging their spouses. They were doing so on the terrace of one of their houses. A bunch of boys who were hanging out on the neighbouring terrace caught it on camera and released it as an MMS, much to the consternation of the bourgeois populace that promptly ostracised the couples.

Soon, more people were caught committing adultery. Men and women, who were strangers, began to get together and copulated like dogs in heat. Middle-aged men who were perfectly respectable and moral, went around sporting huge erections, chasing after young, nubile girls returning from school. Aged men who had given up carnality, began to harass women on the streets. Adolescent boys who were in the process of being socialised, and had formerly been strictly surveilled by their parents, were running amok in the streets chasing after girls who were all too willing to sleep with them now that their parents themselves were engaging in debaucheries of their own. Even women who had always been chaste and virtuous, began calling in men in the absence of their fathers or husbands, and made love freely to whoever came. In case of pregnancies, it became impossible to determine whose children the women were bearing.

Such unbridled carnality in a conservative place was bound to cause mayhem. There were scuffles, beatings, murders, lynchings every other day. Men were beating up men who had slept with their wives, or the wives who had cuckolded them. Women who had been cheated on were going through the streets narrating tales of their husband's adultery. Some began hounding after the women who had seduced their husbands. One woman cut of her husband's genitals in anger.

The age old morality that had ensured a smooth social existence had suddenly disappeared. When asked why this was happening, the adulterous couples said they had confused the 'smell' of their partners, and that the people they had been with had smelt like their spouses. They said that the scent had not only confused them into believing that it was indeed their partner, but had also somehow hypnotised them into having sex…they also said that they had felt an acute desire to make love—a kind of desire they had never felt before. It was all too mysterious.

The people, bewildered at first, soon began suspecting the rickshawwalla who had once been the attarwala of Gulabi Gali, and whose father, they remembered, could make the most potent aphrodisiacs as scents. At the time it was even said that his grandfather had made a pact with the devil and could trap the scent of human beings, stripping them of their essence.

What would a neighbourhood, on the brink of anarchy, do in such a case?

A man-hunt ensued for Abdul Ali Baccus. Men and women with flaming torches and metal rods marched through the chowk in the wee hours of one morning in December when the whole city was shrouded in fog. Blood-thirsty cries of anger and revenge rented the skies, waking up dogs on the streets, and rousing those who were in bed, still unsuspecting of the evil-doings of the attarwala.

Slowly the crowd winded along the lanes of Gulabi Gali. They knew it was the dilapidated house that was located at the far end of the street. They uncoiled towards it, like a serpent of fire, hungry for the flesh of the man who had traded with the Shaitan…

✦

I stood under the tree that had grown in the debris of the house belonging to the Baccus family, smoking and sipping tea. It was 3 p.m. and the day was miserably sultry. I was soaked with sweat. But, at least, I had gathered enough information to wind up the story.

It had already been a week of a crazy, wild goose chase, and I was exhausted. As I stood there soaking in the details of the neighbourhood, and the house before me, I felt that the Baccus Haveli looked absolutely like any other decrepit, semi-demolished house of Chandni Chowk, but for the large tree growing in the middle, and which the locals said (much to my incredulity again), had cropped up within a week of Abdul Ali Baccus's disappearance.

Apparently, the night when the mobs had landed in front of the house with the intention of setting fire to it, they were assaulted by a strong scent (which not surprisingly, none of them could describe coherently). Silence had fallen over them immediately, and their raised torches, flaming with the kerosene that they had dipped it in, began to fizzle out in the gentle morning draughts. Eventually, one by one the men and women turned away and made their way slowly back to their homes.

The onlookers who were peeking from their windows said that they had looked as though they were possessed. Or perhaps hypnotised? They couldn't quite tell. A thick layer of fog had wrapped itself around them, obscuring their vision. And there was a faint scent in the air...

No one quite knows what really happened that day. All I was told was that the scent had hung over the neighbourhood for a week. And when it dissipated, Abdul Ali Baccus had disappeared from Gulabi Gali. The mystery was never solved.

That was the resolution of the story. My rational mind churned it over and over again to make sense of it and create a decent story, but there was too much of hocus-pocus in its core that no matter how hard I tried and how deep I dug, I couldn't bring together a logical explanation.

And so I decided to give credit to hearsay and end the damned fool's errand.

Of course, my editor was more than happy to print

the god-awful canard. I even got a promotion soon after (which I really hoped was not entirely because of the story on that Abdul chap, although I knew it was partly because of it—I realised I could write shitty whodunnits well!).

But what I couldn't understand was why there was always a lingering scent around me now. It followed me everywhere. The scent of what seemed like…freshly mowed grass bleeding dew in monsoon someday…or raat ki rani blooming in late September…It was really quite peculiar.

PANDOOBI

The horizon turned golden as dawn approached, and the subtle rays of the morning sun leaked through the clouds. Gokul paused from his work and scanned the eastern skyline for signs of rain, his coarse fishnet in hand.

As it brightened, he could hear the slow strain of voices carrying over the water to him from the banks. The fishermen woke before daybreak, while it still looked like night time and the water was as inky as the sky, and began their day's work. Sometimes before work, the nets had to be stitched; sometimes the boats had to be fixed if the aluminium was giving way or the wood was rotting. They did not have time to eat before the early morning catch. They had to cast their nets before the city awakened.

Gokul flung the net wide over the surface of the water and watched it sink. The Kalindi Kunj stretch of the Yamuna was unpredictable. On some days, the nets would be full, writhing in the boat, glinting like a sack of silver coins in the afternoon sun. But on some days they would have to go beyond the Badarpur border to catch even a few kgs to bring back to their contractor. The past few years had been difficult because of the poor fish variety in the Yamuna. The river was dying. It was once bounteous—the fisherman's Amrapali—but it no longer obliged them. The water was getting filthier by the day and people didn't want to eat as much fish as before. The fishermen families that had moved to Delhi from Bihar and Bengal had begun returning, and the ones who had stayed behind could hardly make ends meet.

Gokul was amongst the few who had refused to go back to Murshidabad, his place of birth. He had lived in the city for nearly fifteen years, and even if there was barely anything to call home, the city was familiar, and the river where he fished, like a mistress he kept going back to simply because it felt comforting to be engulfed by it. His wife, Sharada, worked as a maid in people's homes, and if work was good, earned about ten thousand rupees every month. She refused to give it up and move back with him. His twin brother, Mukul, who was a rickshawwalla, as he had been initially, also lived in the city, in Patparganj. He seemed to be doing well and lent him money whenever he needed, especially after Sharada took their sons and began living with her sister in Janakpuri, where she worked.

Without wife and children, Gokul had become something of a nomad, living in makeshift tents as the water receded after August.

Last year when it was a particularly bad season, Mukul had suggested he start rickshaw pulling again. But his heart was in fishing and he wasn't prepared to give it up yet. They had been jeledera for generations. He couldn't be a rickshawwalla navigating roads when he could be in a boat, rowing, swimming, casting nets as he had seen his forefathers do for generations.

He stood still for a moment, letting the morning air permeate his skin. He always woke up while it was still dark like night. It gave him satisfaction to observe the river, peaceful as it was at that hour. Before the city sounds rose around him, the river's serenity was all-permeating. The slow churning river touched him deeply, as it sang to him its own melancholic song flowing through eternity.

It was only in such moments that he truly felt connected to his surroundings—as if he could communicate with the land and the water in the rolling silence. It was only during such moments that his senses were at their sharpest, and he could feel the life underneath, swimming in the waters, as his boat bobbed along.

Gokul closed his eyes and breathed. It was only then that he could truly feel the river.

A fisherman called out to his mates, breaking his reverie. He turned to look towards the bank again. The men were beginning to get into their boats. But it would take them time to reach where he was.

He took a deep breath and dived into the water, still gripping one end of the net. There was time for one last catch.

✦

Gokul sat on the banks of the river, watching the rain make millions of little dents on the surface of the river. It was one of those evenings when the sky was pale yellow and everything looked like it was being viewed through yellow cellophane.

The riverbank was empty. People had taken shelter inside their makeshift houses, and he could see men struggling with the tents, trying to keep them upright in the sluggish ground as the winds lashed against them, threatening to tear the plastic away. Gokul looked towards the river again. He could see fish jumping out in the middle of the river as the water churned aggressively. If he went in now he was sure to get a good catch.

But the current was too strong. The wind kept changing direction as it slapped against him this way and that. He edged closer to the water. It was frothing up as it swirled by, licking his feet. He was tempted to go in. He had his smallest fishing net and there was no one around. No one would notice if he was gone for an hour or two.

He twisted one end of the net around his waist and began fumbling with his lungi. The silvery gills of a fish that jumped up from the water close to where he stood caught his eye. He was about to step forward when someone called out from behind.

It was Kishor Haldar. He was walking on the dirt track towards where he was. Gokul hastily tucked back his lungi and turned towards him. His heart thudded in his chest for some reason. What was he doing out in the rain? He had almost not heard him over the thunder.

'Kishor Da, what are you doing here?' He tugged his fishnet, pretending to adjust it.

'I can ask the same,' he replied. 'Why are you out in

the rain? And why are you standing so close to the edge? Do you want to get swallowed by the river? Come away quickly.'

Kishor Haldar was only about ten years older to him, but always acted like his father. He was from Kakdweep, and had come to Delhi some years ago. He was a quiet man, a widower, and Gokul had enjoyed his company on many a sleepless nights in the past year. He had even taught him to play cards, and they often wiled away dry summer nights playing bridge when the heat, hunger and mosquitoes kept them awake.

'Ye-yes,' Gokul stammered, and stepped back from the waters, treading carefully on the slippery ground. There was no way he would be able to get rid of Kishor da now.

The rain suddenly slowed, and the noise fell, as though someone had turned down the volume. As they turned to walk towards the settlement, the sun came out. The scales of rui frolicking in the waters were pearlescent in the yellow glaze. Gokul sighed to himself. It could have been a good day.

✦

The rains did not stop that day. After Gokul came away from the bank, the fishermen decided to go to the river after all and try to catch fish for their evening meal. Their contractor was absent but his helpers were there, inside Kishor Da's tent, not wanting to get drenched in the rain.

'Don't get in the water, brothers,' Gokul warned them. 'The current is stronger than ever today. It is risky.'

But the men did not listen. Their stomachs were

empty and their hearts yearned for the katla and ilish of their dreams. They gathered around near the bank and loosened their boats. Fishnets in hand, they began to row out, struggling to keep balance in the choppiness.

Gokul's chest heaved. He knew the waters were being mischievous. He could feel their glee as they tugged the boats and made the men topple. Gokul breathed heavily and closed his eyes. He could feel the mirth of the water increase as the men struggled. They were shouting out to each other.

'Let's go back! It's too strong. Let's go back!'

'Pull! Pull! Pull!'

He could hear the laughter of the river as it cascaded towards the next dam. But would the dam be able to restrain it? Gokul looked in the direction from where the river was flowing. Surely, it seemed thickened more than he had ever seen in the past many years. Had they opened up dams upstream…?

Just then there was a loud cry. One of the five men had fallen into the river. His head appeared once or twice above the surface then disappeared.

Without thinking, Gokul jumped in.

✦

The water was biting cold. For a while, Gokul could see nothing but murky greyness. The current was strong and he struggled to steady himself. But the river tossed him around. He could barely get a sense of direction.

Then he felt the body. The man was near him, he could feel his human heartbeat pulsating towards him—rhythmic, but fading. Gokul closed his eyes and swam towards him. The current remained strong but he had his balance now. He swam towards the man, unable to see him yet but feeling his ebbing heartbeat. Above them, the boats were shifting. They seemed to be going back towards the riverbank.

Gokul looked around. He saw the dark form of the man, clinging to the net of the boat he had fallen out of. He swam closer. The man was unconscious but the net had entangled him, preventing him from flowing away. But it also kept him from resurfacing. Gokul tugged the net to release him, but the current made the net twist out of control and entwine the man further.

With a heave, Gokul clutched the man with one arm and with the other, pushed away the net. It came loose all of a sudden. The man who was holding it had let it go.

Gokul pushed off against the current, and began swimming towards the bank. The man was dead, and his body was getting heavier as water filled in it. Gokul strained as he swam, trying to maintain his grip.

The fishnet kept coiling in the current threatening to ensnare him, then flowed away.

✦

The fishermen community in Delhi was not as close-knit as they were in Diamond Harbour where Gokul spent all his wakeful days in childhood with Mukul, helping their parents sell fish all day. But they were superstitious and never forgot strange incidents. Gokul had been seen swimming underwater for a good ten to fifteen minutes before he surfaced with the body of the drowned man. When he came up and swam towards the bank, he could already see the looks of shock and disbelief on the people's faces. Two of the men came forward and pulled up the body, but were looking at him oddly.

Later, he tried to tell them he had come up for air several times. But they were not to be fooled. 'We saw you go underwater. At that time the boats were still there. It was several minutes after all the three boats had returned to the bank. You came up when we had already reached the bank…'

'Don't be mad, brother. How is that even possible?'

'We saw it with our own eyes. You were underwater longer than any man has been known to!'

'That is absurd, brother,' Gokul tried to shrug it off nonchalantly. 'It was raining. You probably did not notice.'

'I saw it with my own eyes,' Ghanshyam Kumar said, coming forward, his broad shoulder spanned out as he spoke. 'Don't try to fool us.'

Gokul narrowed his eyes. He had once got in a fight with Ghanshyam when he noticed that his wife was making eyes at him. Later, he had accused him of seducing her. Gokul wanted to laugh at this. Little did anyone know that he was in love with Mariam. 'Fool you?' he said, feigning outrage. 'What would I get out of fooling you? You men should be grateful to me for risking my life and bringing back the body. You had abandoned him!'

'No one can change the force of destiny, my son,' Mirza Khalid said. He was an old fisherman who had come from Dhaka nearly fifty years ago. Everyone called him 'Mirza

Miya'. 'Rahul was a foolhardy boy. But his death was willed by Allah,' he said. 'And no one can stop the will of the Almighty. But Gokul, you must tell us the truth about yourself. What nefarious magic taught you to swim underwater longer than any land creature?'

'Miya, these men are mistaken. I did no such thing.'

'He is lying,' Ghanshyam spat. 'I saw it with my own eyes. And my eyes never deceive!'

Gokul sighed in exasperation. Luckily, the other fishermen knew about Ghanshyam's grouse against him and the attention shifted to their personal conflict. A scandal was much more interesting. Besides, the dead man had to be taken to his family. They stood there staring at the body, wondering what to do. The rain was subsidising, as though satiated after claiming a life. The river seemed unchanged.

✦

The rain grew heavier in the next few days. The banks had turned soft and dangerous, and the fishermen were forced to move to thicker lands. Dams had also been opened up, and the flow of the river seemed more than the week before.

Gokul went and sat at his usual spot on the bank and watched the water swirl. The usual stench wasn't there but he could see debris and waste being carried by the river. In the corners, there was the usual muck between rocks. He saw a used condom lying at his feet and moved away in disgust.

The river had changed so much over the past few years. He wasn't sure how long he would be able to eke a living this way. There were too many fishermen too few fish.

Gokul rose, his eyes still on the waters. It had begun drizzling. The clouds were low and dark, and there were occasional rumbles. It was going to be a rough night.

'Gokul...'

He turned to see Mariam standing a few feet away from him. She had wrapped a black cloth around herself but her bare knees were visible.

'Mariam, why did you come before dusk?' He turned to look in the direction of the tents. He could see people walking about still.

'I couldn't stand to see you sitting here alone looked so morose,' she said tenderly.

'Go back. I'm fine. I will see you after sun-down.'

But the sun was already ebbing. The orb was dull red when it finally dipped into the building-studded horizon. Then in the semi-darkness, he turned to Mariam and undressed her. Before them, the river gushed ahead on its course. The swirling water always kept their secret.

✦

Ghanshyam had been keeping a close eye on Gokul. He knew about his adulterous affair with Aminuddin's young wife, Mariam, but that wasn't what he was after. He did not care for such trivialities. He wanted to discover Gokul's secret to swimming underwater unlike any man. He was certain that it had something to do with his generous catch every day. No other fisherman managed to catch as many fish as he did.

One day, he hid behind Gokul's tent and followed him when he woke up at 4 a.m. while everybody slept. He saw him walk towards the river, his net in hand.

It was an overcast night but the lights from the nearby factory shone upon the spot where Gokul stood and undressed. A few moments later, there was a low splash. Ghanshyam came out from where he stood and gazed into the inky darkness. Just then the clouds moved and the river was illumined. Ghanshyam scanned the surface to see when Gokul resurfaced for air.

Nearly half an hour passed when he finally came up. The net in his hand was full and moving. A fish escaped from the pile and flapped about on the river bank. The ilish would fetch him more money than anybody managed even on the best days.

Ghanshyam lay still in the cluster of brambles as Gokul passed by and went back to his tent. His heart burnt with envy.

✦

At first, nobody had believed Ghanshyam. They laughed off his story and called him a jealous and resentful man, thinking he was trying to pester Gokul as he always did. Then one day Ghanshyam decided to prove his words. He convinced four other fishermen, Ravi, Sompal, Lakhan, and Sonu, to help him, in exchange for a hundred rupees each. That night, Ghanshyam snuck inside Gokul's tent and drugged him. Then he and the rest of them dragged him to the river. They tied him in a net, and rowed to the middle of the river. The current was slow, and they didn't have trouble throwing him into the water, unconscious as he was.

'Let us start with five minutes,' Ghanshyam said.

They pulled him up five minutes later. He was breathing.

'Throw him again,' Ghanshyam growled.

They lowered him again. After a full ten minutes, they pulled him out. He was still breathing. They lowered him again.

'Let's pull him out, brother,' Sompal said, after several minutes.

'Yes, let's pull him out. We don't want him dead!'

'No!' Ghanshyam's eyes blazed. He knew what he was doing. He had seen him swim underwater for nearly as long the other day. 'He won't die.'

After about half an hour, he told them to pull him up.

Gokul was still breathing.

✦

The weather improved for some days, but the rains began in the city once again. This time, it was coming down with a vengeance. There were warnings across the city for flooding, and they had already begun evacuating settlements along the river banks.

The murmurs about Gokul were increasing by the day. People were beginning to ask difficult questions, and he had no answers. Ghanshyam regularly beat him up if he refused to give him his cut of the fish from his catch. He no longer felt safe.

Then one night, as he lay in Mariam's arms, he thought of telling her his secret.

'Mariam, people are saying all sorts of things about me,' he began tentatively. 'But you never asked me a single question.'

'I want to know no more than what you tell me of your own accord.'

He looked up at her face illumined by the half-moon that had come out after several days. 'But do you not wonder if what they say is true?'

'I have wondered. But I know you are not…you are not…'

'A Monster? Evil?' he laughed.

Mariam was embarrassed. 'No, I meant…'

He took her hand and kissed it. 'I know what you meant, my darling. You are too sweet.'

She smiled and was silent for a moment. The trees around them whooshed in the wind as if shushing them. They could hear the occasional honking of the midnight traffic from the nearby bridge.

'Gokul,' she said finally. 'Is it true?'

He turned towards her and propped himself up on his elbow. Lighting a bidi, he looked at her straight. Then he took her hand and touched it to the back of his ears.

There was a strange flap of flesh there. Mariam gasped and withdrew her hand. 'Is that…'

'Mariam, even my wife does not know. Only my twin, Mukul, and my dead mother.'

Clouds were beginning to gather above them again. A thunder clap echoed across the sky. Mariam raised her hand to touch it again.

'I was born like this,' Gokul began. 'My mother and father thought it was a birth defect and didn't pay much heed to it. Neither did I. Then one day, my mother had to take the boat and go fishing without our father. He was severely unwell and couldn't move a limb. She woke us up early in the morning and while we were still half-asleep, carried us to the river bank where they docked their boat. There was no one who could take care of us while she was fishing so she placed us inside the boat and rowed a little way along the Hooghly. They wanted to send dried fish to the markets in Uluberia that season. It was a good time for my parents after many years...'

'Go on...' she whispered.

'I don't remember clearly except that as I lay in the boat, I became increasingly agitated. Mother was busy casting the net and Mukul was asleep. But I was wide awake. It was my first time in the water, and I could feel the water churn under the boat...and something else. Something strange. I had never felt it before. It seemed like a presence...of several creatures. I later realised I could feel the life inside the waters. But in that moment, I was confused and scared. I reached out to hold mother's aanchal. That's when I lost balance and tipped over.'

Mariam gasped. 'Allah! You fell into the Hooghly?'

'They found me hours later, downstream. I just remember...I just remember images of underwater, and being carried along. Naturally, I did not tell anyone what I had discovered about myself. I was just ten...I was scared, and it took me some time to understand it...I told Ma and Mukul some years later.'

Mariam was exhaled and looked away. 'I can't believe it...'

'It is the truth.'

They turned to gaze into the river. It was murky and they could hardly see the water except when it glinted in the moonlight. But the river had sounds. It was loud and compelling.

'The river is angry, Mariam. That is the sound of an angry river.' He got up. 'Here,' he said, handing her the clothes. 'We should go now. I don't want you to get stuck in the rain.'

✦

It happened swiftly. The city was suddenly immersed in floods. The fishermen community where Gokul lived had to be relocated and they moved to ITO, into makeshift tents. He decided to go live with Mukul in Patparganj until the river receded and everything went back to normal.

But there was turmoil everywhere. In East Delhi, the river had risen almost to the point where it could roll down into the nearby residential areas. And the fish markets suffered because of lack of supplies.

Gokul did not see Mariam after that night. People said she and her husband had moved to Okhla for work. But Gokul knew Mariam wouldn't have left unless she really wanted to. She was obviously trying to escape him. He was a freak, a hideous monster. And no one except for his twin could stand to bear his reality. Even his own mother had spurned him.

That night Gokul decided to go for a swim. He stood on the bridge connecting East Delhi to the rest of the city and took a plunge. Perhaps he would even bring in a catch for the next day's meal. Mukul and his wife had been generous enough to let him stay for as long as he wanted. The least he could do was to find some katla for their dinner every day.

✦

Mukul was worried for his brother. Each day, he seemed to shrink in size, but not due to any physical ailment. It seemed it was to do with his lack of work. The floodplains around the river were submerged and several of the fishermen had to abandon their belongings and move to shelter tents in the middle of the city. There was a sudden deficit in the fish produce as it became hazardous to even get in the water. There were some reports of deaths in the past few weeks.

As the days passed, more and more fishermen families and farmers who had lands on the floodplains began living on the streets. There was no rehabilitation or management whatsoever. The traffic rolled around them each day as though they had always been there. Because of overcrowding and insanitary conditions, several of them were falling sick.

Mukul was grateful that Gokul had been cautious. He had moved into their house before the flood got worse. When he had turned up at his doorstep, he had simply said that the river had to be left alone for a while.

Of course, Gokul was bound to know when the river got angry. Hadn't he once before, in the Hooghly, many years ago? It was the time before their father died...before the nikari took away everything...before they turned manjhis for a while.

His mother was the only female manjhi at that time. But there was too much opposition in the community itself. Women talked behind her back. Then one day, Mukul spied on his mother cutting off her knee length hair. He clasped his hand on his mouth to keep from screaming but tears rolled down his cheeks. He stood in the dark and watched as she tied her breasts tightly and wrapped a shawl across the chest, transforming into a man.

They moved from Hooghly soon after. It was the year when the rains were coming down in little pellets of ice and fire. It was the year Gokul told them about his gift.

The day was clearly etched into his memory. It was night time when Gokul came to him and asked him to go to the pukur near their house.

'Bhayi, come with me. I want to show you something.'

Mukul had always been subservient to Gokul. He followed him to the pond without a word.

'Stay quiet and don't call for anybody.'

Puzzled, he watched as he dived in.

Gokul stayed underwater for several minutes. Mukul was beginning to panic when he came up, a live koi maach in his hand.

'Now watch me. But don't call anyone, alright? And don't worry because I can do this for much longer.'

Mukul was stunned at first. It seemed strangely terrible. But he was a child, and it thrilled him to discover this magical thing about his own twin brother.

'Adbhut! Tui toh jalpori'r moton jole thakte parish re!'

Gokul had shaken off the water from his hair and grinned.

'How long can you stay underwater?'

'About half an hour.'

'That is incredible…but so strange…can I do it?'

'I don't think so.'

'Why?' he sounded annoyed. 'We are twins. We are alike!'

'Do you have this?' he showed him the extra flesh under his ears.

Mukul touched his ear. The skin under it was smooth, unlike his brother's. 'So it is…and we thought it was a malformation…'

'Mukul, listen, you can't tell anyone.'

'What about Ma?'

'She will scold me.'

'No, she won't. She loves you.'

Gokul thought for a moment. 'I will tell her only if I find a big rui. I'll tell her I can catch fish for her every day. That way she will think it's a useful thing.'

But their mother was horrified. She grieved this unnaturalness in her son and cried all night clutching him to her bosom. The next morning she told them to keep it a secret from the rest of the world for all their lives.

And she forbade him to ever go in the water.

But it wasn't to be. Their mother died a few years later when Gokul and Mukul were still adolescents. Orphaned, they decided to escape to Delhi where they were sure they would find some job or the other. It was a big city after all. They could work at a dhaba or perhaps even a fancy restaurant. They could take their chances.

✦

The water levels were rising steadily and several neighbourhoods were submerged in knee-deep water. The city almost came to a standstill and no one knew what to do. Already, there had been a lot of damage because of the clogging. And it was getting worse by the day. Just a few days ago, seven men died while fixing the electrical line in Ashok Vihar as a live wire fell into the water instantly electrocuting everyone standing in the puddle. A similar thing happened in Okhla and Paharganj just days after that incident.

Gokul was tired of staying home. He was of no use to anyone and a burden on his brother. Secretly, he began to go to the river to catch fish. When Mukul and his wife found out, they tried to stop him. But Mukul knew that his brother knew the river well and wouldn't risk his life. Ultimately, he told Sudha to let him be and do as he wanted.

A month passed this way. The river was swollen, but the storm had driven away the good fish, and there were hardly enough for his net even though he swam around underwater for very long.

Then one day he saw a big fish. It was two feet long and incredibly thick. Probably an over-grown rui. This meant there would be more.

✦

There was chaos in the city. The water had reached the low lying regions around the river in East Delhi. Akshardham was submerged and the water was rolling into the roads in waves now. It would reach the low lying residential colonies around within a few days if the rain did not stop.

Then one day, while fishing, Gokul got swept along. The current was strong, and the rain made it worse. It was hard to remain buoyant. After some struggle, he gave in and went under, thinking he will resurface only when the rain lessened.

By the time he managed to come up, he had already crossed the Okhla barrage. But the current was still too strong. He felt the waves were like hands carrying him like a little child. It was a familiar feeling, being held by a river in that manner. So many years ago, he had felt the same in Hooghly. Before he knew it, he was lulled into sleep.

When he awakened, the rains had subsided. But the horizon remained clouded. He looked around and to his surprise, a pristine white dome-like structure loomed to his left. It was flanked on all four sides with tall minarets. The moon was luminescent and the structure glowed in the dark.

Gokul swam to the bank and lay there in the dark. It took him a while to realise he had reached Agra. He would go back the next day.

✦

Gokul returned late at night the next day to find the house locked up. He asked the neighbours but no one knew where Sudha was.

It was midnight when Sudha returned, her eyes swollen, her clothes dripping wet. Gokul had fallen asleep at the doorstep and she shrieked when she saw him. Then she realised it was him and began wailing again.

She told him Mukul had fallen into the river before her very eyes when they had gone looking for him, thinking he had gone to fish.

✦

Even in the chaos and confusion of the Delhi flood, the media reported the case of the "Pandoobi Aadmi"—the human submarine—who had been seen swimming back and forth in the river for the past few weeks. According to news reports, the man could breathe underwater, or at least, hold his breath underwater, for up to an hour.

A reporter, fresh out of college, decided to follow up on the case and managed to interview some fishermen who had known him before he disappeared. The reporter said that apparently, the man was infamous in his fishermen community for his dubious methods. They said that he had fled when they had begun to suspect him. They were sure that his ability to stay in water for so long was the result of some black magic. Or he was simply not human.

It later emerged that the man was looking for his twin brother's body in the river. Some fishermen who had encountered him had tried to talk him out of it, but he was in a kind of frenzy and did not seem to hear anyone.

Pandoobi Aadmi was in the news for a whole week. But it did not gain much prominence, and even the young reporter forgot about him.

✦

Gokul sat on the ghat near Wazirabad eating his meal. He had burnt a small rui on a bonfire and ate the meat slowly. The acrid taste of dirty fish made him blanche, but he was hungry.

Before him, there was an expansive clump of pure white froth which had collected next to the bank, although it was much lesser than before because of the rains. It was almost twilight and the traffic nearby was at its height. He could hear the blare of the vehicles and the general sounds of evening fauna. Somewhere, people were playing loud Haryanvi music and the fast beats seemed to reverberate on the soft ground underneath him.

After he was done with the meal he decided to begin his search again. He walked up to the clear patch in the river where there was no sewage or froth and was about to jump in when he saw a large fish—over five feet long. It was dead but immersed in water, in a small pool that had formed next to the river. He got down on his knees and pulled it back. The sight of the huge fish brought back memories of the days when his parents would make money from fishing. Everything was good then…

The crickets were beginning to chirp around him as the sky dimmed. A lone tear trickled down his cheek. His brother had drowned and he had to accept that. His wife was a widow with three children, and as the brother of her deceased husband, he should provide for her and the children.

He looked back at the fish. With it he could perhaps make enough money to give to her for a few days, until he found some other work. Or perhaps he would go back to fishing—it was what he was best at.

✦

The macchi bazaar at Ghazipur opens early in the morning. For that the fish sellers begin setting up nearly two hours before. The fish is brought in on trucks, alive, flapping around, and flung inside Styrofoam boxes covered with black plastic. Some of the good fish are cut up to display the fresh glistening meat, and bright blood trickles down the white cardboard like thick sweet syrup. Bricks of ice are used to line the slabs. The fish won't perish for hours this way even in the sultry sun.

The morning azaan had sounded when Gokul reached the Mandi. The autumnal mist was rolling through when he hauled the fish he had found the evening before, through the market. He walked up to the nearest stall and spoke to the man who was busy removing the scales of a large rui. He was a Muslim man with a lurid orange beard, and his pristine white kurta seemed to glaze in the fluorescent morning light.

'Miya, would you be interested in purchasing a large fish?'

The man ignored him. Around him men went about busily, shouting to each other. They were still unloading the fish and setting up.

'I will sell it to you cheap.'

The man glanced at him but waved him away. They weren't interested in purchasing from the fishermen. They only transacted with the contractors.

Gokul folded his hands. 'Huzoor? Please buy this fish. I need to give money to my sister-in-law. She got widowed a month ago when the floods came. I must help them. My brother…'

The man looked up irritably.

'Arre, nikal yaha se. Dekh nahi raha main kaam kar raha hu?'

'Miya, I am a fisherman from Hooghly. Surely you will help a poor fisherman? I made an excellent catch yesterday. It is a huge fish—nothing like you have seen before. Have a look before you send me off.'

Before the man could say anything, he bent down and unwrapped the sack. The man bent forward to have a look.

'Isn't it unbelievable? I caught it at Wazirabad.'

But the man was staring at the fish at his feet in utter horror. Gokul looked at him in confusion.

'What happened?'

Suddenly, the men around them began shouting. Gokul looked around in fear. What was happening? Why were they gathering around? He bent down to wrap up the fish and go away. He didn't want anyone to steal it.

He froze, sack in hand.

The bloated body of his twin lay there. The skin had become leathery and slimy. The abdomen was swollen with water.

In the dawn's light. the empty eyes looked round and large—like the eyes of a fish.

THE FEVER OF RICKSHAWWALLAS

Shabana was squatting before the portable gas-stove at the entrance of their house when Mounir returned home just before dinner time. She was in the direct line of vision of their neighbour's TV set which was about ten feet away, behind their grilled entrance. When Mounir walked up, she dusted her hands briskly and moved the stove so he could enter without toppling it over. Then she moved it back and resumed work, hardly processing the words of endearment he said to her as he helped himself to a glass of water. Her hands worked mechanically, expertly tossing the rotis as she squinted at the TV screen, craning her neck to catch all the juicy dialogues the actors spewed.

Mounir sighed to himself. Shabana sat by the door every day so that she could watch their neighbour's TV because they didn't have one. The neighbour was her fast friend and had aligned the TV in such a way that it was visible to them from the doorway. She had even asked her to keep the volume high enough for her. During the day when he went for work, she spent hours watching one serial after the other at their house. In the evening when the woman's husband returned, Shabana finally came home to begin the day's chores. But at 9 p.m., when the prime time serials started, she went to the spot at the main door, with her stove and other cooking material, and watched serials while she cooked.

As Mounir undressed and went for a bath, the jarring background music of the show grated on his nerves. He could even hear the domestic banter of their house over all the television cacophony. The children were shrieking, and he could hear the woman screaming at them to shut them up. Mounir gritted his teeth in irritation, trying to control his temper. The serial went on, and he could distinctly hear the melodramatic dialogues.

But Shabana seemed absolutely unfazed by all the noise. Her eyes remained glued to the screen. He wondered how she was always so utterly oblivious to his mood. She had not even said a word to him, engrossed as she was in the show.

'Begum, are the rotis ready?' he asked tentatively. He had had a tiring day and wanted to eat in peace. 'I am very hungry…'

'Ssshh!' she hissed at him. Without turning her head, she tossed down rotis on his plate. 'Here!' she snapped. 'Have it now. And let me watch the show. I can barely hear anything!'

Mounir shook his head in disbelief and ate in silence. Her behaviour was beginning to drive him mad. She was his wife after all, and was supposed to be sensible enough to pay him attention during dinner time. It was her duty to take care of him.

But as always, he could not bring himself to complain. What would he say to her anyway? He supposed it was the exuberance of youth—vestiges of a mischievous childhood cut short prematurely by matrimony—that made her so self-involved. After all, she was just twenty-one. And what else did she have to do when he was gone for most part of the day? How was she to spend her time? She repeatedly reminded him that it was his fault that she had to make such elaborate designs to do something as simple as watching TV. If they had the resources to buy their own TV set, she wouldn't have to do any of this.

Mounir partly agreed with this. It was a sore point with him that even after three years of marriage, he still couldn't buy a TV for her as he had promised her on the night of their marriage. And so, if through her own resourcefulness she had made an arrangement which afforded her an easy alternative, who was he to put a stop to it? Besides, it was alright to have a vice or two. In fact, he sometimes found her obsession for TV endearing. Her girlish thoughtlessness had struck him as charming and it was what had drawn him to her in the first place.

And so, every evening except for weekends, he found her sitting at the door watching their neighbour's TV, as he quietly ate his dinner despite the din.

✦

Mounir was from a family of carpet weavers who originally hailed from Malda in West Bengal. In 1976, when he was born, his father had already made plans to move to Kashmir where carpet weaving as a profession was still thriving when it had begun to die out in Bengal. When he turned two, they moved to Najan in Sumbal to work alongside an old friend of his father's, Jamal Ali, whom he addressed as 'Chacha'.

But soon after settling down, his father realised that the newer generations of carpet weavers in Kashmir who had been practicing their craft for years, had begun to lose interest in the craft. The younger men wanted to leave the villages and do other forms of labour. Jamal's own sons wanted to move to Delhi and take up other professions.

The gyres were turning. There was nothing that could be done to resist the onward movement of time. They had to move ahead too. But Mounir's father and Jamal Chacha knew no other work. And not only did they lack other skills, they did not even have the capability at the age of fifty to learn any other trade. The biggest problem was that their families had been weavers for generations, and being a kaleen was a part of their identity. They could not perceive themselves as anything else. Even poverty that loomed large refused to beat the carpet weaving out of them. They simply refused to do anything else. And hence, with time, their families' condition got worse.

'I do not want to go to the wosta, Sadia,' Mounir often heard his father tell his mother. His mother was a kind woman who understood their predicament. She was uncomplaining and never caved under pressure. But their coarse pherans had begun to show tears despite repeated mending, and their half empty stomachs spoke volumes.

One evening, exactly a week before Jamal Chacha decided to move to Delhi, he overheard him talk to his father after dinner.

'The new generation has forgotten its roots, Moumin,' he said. 'My sons have already forgotten their identity. They have forgotten who their forefathers were. They are practical and hard-hearted. There is no sentiment, no emotion involved in their craft when they did weaving. It's only a skill for them—only a form of labour. For years they have been doing it mechanically, without love, without emotion. I say to you, that is the reason why this craft will perish someday altogether…why we will perish. But perhaps it is our fault. We passed on the skill to our sons but we could not pass on the art. And art is only when there is love for the craft. And we failed in invoking that love in them. We failed to create the magic that our fathers created for us when they passed on the art. The art for which we stand here today as true sons of carpet weavers. Moumin, brother, mark my words. Our sons are the lost generation. But we must let them decide their destinies.'

Mounir listened, feeling sorry for his Chacha. But he sympathised with the sons. He himself hardly cared for carpet weaving, and spent most of his free time reading books and writing poems about nature. He was an artist at heart, and he knew he was going to study painting in college someday.

But the valley was burning. It was the turn of the decade—the year 1990. A massive protest for plebiscite broke out in Srinagar and thousands of people took to the streets. The violence and protests escalated in the next few months. And in the month of May, his father, who was more of a sympathiser than an activist, was one of the hundred men killed in a police firing while walking in a funeral procession of the martyred leader Mirwaiz Maulwaiz Maulvi Jamal.

That year, Jagmohan was appointed as the governor after the resignation of Farooq Abdullah. The massacre of civilians in January, when the curfew was broken for a peaceful march, had made the situation dangerously volatile. After the police firing that had claimed his father, Jagmohan resigned.

But there was no peace even then. In the following year, when Mounir's own friends were crossing the border to Pakistan, he stood up as the man of the house and decided to take his mother back to Malda. He had no desire to participate in the politics around him. The cries of protest and the yearning for azadi had not permeated his skin.

He was merely fifteen then. Their life in Malda was not easy. He briefly worked as an artisan, but that only pushed them to the edge of poverty. After a few years, his mother died, and he left everything to move to New Delhi.

In some years, he became a rickshawwalla.

✦

Mounir, rather plain-looking, had never hoped to find a woman as beautiful and vivacious as Shabana Bano. She was fifteen years younger to him, and just eighteen when he married her. Shabana's family was completely impoverished when they gave her away, and kept no expectations from him apart from a significant maintenance. He was already in love with her by that time and would have agreed to anything to have her. Besides, he was aware that she might have married a better man, considering her beauty.

But desire and obsession drove him to ask her hand in marriage, and moved by his spirit, and perhaps girlish fantasies, she relented.

After marriage, they began living together in various small quarters all over Delhi, finally moving to Abu Fazal in Jamia Nagar in their thirteenth month of marriage, in a building that overlooked an enormous garbage dump beyond the university. Although Shabana complained, Mounir was more or less satisfied. He had a house, a young and beautiful wife, and a steady means of sustenance.

Things were going fine until slowly Mounir began to doubt the bliss in his conjugal life. One night when he lay in bed next to Shabana, he moved his hand up her body feeling her curves, when he realised she was lying rigidly, completely unresponsive to his caresses. He let her be, thinking she must be tired.

But soon it dawned upon him that his wife was beginning to grow aloof. He realised that she was not only growing steadily indifferent towards him, but was also beginning to show signs of being extremely vain and covetous—something he hadn't known before. Soon he realised that he had mistaken her for an innocent girl who needed a husband to love and support her. She was, in fact, a woman who was aware of her beauty's worth, and managed to draw the benefits that such beauty afforded to a woman of loose morals. He even discovered, to his great discomfort, that she actively took advantage of her body in ways that he was better off not knowing.

And so when he saw her garish garments, her sparkling mass of artificial jewellery bought off the streets with his hard-earned money, and often provocative undergarments which he was seldom audience to, he became convinced that the woman he had married was a nymphomaniac who fulfilled her desires elsewhere. Still, for his own sake rather than hers, he did not confront her. He was too disgusted, and too afraid to have his suspicions confirmed completely. He decided to ignore everything as long as she remained a good wife to him, in his presence. What she did behind his back was something he was not going to take too much pain to investigate. Besides, she was so much younger than him. He reasoned to himself during nights when he lay next to her, desiring her voluptuousness but unable to draw her out, that perhaps, it wasn't her fault that she didn't want him. He was not attractive or young. And she was too beautiful for him.

And beautiful women were allowed to be fickle.

One night, after weeks of denial, Mounir took her forcefully. To his great surprise, she seemed to like it. But it disgusted him to think of his actions afterwards. How could he have forced himself on his own wife?

And so he eventually stopped trying altogether. Shabana never asked why, or initiated anything herself. They both fell into a complaisant marriage where they lived with each other, without being intimate with each other.

✦

Several months passed. One night when Mounir returned home early, he found Shabana waiting for him in a lacy, bright red panties and bra set. He had not seen her undressed in about six months. The sight of her breasts and curving belly aroused a sudden wild hunger in him that ran through him like a crashing wave. She beckoned to him and spread her thighs.

Mounir was a beast that night.

The next morning, he woke up, with an aching back and a throbbing member. Before she let him have her, she laid a minor condition.

She wanted a television set in the house.

That night Mounir calculated his expenses and came to the conclusion that it would take him about five to seven years to save enough money to buy the kind of TV his wife wanted. He told her as much, and much to his dismay, she began to refuse him in bed again.

'Is this really because of the TV?' he asked her flabbergasted.

'If you truly loved me, you would be able to tell why I am so depressed!'

'I assure you I do, but I do not understand this.'

She sniffled. 'I cannot be your toy and satisfy your urges all the time. I am a human being with needs too!'

'And you will feel better only when you have a TV?' he asked, aghast.

'I really will not answer that. You are my husband. You should know my heart!'

And so the momentary spell of desperate love-making that he had so ecstatically welcomed, fizzled away as suddenly as it had started.

✦

The onset of winter brought with it its own set of problems. Shabana had developed a recurring cold, and he himself had briefly fallen ill. His mates near the campus who began arriving at 6-7 a.m. every day, had also acquired different stages of the common cold and flu.

One day, after taking Shabana to the doctor in the morning, he went to the campus to begin his day's work and saw that the whole place was deserted. No rickshaw lined the pavement as it always did at all times of the day, with men eagerly waiting for passengers so they might earn their day's wages. People milled about, with no rickshaw to hail.

Puzzled, he pedaled to his usual spot and was immediately assailed by passengers who wanted to go this way and that.

He took passengers around all day, without a single break. The sudden disappearance of rickshaws had caused quite a crises and people fought aggressively over his rickshaw. Mounir was perplexed at his sudden monopoly over the area. He couldn't imagine why none of the men had come in that day. Had they decided to migrate to someplace else? Or was there a meeting somewhere? Was there a strike he didn't know about? He was bewildered. They did not have a union. So what was the issue? Did they suddenly decide to make one? He grew concerned. Why had Hamid or any of the others not told him? They couldn't have forgotten to inform him, he figured. Perhaps he should buy a mobile phone like everybody else…Shabana was right. He was a fool to not buy a mobile.

As he ferried people about through the day, all sorts of speculations bounded through his mind. The sudden absence of his men was acutely disconcerting especially because of the sudden surplus of space. But autos soon began gathering and there was a lot of confusion on the road as they quoted high fares for small distances without coordinating amongst themselves.

As evening approached, Mounir grew more anxious. He had seen rickshaws around but none of them were from the bunch that waited around at the stop that he did. He decided to pedal towards the other stop and was surprised to see that it was teeming as usual. What was the matter with the men at his stop then? He had no way of finding out until he got home.

✦

As Mounir discovered the next day, the rickshawwallas of his area were under attack by a particular flu. They were suffering from high fever, sore throat, diarrhea amongst other things. Mounir was flummoxed. All of them had fallen ill at the same time and were so sick that they couldn't come to work for several days. A few of them started plying despite their illness, but Hamid and the others were still too unwell.

Several days passed. The matter did not change. What baffled Mounir the most was that he was apparently untouched by this flu. Only he, amongst the fifty odd men of his stop, was spared. He wondered at strange mercies of Allah and offered namaz in gratefulness that afternoon. He knew he couldn't afford to fall sick. And he was thankful for not being claimed by the flu—yet. It would have easily cost him at least a week's earnings.

✦

December arrived, and the temperatures dropped further. Mist rolled across the city cloaking it with a milky robe, carrying with it bacteria and viruses that birthed pneumonia and tuberculosis.

Mounir's mates at the bus stop had still not recovered. His stand was right next to the Jamia main campus, and the next main stop for rickshaws was near the hospitals down the road. Much to his horror, slowly the men at the next stop also began to fall ill. The one in the other direction, towards Jamia Nagar, saw a sudden dwindling of men too.

People began to call the flu 'Rickshewalon ki bukhar'—the fever of rickshawwallas. Apparently, it was a common form of influenza, but strangely, it seemed to be hitting only the rickshawwallas in that particular area. Doctors said that it was probably because of some virus that was transmitted through a common source of food or water, since it was usual for the men to eat and drink together during the day, from the same sources.

What made matters worse was that the men did not have adequate clothing for the season. The convalescing rickshawwallas who braved the cold and fog and ventured forth to make earnings, wheezed about in their tattered sweaters, and torn and insufficient pants.

Slowly, the flu spread. More rickshawwallas reported sick. AIIMS and Safdarjung reported over-admissions and they soon began turning patients away.

At the end of December, Mounir was the only rickshawwalla left who was untouched by the flu. He began to wonder why he should be spared an ailment that had claimed all the other rickshawwallas of the locality. What was different about his constitution? How had he escaped the illness?

One day while returning to the campus area after dropping a man at Modi Mills, Mounir's eyes fell upon a discarded heap of rucksacks. He was lost in thought but out of some strange and unknown impulse, he stopped his rickshaw and picked up the heap. Then he loaded it into his rickshaw and pedaled directly home.

✦

Mounir spent the next few nights recalling his childhood and contemplating upon his past. Things were still dull at home; Shabana had not relented to him in bed and persisted in her demands for a TV set. Lying next to her every night, he felt the stirrings of desire but refrained from touching her, wary of her reaction.

By then, he had found out about her extra-marital affairs. She had begged his forgiveness after being caught red-handed the first time, but he knew that she was back to fucking the young man who lived downstairs in the same building. Often when he returned home early, she would be in his room on the pretext of cooking food for money. She said it was her 'job'—that she was his cook and housekeeper—but Mounir was not fooled. He knew the real reason behind the sudden inflow of money. Still, he did not say anything to her. She was a sensual woman with needs. And there had to be an outlet. Besides, he preferred for her to earn money herself than leech off him especially since their marriage had become such a farce. How she earned her money was up to her. If she wanted money though sex, he wasn't going to judge her for her morality; although he resented her for cheating on him. But he could not even dare to point that out to her. There wasn't a single argument in which she did not question his masculinity. It was best to keep quiet and turn a blind eye to her philandering.

One night when he lay in bed just having turned off the light, an idea came to him. At first he dismissed it, exhausted as he was. But he was startled by the sudden pang of excitement that reverberated through him. With a burst of energy, he got up and turned the light back on. Shabana squealed in annoyance but for once, he wasn't going to give in to the complaints of an adulterous wife. 'Shut up and go to sleep,' he growled at her.

She immediately quietened, blinking at him in surprise. When he did not respond, she squeaked gently, 'What is it?'

But Mounir wasn't paying attention to her. He was feeling the coarse rucksacks that he had stowed under the bed.

What seemed like ages ago in the valley, his mother used to tell him, 'Mounir, you must cover your feet and chest. That is where cold enters your body from. Don't leave the house without wearing your socks and scarf.'

'Yes, mother. As you say.'

And the bitter cold of Kashmir winters hardly ever affected him. His swarthy face, inherited from his parents who had known the tropical sun of the east for generations, was immune to the dryness caused by the gales that swept through the valley making the other children's cheeks red and sore. The hakeem who came to treat the sick in their neighbourhood, seldom entered their house. The local women said his mother knew kala jaadu and transferred sickness that came into her family to those around them. His mother always laughed off such talk.

'They are too imaginative,' she would say in amusement. 'They say this because we are different. My "black magic" is just common sense.'

Mounir knew what he had to do.

✦

The next week, after returning home from work, Mounir began undoing the sacks. One by one, the sacks came apart and became one long string of yarn which he rolled up in a great ball. When all the sacks were done, he brought more. His hands worked frenziedly, his breath quickened, and his eyes glazed over as he worked, through the nights, refusing offers of tea or biscuits.

Shabana tried to complain about the mounting pile of yarn rolls but stopped when he snapped at her and told her to keep her trap shut or he would beat her up. The spark that had suddenly ignited in his eyes sobered her considerably. For the first time in their entire married life, he had spoken to her authoritatively and it intimidated, even scared her. Had he found out about her new affair? She wasn't sure. Guilty, she did not wrangle any further. What if he actually decided to throw her out? What would she do? She could not understand why Mounir had suddenly taken to un-weaving sacks. And she dare not ask him directly.

Mounir noticed smugly how her tone, over the next few days, grew softer and softer, until finally, it was adequately respectful. Still, he kept his idea to himself. He did not want to tell her about his plans to weave socks and scarves from the yarn, not because he was afraid of her ridicules for doing petty work, but because she would make jibes at his mardangi again if he told her he was weaving clothes.

But he knew he was doing more than that. Every night when he left the house to sit upon his rickshaw chained by the gate downstairs and weave, he knew he was doing what was in his blood.

And so Mounir sat on his rickshaw, weaving by the light of the street lamp every night, making pair after pair of coarse socks that would keep rickshawwallas warm.

✦

Mounir spent the next three years weaving socks and scarves, first from discarded sacks, then from the wool he purchased after the profits from his previous sales began to mount.

He priced his merchandise at an affordable rate, and worked ceaselessly during the nights, ignoring Shabana's protestations—timid as they were now. He weaved through summer, stocking up supply for the winter, and sold them at the onset of the season. During hot days, he sat in the dark, motionless, but for his fingers that drew the same patterns over and over again in the semi-darkness until a perfectly woven piece was made. Mosquitoes spared him—for no apparent reason—just buzzing around him harmlessly. When it rained and it was difficult for him to sit on his rickshaw and weave, he sat in the stairs of the building, weaving by the light of a lantern or a candle. Only winter was uncomfortable for the fog that swarmed around him, obfuscating his vision. But other than these slight climatic obstacles, nothing bothered him. He managed to escape everybody's eye by timing his work and making sure that he wasn't out when the morning azaan sounded at around 4 a.m., or when someone was likely to see him. He emerged from his house at 2 a.m., and wrapped up work by four. Shabana did not know his whereabouts during this time and assumed he went to a mistress, or to G.B. Road to fuck whores. She did not care enough to inspect, and hence, never found out.

And so nobody knew where the knitted items came from, not even her. And nobody saw him; nobody realised that he stayed up every night weaving countless socks and scarves, under their very noses.

✦

Mounir's socks and scarves had become popular right after the first season. All the rickshawwallas began sporting his merchandise, and to everyone's amazement, they did seem to be making them immune to cough and cold.

Soon, there was a rumour that the socks and scarves he knitted were charmed. People began saying Mounir put spells on them to deflect diseases. More gossip floated around him, and people became inquisitive about his life.

They made up bizarre theories about his magic too. They said he got the things from some poor people and then created magic on them.

The only problem was that Mounir's sleep patterns had become severely disrupted. He plied his rickshaw in the day, weaved by night, and slept when he could in between. The lack of rest, intense exhaustion, and the thrill of weaving in secret resulted in an odd behaviour. His face, although already unattractive, acquired a haunted look. And people took this sudden anti-social and forbidding demeanour to be a sure sign of dark magic.

Mounir, who had grown steadily taciturn, could hardly deny the conspiracy theories. Not that there was any trouble because of the rumours. Whatever it was, it ensured that his items got sold. But he wanted it to be kept a secret because he could not be seen doing a woman's work.

Three winter seasons passed in this manner. Mounir soon acquired the reputation of being a warlock with the abilities of a hakeem. Rumour was that his garments could not only fend off diseases, but could also cure them. Soon, people from other parts of the city came flocking to him, offering him more money than he could imagine for a simple sweater or a cardigan.

Mounir himself did not understand it. Did the garments he weaved actually have magic in them? Memories of the old rumours surrounding his mother wafted back to him. They said she was a sorceress...had she passed it onto him, her only son? Was he really a...?

No. It was an absurd notion. And he knew the truth about himself.Besides, no matter what status he acquired—

even if he was indeed a 'jaadugar hakeem' as they called him—he was just a man, in love with his wife despite her infidelities.

✦

Quite involuntarily, due to his exhaustive schedule, Mounir had become brusque and rough in his mannerisms, and rigid about most matters. Before this, Shabana had always held the reigns of their marriage. But now he had become a strange and secretive man who seemed like he would not baulk at physically chastising her if she made a mistake. Ultimately, it worked in his favour because seeing that he was no longer the indulgent and forbearing husband that she had taken for granted since the beginning, she finally began to take him seriously.

In due course of time, Mounir had managed to completely domesticate Shabana. Out of a primitive instinct of self-preservation common to deceptive women, she gave up her old debauched ways and settled into the role of a meek wife.

But giving up wicked ways has a toll on someone who has always been like that. No longer the seductress, Shabana, now had no one to direct her lust towards but her husband.

But strangely, Mounir did not respond to her advances now. He refused her each time she tried to get close, and seemed absolutely immune to her touch. She grew more and more restive as she realised he had developed a wall around himself and barred her out. But how could he resist her? What was she doing wrong?

She gave up soon and begun to grow quieter each day.

She no longer even complained about not having a TV in the house. But her obsession about serials grew now that there was a great void in her life that she had no way of filling. Mounir did not seem to desire her at all, and no matter how much she tried, she could not coax him to have sex with her. Neither was she able to entice him with her body. She had tried everything: provocative clothes, whorish makeup, dancing, oils, tablets, bright jewellery… she had even begged and pleaded and sworn to fuck another man if he did not relent. But he seemed to have grown completely resistant to her. Every night they went to bed, facing away from each other, without exchanging as much as a word.

Only Mounir knew what truly was in his heart.

Time passed quickly. Mounir had aged considerably in just a few years. There was grey in his hair now, and he was bespectacled. The incessant weaving in the dark had weakened his eyes and given him dark circles, and a bald spot.

But the spectacles gave him a kind of gravitas that was attractive. Shabana, after two years of sustained chastity, began to find the husband she had cuckolded so many times, appealing. She seemed to really want him, even after he refused her each time she tried.

One night, after four years of a sterile marriage when he returned home from work, he found her stark naked in bed. But he did not want to have her only because of what he knew was her submissiveness towards his new dominating personality. He wanted her heart.

And so he deferred their consummation. He had been

patient for so long. He could go on for a little more. It was a question of a little more time after all. He had all the money now.

✦

As it turned out, Mounir had accumulated enough resources to buy a flat screen TV set for his wife. But the week he brought home the TV set, was the week he lost his eyesight.

The doctors called it Anterior Ischemic Optic Neuropathy (AION). The main cause of it was sleep apnea—lack of sleep. Apparently, his blood vessels had inflamed to the point that his optic nerve got damaged from insufficient blood supply to the eyes.

He couldn't explain this to his wife. It was attributed to poor health and age.

But Shabana seemed to be strangely at peace now. In the room, facing their main door, now sat a brand new four feet wide TV.

ACID

It was late afternoon. Laxman sat on his bright red rickshaw at the exit of the Mayur Vihar Metro Station. There were hardly any people to ferry at the hour, and the other rickshawwallas like him, relaxed in the shade, slumped on the backseats of their vehicles. As soon as it would strike five and passengers would start coming, the other rickshawwallas would sweep in and crowd the place. They had to gear up for the rush-hour hustle.

Laxman leaned back into the backseat and stuck his legs out from the side so that his back was flat on the seat. Around him, more rickshaws had begun to gather already. Why did there have to be so many in this area? Just about a year ago, there were hardly ten or twelve men who would station themselves at this particular metro exit. It was smooth and peaceful. They had an unspoken code and took turns to go. No one tried to snap up another's passenger. But ever since the men from the next metro station discovered that they had a nice little lucrative spot at Mayur Vihar Extension, they had gathered in, like flies to cut fruit, ready to grab what they could. They did not even follow the rule of waiting for their turn and quarreled loudly, hurling abuses at each other. Laxman did not intervene even if things got heated between the men. He watched quietly, keeping as much distance from the new rickshawwallas at all times. They were intruders.

But there was no actual way to mark one's territory. There were no official rules. Those men couldn't be asked to leave or be ousted in any way.

Laxman kept his gamcha over his eyes, and drifted off to sleep.

✦

Laxman had become friends with Hari about a year ago when he had moved into the building in Trilokpuri. He plied his rickshaw in the same area and was the most garrulous of the lot that stood outside the Mayur Vihar station. Initially, Laxman avoided talking to him. But Hari was not someone you could ignore. When he saw that Laxman did not bat an eyelid at anything he said, he took it upon himself to make him a part of his gang. Laxman maintained his indifferent attitude nonetheless. Then one day, he got into an argument with another rickshawwalla and Hari intervened in his favour. Since then, Laxman became more open towards him. Very soon, he was introduced to two more chaps, Gopal and Harish, who were also rickshawwallas who plied around the same area. Before he knew it, he had become a part of their group.

It was not long before the three introduced him to

drug peddling. Hari had broached the subject casually once while they were drinking in his flat. Laxman was shocked at first, then it all made sense to him. Their clothes, the expensive booze, the flat where they lived. He had always wondered how they afforded it. When they offered him a task, he was reluctant at first, but relented when all three teased and cajoled him.

The work turned out to be surprisingly easy. All they had to do was take the stuff from the dealer to the customer at their house, or whichever place they asked, and receive the money. All they had to make sure was that they were dressed up in a way that they would mingle in the posh areas where they dropped off the package. These customers were regulars and the dealer had had long associations with them so there was no risk of being attacked, robbed, or ratted out. The only trick was to remain inconspicuous, which wasn't so difficult in this overpopulated city, if they dressed the right away and had the right cover-up.

They usually went in twos, and Hari became his mentor, teaching him how to carry out the transaction in a safe way. The first time he went for a delivery all by himself, to a hotel in Khan Market, he almost refused. The customer was a diplomat who had proven to be a very good customer over the years. He had to be extremely cautious because the man was very well connected and a rather prominent figure. Besides, Khan Market was a heavily surveilled area.

It was supposed to be a one-time thing for Laxman, but it turned out to be addictive. He had never seen so much money in his life. They were given good clothes, a bike to make deliveries, and the best part was the easy access to crack, heroin, hash, marijuana and acid. Hari even said that they could nick some stuff from the packets every time they made a delivery, if they were smart enough to not get caught.

As things went smoothly, Laxman gained confidence. If there weren't too many deliveries in a month, it didn't feel too dangerous. And there was a thrill to life which wasn't there before. It was the first time he owned proper clothes. Eventually, with the money that came in, he also purchased a leather jacket, a pair of shiny leather boots, sunglasses, and a thick glossy leather belt. If anyone now saw him on the roads in the posh neighbourhoods where he made the deliveries, no one could guess he was a rickshawwalla by day.

✦

Sighing to himself, Laxman adjusted himself in the rickshaw and tried to catch a nap. He was stationed at his usual spot waiting for passengers, but there weren't any around. He could barely sleep a wink because of the loud construction work going on for a new parking space and cursed everyone. He was craving a cigarette. But if he was to take out his pack of Navy Cut and his skull-shaped lighter, the faces of the rickshawwallas around would be worth seeing.

He spat in disgust. It was hard to play the role of the rickshawwalla despite having decent money now. But the seth insisted that they keep up the facade so they wouldn't raise suspicions in the area where they lived. Of course, the seth would never want them to quit the work of rickshaw-pulling. It was all too convenient to have men who worked as rickshawwallas double up as peddlers. No one in the locality could question them because everyone knew they were hardworking men who plied Mayur Vihar daily. They even lived in the building where bachelor rickshawwallas lived. But this double life was getting burdensome and he wanted to save enough money and quit, and then buy an auto-rickshaw once he was out of the area. He would go to South Delhi. He was not going to peddle drugs all his life. He knew Hari and the rest didn't have any qualms but he did. Besides, they were afraid of the seth. He had threatened to have them jailed if they tried to leave. Once you were in, there was no leaving until the seth decided. But he was not a coward like Hari and the others. He wanted to get the auto rickshaw soon, and eventually, a car so he could become an Uber driver by the time he got a wife.

The bidi tasted acrid. Laxman sighed and leaned back into the seat. Soon, people began to trickle out of the metro, and the crowd around the station thickened. The rickshawwallas made off one by one with the passengers seated, even as the others pulled in to rejoin the queue. Fortunately, there was no scuffle over passengers that evening. Laxman felt he would not be able to tolerate another episode in the mood that he was in.

He took one or two passengers for appearance's sake, then napped in his rickshaw. After 9 p.m., the number of rickshawwallas dwindled as the stream of people coming from the metro also lessened. Laxman had to work until ten before reporting to the malik. He was tempted to go back at nine itself, but it was imperative that he didn't do anything out of the ordinary. Peddling was not an easy task. The cover up and alibis had to be impeccable.

✦

Several months passed. Laxman, Hari, Harish and Gopal were in their boss's office in Laxmi Nagar. A week ago, Harish was almost caught while delivering a packet of crack to an NRI in Sainik Farms. He was chased for nearly ten kilometres and had somehow escaped but they had traced him to Trilokpuri. Before they could even devise a plan, the police raided their flat. Thankfully, their cover was flawless and the police could not find any incriminating evidence against them. But the expensive cigarettes and alcohol in Harish's room had aroused the inspector's suspicion. He was a young fellow, a Chowdhury.

'I'll have my eyes on you, remember that,' Chowdhury warned him, slapping him on the back. 'One foul step and you'll be in.'

Harish laughed off the insinuation and swore that there was a mistake, cracking jokes to placate the cop. But, inside he was panicking. It was a stroke of luck that he had no cash in the house. The payment for the previous delivery had not come in, and he had exhausted his stash after hiring an escort for the weekend. But a Rolex purchased from the black market hung on his wrist and his knees were trembling as the inspector spoke to him, praying that it goes unnoticed. They had bribed the man with whiskey bottles and twenty thousand rupees, but it would not be enough if drugs were found in the house. That's when they decided to quit and move to another part of Delhi, or at the very least take a break for a few months.

Hari, Harish and Gopal watched Laxman as he talked to the seth behind the tinted door marked 'Lakshmi Properties'. He was gesticulating keenly, while the seth sat leaning back in his chair, looking disinterested, and smoking one cigarette after the other. He looked like the classic lala, dressed in a white safari suit with double breast pockets and shiny buttons which were straining to contain his humongous paunch. He had golden-rimmed glasses on, a couple of thick gold chains around his neck, and a shiny golden watch that glinted in the fluorescent light through the blue glass. When he brought his cigarette to his lips, all three of his gem-encrusted rings that he wore in his fingers for astrological goodness, glared at them as if leering at them.

Smoke was beginning to gather in the office. It was clear that whatever Laxman was saying was bouncing right off the seth's skin. He remained expressionless as Laxman went on, stubbing out his cigarettes and lighting another. When Laxman was done talking, he mumbled something and then picked up his mobile phone. He spoke briefly into it, and then nodded, listening to whoever was on the line. Laxman remained standing, waiting for him to be done, his shoulders stiffened, his posture clearly indicating suppressed desperation. Finally, the lalaji hung up and said something to him. Laxman turned to exit without responding. It was evident that he hadn't managed to get what he wanted.

'Let's get out of here,' he told the three.

'What happened? What did he say?' Hari asked.

'Let's get out of here first.'

'Brother,' he hissed in reply. 'Don't do this. Tell us. Did he agree or not?'

They had walked down the stairs. Once they were in a crowded place, they could talk properly.

'He says we have to do it the whole of this year, that haraamkhor. If we don't, he will ruin us.'

'This whole year? You mean, for three more months? That's mad! I cannot do this for so long. It's getting too risky. We have to lie low for some time. Or we need to move out and go somewhere else.'

'Yes. With the police already onto us, it would be suicidal to do another delivery. And frankly, we don't get paid so much that we would risk it in such circumstances.'

'It's not like we have a choice.'

'Oh, we do. Let's kill that bastard and we'll be through,' Hari spat, letting loose a stream of red spit.

'Don't be an idiot. And stop mouthing such nonsense all the time. Do you have the balls to even touch that guy?'

'Look Laxman,' Gopal interjected. 'What do you want? Should we let this bastard get us in jail? I am an honest man. Yes, I am greedy for money, but brother, I cannot take such risks. After what happened last time, I don't have the guts to do it again frankly…Gaand phat rahi hai yaar. If we ever get caught…' he paused trying to guess what the penalty would be. 'Look, I have to marry Sheela this year. Otherwise she will leave me.'

'Saale, she will leave you anyway,' Hari quipped. There was a pause as they looked at each other. Then all of them began laughing.

Laxman laughed forcefully. The lalaji's words echoed in his head. 'Tu launda toh accha hai. Kaam kar theek se. Sirf kuch ek deliveries hi toh hai. Abhi mehnat kar, mehnat. Samjha? Kisi din mere jaisi kursi pe baithega.'

✦

'Brother, I say we make off with the stuff,' Hari was saying as he smoked his bidi that evening. He was already drunk on the tharra he had purchased from the theka nearby and was intent on getting drunker. He took another long swig from the bottle and set it down on the floor with a loud thud.

'Easy, brother, easy,' Laxman said. 'All that money and you still drink tharra. What is wrong with your head?' They were in his room. Gopal had just joined them after returning from his girlfriend's place. They were waiting for him to return before rolling a joint.

'Arre Laxman, you take it easy brother. Nothing is going to happen. Desi daaru is the best. I would drink tharra even if I had a swimming pool of English whiskey.' He grinned. 'How is my idea by the way? Should we make off with the damn packets? Imagine how much money we will make!'

'You have lost it,' Laxman said, trying to check his irritation.

'What is it, brother?' Hari asked, looking suddenly serious. 'You don't seem too interested in us these days.'

Laxman was taken aback, but recovered quickly and gave Hari a bored look. 'Saale, gaand mein le le. You're always talking nonsense. He leaned back trying to look nonchalant. When nobody replied, he went on. 'Did you see the seth's face that day? Kameena bhenchod...we are in this shit forever.' He glanced at Hari to see his reaction.

Hari was far from suspecting anything. 'You know…' he said dreamily. '…I get the feeling we will have to do this as long as we can. Then we will get caught and put into jail to rot away. But I don't mind it. At least now I never go hungry. And I have liquor and heroin and ganja whenever I want it. Plus, I have enough money to buy my own bike…' He drifted off. 'But saala, the irony is, I cannot buy it because it will blow my cover…still, at least I get to send good money back home.'

Laxman remained quiet. Hari continued. 'Do you think we can talk about at least changing our occupation? I wouldn't mind posing as a salesman…I have been plying the blasted rickshaw for five years now. I am sick of it!'

'Don't say that,' Harish said hardly looking up from his mobile. It was a new Chinese android and he was watching porn on it with one of his earphones on. The other ear, he kept on the conversation taking place. 'Being rickshawwallas is the best cover there can be, believe me… everybody pities us. No one is going to guess we are rolling in money.'

'Abbey, we are not rolling in money,' Hari interrupted.

'But he has a point. Rickshaw pulling is the safest bet,' Gopal mumbled. He was lying on the mattress, resting with his arm over his eyes.

'Aur kya!' Harish said. 'Hari, yaar, why are you always so sour? Here watch this.' He turned the screen towards them. A big breasted woman was sitting with her legs parted, touching herself. 'Yaar, this internet thing is so amazing. I love it. Blue film anytime.'

'Don't show us all this vile stuff,' Gopal said, pretending to be scandalised. 'Aurat devi hoti hai, kutte.'

'Yeah, but this one is surely the devi of kama,' Harish grinned, revealing his ugly set of decaying teeth. 'Look at her playing with her tits. Man, I wish I could grab them and…' He raised his hands to a pair of imaginary breasts and made squeezing actions.

Hari began guffawing, spilling his tharra on the floor. He had clearly forgotten about the conversation. Laxman was glad. He might sense he was up to something, or that he had a plan. He was smart that way. He could intuit things uncannily accurately. Besides, Laxman was a poor liar.

'You will clean the mess before leaving,' he told Hari.

Hari laughed harder at this. 'What's the matter with you tonight? Can't get it up or something?' He was on Harish's team now. 'How can you not be affected by the yellow-haired beauty? Look…look at how she's sucking his cock…saala, these goras have such huge dicks.'

Laxman did not respond and went and sat on the chair next to the window. The October wind was getting nippy and he felt goosebumps on his arms. Behind him, the three men continued to pass lewd comments about the white woman.

Just then the electricity went out. Harish, Hari and Gopal began hooting in unison, laughing and slapping each other's backs like little children spooked in the dark. From the houses around, similar shouts of glee echoed. Laxman leaned out of the window to look around. For a moment, he could not see anything. Then slowly, his eyes adjusted to the dimness of moonlight. None of the houses in the vicinity had electricity. The tall lamp posts beyond Chilla Gaon, in Mayur Vihar where the society complexes were, were also dark. But already, orange dots had begun appearing on the tall multi-storied building next to the Sai Baba temple. Those societies had automatic power back-up. Some moments later, the distant rumbles of individual generators starting off in the nearby houses also reached him. Lucky bastards, he thought.

He kept leaning on the windowsill for a while. It won't be long before everybody in the neighbourhood went to bed, unable to watch their prime time TV shows after dinner because of the load-shedding. He was glad. It would be safer to sneak out and carry out the delivery. How convenient it would be if load-shedding occurred in areas where he had to take the stuff to. He was guaranteed to never get caught.

✦

The party was in full swing when he reached the bungalow near Khan Market after midnight. This was his third delivery that week to the same house, and he was getting a little jittery because now the owner—a strapping man in his thirties—had come to recognise him.

'Lucky!' he had exclaimed the previous week when he had gone to make the delivery. 'You are here again to delivery my poison? Bravo, bravo! You are good boy. You know I specifically asked for you when I called sethji? I can recognise an efficient man when I see one. Do you want to eat something? We have lots of food!' He had blabbered in a strongly accented Hindi as he fumbled in his pockets for the payment.

But today the party was not a sophisticated one. He

could hear the muffled sound of DJ music coming from the bungalow the moment he turned to enter the street. He passed by, making a couple of rounds on the street first to check if it was safe to enter. He was worried that all the lights and music was going to attract attention. What if the police came to inspect? Laxman paused, trying to make up his mind. Just then, someone turned down the music and the lights in the front lawn were dimmed. Laxman could still hear the music but it wasn't as loud as before and wouldn't be enough to make the neighbours call the police. He looked around to check if anyone was coming up the street. It was well past midnight and hardly any car drove by. Quickly, he parked the bike and walked towards the house.

He could hear people's voices now. He rang the bell and stood waiting. No one came. Where were the guards anyway? He rang the bell a couple of more times and then finally, someone walking towards the parking spotted him from inside and called out the sahib.

He appeared at the gate moments later, dressed in a light cotton shirt and blue jeans. His hair was greased and swept back, revealing a handsome forehead. He was holding a glass of whiskey. 'You have the stuff?' he asked. There was no smile, none of the fake pleasantries this time. He was probably high the last time he met him.

Laxman showed him the packet he was carrying. It was marked strategically as 'Paschim Sweets'. Inside it was a yellow cellophane-wrapped cardboard sweet box, a reliable way to hide the cocaine and LSD.

'Come.'

Laxman walked in after him. They went through the lawn, to the entrance of the bungalow. A blast of music which was subdued because of the tightly shut door, met them with force as they entered.

They were in a small space with the stairs leading up to the upper floor of the house. It was dim and smoky, and the glass vibrated due to the music. Laxman was wary of the thick mass of jumping and gyrating bodies dancing on the smooth marble floor in the hallway just beyond. He tried not to look but from the corner of his eyes he could see tall and slender women in shimmering dresses. He was trying to resist looking, but the diplomat was unconcerned. 'You stand right here,' he said, and went upstairs.

Laxman stood awkwardly. The loud music was making him restless. He shuffled on his feet and tried to focus on a painting on the wall. Then his eyes flickered towards the dancing crowd despite himself. The women were heavily made up, their bleached hair done up in fancy styles, their creamy legs going well with their short outfits. There were a few foreigner women too. They were dressed skimpily and their tall and sturdy frames stood out in the crowd. They were snorting cocaine by turns, leaning against a table with little lines of the white substance. There was a pile of loaded syringes too. The sight disturbed him somewhat. He didn't want to be a witness to all this.

The music changed. It was a softer number, and people relaxed, collapsing on the chairs and couches. They were walking in and out of his line of vision. The ladies looked heavenly, with their dresses swishing around their slim legs. How the boys would drool over them if they were there,

Laxman thought, almost grinning. Harish would simply lose it. Not all houses were as exciting as this one. And he was visiting here for the fourth time in two weeks, and each time there had been some sort of a party going on. The sahib must have a lot of money. His was always the biggest order. Laxman exhaled, processing the information. These rich motherfuckers…

A door on the upper floors opened and shut with a bang breaking his reverie. He heard quickened footsteps—heels clicking on marble—and a lady in a sheer, skin-coloured saree with a shiny blouse that revealed a beautiful cleavage, came in view. He was standing at the foot of the stairs so she could not hide her face from him, and he saw that her kajal was entirely smudged and her face red and blotchy. She paused when she saw him, then breezed down the remaining steps, clearly upset. Just then the door upstairs opened again and the sahib came down after her. He rushed past him, grabbed hold of the woman's hand as she was about to open the front door to leave the house, and dragged her back a few steps. She struggled against his grip, and then all of a sudden, slapped him on the face.

The music blared on, but everyone froze as if they heard the sharp clap on his cheek through the glass. The sahib looked stunned for a moment, then recovering, grabbed her wrist and began dragging her back again. The woman began shrieking, struggling against him in anger. The guests stood staring, uneasy but not intervening. Laxman looked away, shuffling from one foot to another. He did not want to see any of this. He had to get out of there and quickly. If there was any trouble and the police was called, everybody at the party would be busted. He debated going back without the money. He would come back tomorrow, he thought.

But the sahib had already dragged the woman back to the staircase landing where Laxman stood. Her face was twisted in a grimace as he clutched her hand roughly. Laxman tried to not look at her. The sahib was about to pull her upstairs when he spotted him. His expression changed. He seemed to have forgotten about him in all the chaos. Hastily, he stuffed the money in his hands and pushed past him, pulling the woman with him up the stairs again.

Laxman turned on his heel and almost ran out of the premises. The music had died down by then.

✦

Visits to the diplomat's house stopped abruptly after that night. A whole month passed without an order. Then when he thought that the sahib had probably moved away or found another dealer, the seth called to tell him to make a delivery on an urgent basis to his house. It had to be done the same night. Laxman was expected to pick up the stuff and deliver it by midnight.

That evening after work, he went for a shave and dressed up in a nice outfit. Then he went to the seth to pick up the packet of crack, and drove towards Khan Market.

There was no traffic and he reached the house fairly quickly. He parked the bike on the end of the parallel street and walked up to the bungalow. If he was ever chased by the cops they were sure to get him before he could reach his bike. But it was a risk he had to take. There were clear instructions about not taking the vehicle too close to the delivery location, in case it was tracked or recognised.

The streets were quieter than usual. The orange lamplights made the area look eerie in the wintery mist. The sahib's house was completely quiet. For the first time in the past few months, he was seeing it so deserted, and without party lights hanging from different places. It looked rather gloomy like this.

The gatekeeper ushered him in and told him to wait by the stairs. He went and stood there, not sure if he should ring the bell or not. The curtains were drawn so he couldn't make out what was happening inside, but through the small gap, he saw that the living room was unlit and there was no one there. Just then the door on the upper floor opened with a click. He heard footsteps descending and he could make out they were a woman's. It was the same woman who had slapped the sahib the last time he was there. She was clearly the missus of the house, not some escort he had brought in that night.

Laxman watched as she descended the steps slowly, her satin night dress that barely reached her knees, swishing sideways to reveal more. She was speaking on the phone.

'Yes…yes, he is here. What should I do? Yes, okay… okay. So I should just hand him the money?' She paused, listening. 'All right. You sure I don't need to check?' She paused again, glancing towards him. 'Fine…fine, I got it.' Then she hung up and faced him. Even in the darkness he could see her flawless skin accentuated with makeup. Her eyes were perfectly outlined with kohl, and her lips coated with a rich shade of maroon.

'You have it?' she asked in a bored voice.

'Ji, madam.'

'Show it.'

He produced the packet.

'Here is the money. Sahib said he will talk to sethji.'

He nodded, turning away to leave.

'You were here the other day, right?' He was about to deny it when she turned away and said, 'Never mind, you can leave.'

He managed to steal a glance at the back of her bare thighs as she climbed higher and disappeared on the upper floor.

✦

'Sometimes I feel that we should all get together and kill that son of a bitch…'

They were in Laxman's room after dinner. It was already past midnight and Laxman was growing tired of Hari's ranting. He had hardly slept after making the delivery the previous night and all he wanted to do was for them to leave so that he could get in bed.

'That would solve all our problems. And then these rickshaws will be ours. We will even get to ply them without paying a charge…maybe I'll buy more rickshaws and rent them out. That would give me enough income every month. And there would be no more deliveries to make.'

The rest of them listened to his banter quietly. Harish was watching the India–Pakistan match on his mobile. 'Hari, brother, shaanti se baith ja. Let me watch the match in peace,' he said.

'Saale chutiye, I won't shut up. If you have a problem, go somewhere else.'

But he went quiet for a while. The commentary went on in the background.

'I say, let us smoke some of the shit right now,' Harish said suddenly.

Laxman turned around. 'What?'

'Yeah. Let's try the stuff.'

'What do you mean?'

'I mean that let us do some right now, what else. You haven't done it ever. It's a great experience. What say?'

'Gaand mein le le,' Gopal said. 'I have to meet Sheela.'

'Abbey, isme kya badi baat hai? Thora sa hi lenge. I have a lot stowed away. Mera Noida wala customer toh kabhi dekhta bhi nahi hai kitna diya hai.'

'Yaar Hari, will you shut up or will I have to break your face?' Harish said.

'Laxman,' Hari turned towards him. 'Bhai, fuck them. Let us do it. What is the big deal anyway? We will just take one snort each. That will be enough! I bet you don't even know what it feels like. It's not like the cheap stuff we take. It's some other deal altogether. All you have to do is inhale it in the powder form. Like this.' He made a sniffing gesture, pressing one nostril with his thumb and inhaling deeply. 'And then there is pure bliss...' He closed his eyes and said, 'You will feel like you have achieved everything in the world. Absolute euphoria. Everything around you will make absolute sense. And your senses will be so sharp. It'll be amazing!' His eyes were glinting in the dim room as he gesticulated.

Laxman ignored his rant and went and sat near the window with his back to them. Hari was still talking. 'Crack is different. It is much more potent. There was this one time I was delivering it to a lady in Safdarjung. What maal she was yaar! Her blouse was this deep…I could almost see her tits. She offered me some of the crack I had delivered to her because she didn't have enough money on her. I told her that if she let me fuck her I would give her a discount. Bhayi, she agreed! God, what a fuck it was! Her pussy was soft like a little girl's! Of course, I still made her pay. She was angry at first but I fucked her so good that she paid me more to visit her again. Obviously I didn't go again. I was tempted, sure, but I'm not a gigolo…'

The fantastic tale continued. Laxman tried to block his voice out and leaned out of the window, taking in the view of the tall buildings around. Those houses were so much prettier than the dingy room he lived in. How he wished he could have a proper apartment with a proper balcony and a bathroom…

A blast of guffawing roused him. He had fallen asleep with his arms on the sill, his head resting on his forearms.

'What the hell are you creating such a ruckus about?' he grunted in annoyance.

'Harish wants to do cocaine but Hari wants to do crack.'

'We have both,' Hari said.

'What do you mean we have both?' Laxman asked in irritation. 'Where did you get it from?'

'Brother, I always take some out from the packet that goes to the buyer at Sainik Farms. He never checks because he buys every other day. And he's filthy rich. I have quite a stock now. You guys are so phattu so I never told you.'

'You have gone mad,' Laxman said curtly. 'Don't even think of doing any of it here. Go to your houses.'

Hari began laughing. 'See!' he gesticulated to the rest of them. 'I told you this Laxman is a phattu!'

Laxman remained quiet. He had to make a delivery to the sahib again that night. The lady who had slapped the sahib received all the deliveries now. It seemed like her husband was away on work. The first few times he went to make the deliveries, there were none of the parties that happened when the sahib was there. Then a few weeks later, he saw the house lit up again. It seemed like the diplomat was back.

But that wasn't so. The wife came out to receive the packet from him. She was dressed in a low cut dress that barely covered her thighs. It was made of some velvety material and looked luxuriant against her fair skin. She looked tipsy and Laxman felt his senses tingle as she leaned in to examine the packet. Then she looked him up and down and asked, 'What's your name?'

'Lucky,' he quickly said.

'Lucky...' she drawled. 'All right. Here is the money,' she handed him an envelope full of cash. 'Count it. My husband will talk to sethji.'

Laxman counted the money and left quietly.

That night he lay in bed recalling the sensuous curves of her body. Her skin had shone in the dark, and the glitter she had applied on her chest and cleavage had made it hard for him to look away.

✦

The woman's name was Mallika Prasad. She was the daughter of an MLA, and had very recently married the diplomat. From what Laxman had found out, she could not be more than thirty or thirty-one years of age.

It didn't take him too long to figure out her daily routine. She went to the gym in the morning, then a yoga session in the Lodi Gardens with some of her friends. Then she either went home, or to the malls in Saket. She usually came home by evening for another yoga session at home, and then stayed in unless there was a party at night. Once or twice every week, she spent about two hours at the spa and salon. Laxman also found out she was having an affair with someone, and called him over sometimes, or went out with him to hotels.

Since the night she had asked him his name, he had sensed a change in her tone and attitude towards him. At first he could not comprehend why she would speak to him in such a familiar manner. But it felt pleasant. She was so desirable and beautiful. And she clearly did not care about his background once she was drunk and wanted crack. Besides, he didn't look poor in his peddler clothes.

His visits to her house had become regular now. One delivery per weekend was guaranteed.

✦

One Saturday night, as usual, he parked the bike in the usual corner of the street and walked up to the house. A party seemed to be underway. He went up to the gate and walked straight in. The guards knew him now and did not stop him. Once inside, he took out the package from the pocket of his leather jacket and rang the bell.

Mallika opened the door and stood before him in a shimmering golden dress, looking like she was walking the red carpet at the Filmfare Awards. The gown had impossibly thin straps that dug into her shoulders, and was cinched at her willowy waist. Her eyes were darkened with make-up and her hair was in curls that day.

'Luck-kyy!' she exclaimedd shrilly. 'You are finally here! Come in, come in!' Her breath was stale and her pupils dilated. Laxman wondered what substances she had taken this time.

'Nahi madam,' he said, holding out the packet. 'Apka parcel.'

'Parcel lene se hi andar aoge?' she asked in stilted Hindi. Laxman was surprised. She was asking him to enter the party?

'Nahi,' he said carefully, trying to understand what she wanted. She had been snorting too much. The junkie bitch, he thought in annoyance. She was sure to get him in trouble.

'Oh forget the parcel, darling,' she said airily in English. 'Come on in,' she said and without waiting for him to respond, she pulled him in by the sleeve of his jacket.

It took him a while to make out what was happening. As soon as they were in, they were surrounded by people dancing, drinking, and smoking. The hall was completely darkened and hazy, and the only source of light was a few blue lights blinking here and there. The music was a strange, pulsating rhythm that shook the insides of his chest.

Before he knew it, Mallika had put a glass of whiskey to his lips, splashing it on his t-shirt and jacket. He gulped it down and shook his head. The people around kept gyrating, unbothered about the new entrant who was so different from them. Mallika, high on booze and drugs, was moving sexily to the music, grinding with another female who had thrown her arms around her shoulders. Then she turned around and grabbed another drink. 'Lucky, here!' she said, and brought it close to his lips, her other hand pressing against the nape of his neck to encourage him. He gulped it down too and laughed. The stuff was rich and strong. His throat burnt.

'I should go…' he tried to say. But Mallika had taken his arms and kept them around her waist, swishing her hips so that her crotch grazed against his with every move.

He gave in. She was dancing like a crazy woman, and he was getting more and more aroused by her. She made him chug another glass of whiskey, and he collapsed on the sofa coughing as she plopped on the cushions next to him.

Then they were both laughing. He saw her face in the light coming from the window and he knew she wanted him to take her.

'Let's go inside,' she said. Laxman barely heard her but understood. She got up and pulled him, then began to manoeuvre him through the crowd. They managed to cross the hallway and reach the kitchen. It was in a mess. People were gathered around the marble slab snorting cocaine. A half-dressed woman was leaning over the slab, holding a rolled up note. He watched her snort up a line and remove her shirt as the people erupted in a cheer, including Mallika. The woman shook her breasts laughing hard and began dancing. Lucky noticed most of the people were partially undressed like her. They were playing some sort of a game. He turned to look at Mallika to tell her he wanted to go inside but she pushed him forward towards the slab.

'Everybody meet Lucky! He will try some cocaine with us!'

Everybody hooted, as though all of them knew him and were all such great friends. Laxman hesitated. He had smoked ganja once or twice before and it wasn't too good for him.

But his head was swimming and the people were cheering him on. Then they began chanting his name. 'Luck-ky! Luck-ky! Luck-ky!'

His head was spinning slightly with all the whiskey and smoke.

'Luck-ky! Luck-ky! Luck-ky!'

He did not even know how to do it. He stumbled slightly, unsteady on his feet. He looked towards Mallika in a plea for help. He didn't really know how it had to be inhaled. But she wasn't bothered. She had already bent over the slab and was snorting up the powder. Suddenly, he felt a woman's hand from behind, holding him around the shoulders. He turned to her and was welcomed by a whiff of her perfume. Before he knew it he was holding a roll of note and was being half-held down to the table. The people were still hooting his name.

He closed his eyes and sniffed hard, feeling the substance run up his nose.

Jumping, laughing, grinding bodies all around. He felt like he was floating. He was holding onto whoever was next to him and laughing away with the rest. Mallika had disappeared, then appeared out of nowhere and hung onto him, dancing roughly pressed against him.

'Do you want me?' she asked in English.

He could not understand but she didn't seem to care. She led him out of the hall, towards the door where he always came to deliver the stuff, up the stairs to the floor where the bedrooms were.

They went through another door and came into a separate establishment. There was a similar hallway and several doors on the far end. The living room was entirely white. The floor was tiled and had luxuriant fur carpet covering most of it. The sofas were white leather, and all the furniture was dark wooden in colour in stark contrast with the whiteness. There were large paintings on the walls, and several chandeliers hung down from the ceiling. It was the world of the rich and beautiful. But he did not care that it wasn't his. In that moment, it felt like he was the master of everything. The house, the rooms, the woman—they were all his.

'Quick, come on inside.'

And they ducked inside one of the rooms. It was beautiful, very red, and lit dimly. Laxman could barely see anything but he could make out the luxuriant bed covered in red satin and the lovely tapestry—something he had only seen in films. The carpet under his feet was red fur and he quickly took off his shoes and lay down on it. Then he clambered up the bed and plopped down on the pillows lined up against the velvety headrest. Mallika was laughing at his antics as she undressed. Underneath her shimmery dress was a lacy bra and panties through which he could see her nipples and vagina. He felt his penis grow hard inside his jeans. He said hoarsely, 'Take off everything.' She shook her head and began wrapping a gown around herself. He pounced forward and snatched it away sending her into another fit of giggles.

'You are liking this, aren't you? How is the stuff?'

'Amazing. Take off your clothes.' She began to laugh again. 'Take off your clothes if you want to be fucked,' he told her.

'Wait, boy.' She lit a cigarette. 'Here. Take this pill. I bet you've never tried it.'

He extended his arm and took it from her and swallowed. Somewhere at the back of his head he could hear voices. The music from the floor underneath was still in his ears. There was a sudden splash of colours in front of his eyes and he jerked forward on the bed and rolled over, falling down onto the carpet. Mallika was laughing at him again, cigarette in her hand. She came and tried to pull him up but he dragged her down next to her and tore off her panties and she squealed. Then he got on top of her and fucked her.

She began screaming suddenly. He was still on top of her so he slapped her across the face and turned over so that she was now on top of him. 'You whore, shut up and ride me!'

She obeyed, moaning in pleasure like a cat in heat. He slapped her a few more times, loving the cries of pain and enjoyment. 'You bitch,' he said through gritted teeth. 'You like it like this, don't you?'

He climaxed while he was still inside her and then threw her off. She was laughing and moaning his name as she rolled over and stood up, her panties torn but still clinging to her thighs. Her bra was lowered revealing her beautiful breasts. They were as delicious as he had imagined them to be.

Laxman stood up, looking around. It was a darn good house. There were so many things he wanted to take back with him. Would Mallika let him live there? He had fucked her. He could do it every day.

He walked around, feeling the cool marble under his bare feet. The bathroom was on the right. He walked into it and almost slipped on the tiles. There was a bath tub there. He climbed inside and turned on the shower. Cold water. It hit his face with force and he let himself be drowned in it. Where was Mallika? 'Mallika!' he screamed. 'Mallika! Mallika! Mallika!' He went on screaming. 'Come here! Mallika!'

He climbed out, dripping wet. He saw her lying in bed all naked. She wanted to be fucked again. He grabbed her by the leg and pulled her towards him. She groaned in surprise and let him part her legs and suck her. Then he flipped her over and penetrated her anus.

She was gasping for breath. He grabbed her hair and fucked her harder until he had ejaculated all over her buttocks. Then he pushed her away and slapped her ass until it was red and she screamed his name.

He felt like the king. He looked around to decide what to do next. There was another door towards the far end of the room. What was in there? He ran towards it and yanked it open. It was the closet. He had never seen so many clothes in his life! There were rows of shirts and trousers and shoes and bags. His eyes glided over the satin dresses and glittering jewellery in one corner. He pulled the chains and earrings off the hooks and threw them in the air, watching them fall down around his feet. Then he pulled out the shirts, stack after stack, letting them fall on the floor in a bundle, before falling on them and lying there. Then he got up and put on a shirt and a pair of trousers along with a pair of shiny leather shoes. They fit perfectly. He looked at himself in the mirror. He didn't look like himself at all! He looked like a sahib. He was THE sahib, owner of the house. All this was his. Mallika was his. She would give him everything because now he was her lover.

She was calling to him from the bedroom. He walked out of the closet, dressed as he was. She was smoking again. He took the cigarette from her and sank into the sofa next to the bed, taking deep drags. Mallika crawled up to him and began touching his organ, cigarette in the other hand. He took it from her and made her bend over. Then he pressed the cigarette against her ass until it left a mark. She was crying in pleasure so he took her again.

He was about to climax when there was banging on the door.

'Who is that?'

She did not reply. But he was alert. Was it the guards? Was it the sahib? Did he know he was in the room? He was wearing his clothes. He had fucked his wife. He would kill him. But no, he wouldn't dare to touch him. He looked rich and powerful in the clothes. He was a proper sahib.

He should just act cool. He couldn't act like a coward in front of Mallika.

But the banging increased. He jumped up, screaming. Was it the police? Mallika turned to him in alarm but stayed where she was. Bloody bitch! This was all because of her. He looked around. Where should he hide? Should he hide in the bathroom? He could lie in the tub. He ran towards it and jumped into the tub. But there was water everywhere. His clothes had got soiled. No, he would hide in the closet. But they would look in the closet if they searched the rooms. The balcony! He ran towards it and pulled open the doors. The cold breeze hit his face. It felt nice to be out in the open again. He would just hide there until the knocking person gave up and left. Through the mesh doors, he called out to Mallika and made shushing sounds to tell her to keep quiet.

But there were people in the room already. The fucking bitch had let them all in! He quickly ran and locked the door from outside. But now he was trapped in the balcony. He ran to the railing and looked down. It was just one storey. There was a bed of grass right under. He could just jump and then run towards the gate. It was wide open. He would take his bike and run.

Through the door, he could see shapes of people moving around the dark. Suddenly, the diplomat appeared and saw him. Before Laxman could react, the door was smashed open. The diplomat staggered out and faced him. He looked dishevelled and wild, and his eyes were red-shot. He was high on substance. 'Lucky, you bastard,' he growled. 'Fucking my wife, huh? Saala haraami.' And he took out a gun.

The metal gleamed in the streetlight next to the house. Laxman eyed it, knowing he wouldn't fire it. It would spell doom for his career. There were too many eye witnesses who would testify against him.

'Ab kaha bhagega?'

Laxman edged closer to the railing and looked down. The diplomat was laughing.

Then he heard the muffled crack of a silencer.

A red spot appeared on his shirt and spread quickly. Laxman touched it lightly. The blood was sticky on his fingers. He was fascinated by the viscosity and stared at the puddle of blood that was swiftly collecting on the pristine marble floor before him. His vision blurred slightly.

Then with a loud cry, he grabbed the railing and swung over.

He landed on his feet and began running. The police would be there soon. They would raid the house and arrest the diplomat. Then they will try to find him. But they will probably not arrest him because he was almost killed by the diplomat. They might penalise him for peddling drugs but what was that in comparison to being shot? They should, in fact, make the diplomat pay for his treatment.

Laxman began running faster. He could hear the police siren by the time he ran out of the neighbourhood. His wound was hurting dully, but he ran hard, onto the main road, past the deserted Khan Market, past Pandara, and turned onto the long stretch of road towards the Old Fort.

He ran through the empty night. A few cars went by, honking wildly. The road shrank and distended as he ran. Then it swayed from one side to another. The orange street lamps were getting brighter and brighter. The flashing red of cars and the luminescent billboards were dizzying. But he was running fast, as fast as a car.

From a distance, he saw the Fort—calm, illuminated. But the police siren was still sounding. They were drawing closer. He ran towards the fence and with a swing, climbed over. The lake was sparkling in the moonlight, glittering like the dresses the women were wearing at the party. Beyond the liquid inkiness stood the ruins of Purana Qila. The chattris were silhouetted against the grey sky.

He ran towards the dark corners where he knew the steps leading up were.

The city was glittering in the darkness. A soft wind was caressing his wound. He sat under one of the chattris, and faced the road. If any police vans approached, he would have ample time to escape.

He sighed to himself. Once the diplomat was arrested for shooting at him, he would go back to Mallika and marry her. He would live with her in the same house and get everything, including the cars, signed in his name. Then he would throw parties like the diplomat used to, as her husband and owner of the property. He would get cocaine and acid from the lalaji, and boys like him would call him 'sahib' when they came to deliver the stuff.

He was going to be a rich man and his days as a peddler-cum-rickshawwalla would finally be over.

Turning to face the night, he clutched the wound on his chest as it oozed. The lights inside the compound were starting to blind him. The sirens were drawing closer. He stood with a heave, clutching the pillars. The lake beneath sparkled seductively. He could easily hide in the water if they came. The cops would never be able to guess.

THE CULT OF LUNDUR BABA

It was a cool, cloudy morning in August. Jugal was sitting in his rickshaw outside the Janakpuri Metro Station, waiting for the usual swarm of college-going students to start coming in. The new semester had only just begun, and work had picked up after nearly two months. Some new coaching centres had also opened up nearby, and when passengers for the colleges dwindled around mid-day, the constant flow of the institute-going students kept him busy.

The rush around the station was heartening to see. The summer vacation lull had been too hard on all the rickshawwallas in the area and while most of them had returned to their village farms to eke a living there, he and several others had no choice but to peddle through the streets in the sweltering heat every day in the hope of finding enough work. Most of the days, they managed to get by. But sometimes, the daily earnings were not even enough to have a proper meal in the evening after paying the malik.

Jugal leaned back and eyed the phat-phats that had begun to gather around. The drivers—young boys who aggressively snapped up passengers for half the price rickshawwallas did—were hurling abuses at each other as they manoeuvred their vehicles in the narrowed lane trying to take the better spot. Some of the phat-phats were already filling up with passengers whereas hardly any rickshaw had managed to make even a single trip. Jugal sighed to himself and waited, occasionally beckoning to the people who came out of the station. But they always made a beeline for the phat-phats because they were cheaper and faster.

Finally, three girls came up and got on his rickshaw, chattering busily amongst themselves. He knew them by name: Rashmi, Guriya, and Devika, who went to the women's college nearby. They were his regulars.

Jugal pulled out of the metro parking at his own pace and began pedalling towards the campus, listening to their banter. They seemed to be in no hurry. College girls were his best passengers. They did not complain if he pedaled slowly, and they did not haggle over the going fare. They never even spoke to him roughly, mostly addressing him as 'uncle'. Jugal was happy with that kind of respect. People usually did not bother so much.

There was a flurry of girls around the college when they reached the gates. Several rickshawwallas were already stationed there, eyeing the students as they milled about. The three girls got off and paid him, then breezed through the gates, still engrossed in their conversation. He watched them walk away and smiled at their girlish springiness. They reminded him of his own daughters, Bulbul and Chulbul.

Jugal turned his rickshaw to go back to the station. If he was lucky, somebody would hail him on the way and he wouldn't have to join the queue and wait for his turn again.

As he pedaled, the sky cleared up. The sun was right behind him and beat down on his back until he took a turn to enter the residential colony for a short-cut to the main road. It was one of those days when the monsoon sun dried up all the rain puddles. He was getting a heat rash again and his back felt extremely itchy.

✦

Jugal had migrated from Baka to Delhi about six years ago, with the specific aim to become a manual labourer and earn enough money so that his wife and children could move to the city and live with him. Their village, which was his home for nearly two decades, had ostracised him and his family after one of the main landlords had raped his elder daughter, Bulbul, and then his younger daughter when he tried to file a case with the police. Soon after the incident, he and his wife and children were forced to flee the village. They took refuge in a nearby village where his sister lived with her husband. But it proved too difficult to begin life from scratch. To add to their miseries, his sister's husband humiliated them after he heard what had happened to the girls, and threw them out. After that none of his other siblings offered to shelter them or even gave them a loan.

After a year of struggle, Jugal decided to leave for the big city. He planned to accumulate enough resources for his family to leave Bihar permanently. He sent his wife,

Padma, to her elder brother's house where she was given a corner to live in as long as she and their daughters served the family. He was a rich man and his wife needed maids to maintain their big house in Patna. And Padma and the girls were resourceful and skilled servants. It was to be a temporary arrangement and seemed fine until his elder daughter, just fifteen, got pregnant. It was discovered that one of the sons of Padma's brother who was studying in Kolkata, had raped her continually for a month while he was visiting during his college vacations. When Padma found out, she knew they were doomed. Her brother's family was sure to blame the girl for seducing the boy and would have them thrown out. Everybody knew about the previous rape incidents.

Jugal was supposed to visit them the following month. He called them every now and then from a telephone booth for an update, but it was very rare that he would call more than twice a month. Then one day, while pedalling around near the college, he had a sudden intuition that something was wrong. Immediately, he went to an STD booth and phoned them on the residential landline.

Her brother was dismissive when he answered the call. Without saying much, he hung up. Jugal called again, but there was no answer. There was a sinking feeling in the pit of his stomach. He tried calling a few more times, then rushed to the Nizamuddin Railway Station knowing for certain something bad had happened to his wife and girls. But he did not have the money for a ticket. Luckily, there was a train going to Patna stationed at the far end of the platform, and when it began moving, he jumped in and snuck inside the toilet. He was caught twice by the TT and thrown out at stations he did not recognise. When it happened the third time, the TT threatened to have him arrested if he caught him on the train again. Then he pushed him out on the platform at the next station. No amount of begging swayed him.

But Jugal was determined to reach Patna. Just when the train started moving, he grabbed the window bars and clung on. The people on the platform stared curiously, but said nothing. Soon, the train picked up speed, and Jugal closed his eyes as the train sped towards Patna which was just about a few hundred kilometres away now. It was still early morning and the people inside the carriage did not see him hanging there. They passed paddy and yellowed sesame fields, and several towns and villages. The sun bathed the countryside in the mellow light of midsummer dusk. Once or twice they passed through barren fields where men and women were squatting to shit. They looked at him in surprise as the train went past. It was a fleeting but bizarre sight.

Finally, when the train reached Patna and slowed down, he jumped off and ran across the several parallel tracks, through the overgrowth, and into the main city. He took a bus for his brother-in-law's house, and ran all the way from the bus stop.

When he reached, he was not allowed to enter.

'Your wife is a whore,' his brother-in-law's wife shouted from her room upstairs. 'She ran away with her lover days ago. And your daughters have run away too. Haye, haye!' She beat her forehead. 'They have probably become prostitutes. They always had that streak. My love and affection could not prevent it. They were ungrateful little bitches. I gave them so much and this is how they repaid us! Ensnaring my poor, innocent son! I had to send him away sooner because of your wanton daughter!'

Jugal knew in his heart that his wife and daughters had not run away. These people had done something to them—probably sold them off across the border, or just turned them out to fend for themselves. He went to file a complaint at the nearest police station but was turned away even before he could finish his story. His brother-in-law was a powerful man, and the police wouldn't lodge a case against him. Jugal persisted for days, until the brother-in-law's gundas beat him up and forced him to take a train back to Delhi.

Jugal allowed himself to be sent back. He knew then that he would never meet his family again.

✦

It was late evening when Jugal, tired from ferrying passengers around, decided to go and take a nap in the public park across the road from a college campus. He had just had lunch at a Jan Aadhar and was extremely drowsy after eating a full meal.

The park was nearly deserted at this hour. A bunch of boys were playing songs on their phones in one corner of the park and the words reached him mutely where he lay under a tree.

'Aashiq banaya, aashiq banaya, aashiq banaya aapne...'

✦

Loud rough voices suddenly roused him with a jerk. He had rolled under the park bench in his sleep and for a moment, couldn't tell where he was. The voices could still be heard although they were low now. Hastily, he scrambled out, trying to see what the commotion was about. It was dark, but he could make out shifting forms. About nine men were huddled near the guard room on the far end. Jugal peered from where he sat. He could hear thumps and shuffling of footsteps on wet grass.

His hair stood on its end. He knew that the men were doing some unlawful.

The voices continued. Occasional laughs reached him where he sat crouching next to the stone bench. Careful of not making a sound, he shifted slightly, squinting to see properly in the dark. All around him, crickets were chirping.

Several minutes passed. The rusty door of the guard room creaked shrilly in the night making him start. Just then one of the men moved, and the streetlight fell on a form on the ground. A man on his knees moving jerkily, as if convulsing.

With a pang Jugal realised what he was doing. He could see a naked girl lying unconscious there.

Jugal stared in horror. The man finished off and rose, stuffing his penis inside his pants and buckling up as the next one dropped his pants and bent down over the girl.

For a moment, Jugal felt that he would not be able to react. Then as if in a daze, he gave a loud howl and went charging towards the men, shouting loudly.

'Police, police, police!'

Before he could even reach the man who was raping the girl, the others grabbed him and clasped his mouth shut. Then one of them punched him on the face.

Jugal buckled as he blacked out for a moment. Warm, sticky liquid was dribbling down his chin. His vision was swimming. He fell to his knees.

'Ye kaha se aya!' one of them hissed.

'Bhenchod, maar daal!'

He saw the face of his assailant—a dark, stout man who looked very familiar…the other man who had grabbed him too seemed familiar. He squinted in the dark to look at the other men. They had left the girl and were facing him now. He recognised all of them.

Jugal struggled against his captors. 'Police…police!' he gasped.

'Aur maar saale ko…' came a voice from behind him.

'Police toh nahi aa rahi?' someone else asked.

Just then he felt a sharp searing pain on the side of his head as a loud clang echoed in the night, and everything turned upside down.

✦

The girl who was raped in the district park near the college was identified as Sheetal Sachdeva, a second year student of the girls' college nearby. She used to live in a flat with four other girls who were her classmates. All but one of her roommates was in on the night of the incident. The girl testified that she had gone to the market in the evening and had stayed out late. When she came back, she entered the house with her own set of keys and did not think of checking who had returned.

It was not until late that evening that they had noticed Sheetal was gone. By then her family had called to enquire where she was, after trying her number in vain since morning.

Within a few hours, the police was conducting investigations in the PG and the nearby areas. Several PCRs were lined up on the streets and the place was filled with khaki-clad men marching from one place to another.

It was the first time something like this had happened out in the open, that too so close to the Tihar Jail. The SHO was getting calls from everywhere. The media was sure to get involved.

✦

Jugal gained consciousness in the wee hours of the morning, found himself shoved behind the bushes next to the boundary of the park, and had to struggle to stand up. There was dry blood at the back of his head and face, and his clothes were torn and bloodied. The moment he recollected what had happened the night before, he ran towards the guard room to see if the girl was still there.

The room was locked, and a heavy iron lock leered at him in the light of dawn. Nothing gave an indication of what had happened the previous night. Not even the grass looked like it had been trampled upon by seven brutes who had gang-raped a woman. He peered inside through the grimy window and saw it was empty. There were rods and metal bars lying in a heap, next to which was a pile of rags. The room looked as if it hadn't even been opened in very long.

Jugal walked to his rickshaw still parked next to the entrance of the park, and returned home without going to the police. He knew they wouldn't believe his story even this time. What they had said to him so many years ago when he had gone to report his daughter's rape rang in his ears as he pedaled slowly on the empty road.

'Aisi ladkiyon ka rape toh hona hi chahiye. Nikal yaha se varna tu bhi nahi bachega.'

And then they had guffawed and slapped each other's back in mirth.

✦

Jugal was leaning back on his rickshaw and watching the phat-phats gather around the metro station. It was a little after 6 a.m. The early morning mist had not yet lifted, and there was a sharp nip in the air. Jugal adjusted his muffler over his face to conceal the bruise on his face. He remained unmoving as he scanned the men jumping off the phat-phats, hollering at each other and laughing amongst themselves. Seven of them, he knew, were the men who had raped the girl. He recalled their faces clearly and knew they were the phat-phat drivers who plied in the Janakpuri Metro Station area.

The girl's body had been found in one of the gutters inside the park, tied to bricks, so it would sink all way to the bottom. When the park was first searched, nobody thought of looking inside a sewage-filled drain. It was only when the drain dried out that a young couple kissing behind the bushes discovered it, several weeks later. There had been an unusual number of flies buzzing around and when they went to check, they saw the fluid-filled body lying in the dark.

The story was all over the news. For several days, media vans lined up around the college where the girl studied, and the whole road in front of it remained busy as journalists drove in and out. The gruesome details of the rape and murder were splashed all over the papers and news channels ran the story over and over again. Police vans were stationed around the metro station in front of the college and the DDA park. They patrolled the streets at all hours.

To Jugal's surprise, the seven men were nabbed by the police in the following weeks and put behind bars. The city rejoiced over the quick work of the police. It came out in the local newspapers, and the news channels were at it like hungry dogs to a bone. But Jugal knew that the media would lose interest soon and the neighbourhood would return to its previous state soon. The debates about rape cases would end quickly too.

As he expected, the rapists were locked up for six months and let off. Jugal wondered if he should step forward. But he did not trust the system.

✦

It was after midnight when Jugal began tailing Prakash, one of the seven men who had raped Sheetal Sachdeva that evening. All of them had been released a few days ago, and Jugal, who had kept track of the time of their jail time, had immediately begun planning his move. He had already identified Prakash a few days ago at the metro station, driving a phat-phat like before. It was a wonder how he did not seem to have changed in the past six months. He had cleanly picked up from where he had left off. Jail was as though a tiny blip in the man's life. He simply went back into his previous existence, and without a day's break. Jugal was astounded at how he got away so easily.

They were in Mongolpuri and the streets were deserted at the hour. Jugal looked around to see if anyone had noticed him in the neighbourhood, but not a single soul was in sight. Suddenly, Prakash began singing loudly and Jugal was afraid that someone might wake up and look out of their window. But there was no flicker of movement in the street they were in. The windows and doors remained shut.

Jugal followed Prakash for several more metres. Prakash was now dragging his feet lethargically, and the 'khssh-khssh' of his shoes grazing the dusty road in the still night jarred on his nerves and made him edgy.

They were about to reach the end of the street. Jugal could see that after the turning there were no streetlights. Carrying out his task in the dark would be tricky. He would have to make the move now. With a lurch, he bolted forward and with a swift movement, struck him at the back of his head with a wooden plank, knocking him unconscious.

There was a loud clang as the plank struck his skull. Jugal dropped it in a heap of cement nearby and looked around to see if anyone had seen him. But the streets were absolutely still.

The man lay supine on his face. Jugal turned him over with his foot and took out the blade he was carrying. Then he tore open the man's pants and without another thought, sliced off his penis.

Blood spurted everywhere. Jugal held up the organ and let it ooze. A pool gathered under him. He backed away and ran out of the colony, the sticky member still in hand, leaving a trail of blood that looked like black ink on the gravel.

✦

Janakpuri had nearly forgotten about the gruesome rape and killing of the Delhi University girl, but when one by one, all seven of her attackers were ambushed in different parts of the neighbourhood, it caused a stir.

Initially, the victims of the mysterious castrations and killings were not linked. Then one day, when a young reporter who was involved with a girl who was friends with Sheetal Sachdeva, realised that the seven men were the ones who were the convicted rapists and killers, the rape case began flashing in news channels with renewed vigour. Sensational versions of the attacks on the men were presented with such alacrity that they seemed more realistic than theoretical.

But the connection was exhilarating. Was it an angered family member who had sought revenge on the culprits? Or was it an unknown lover of the girl who had avenged the brutal killing of his sweetheart? The city reeled with the possibilities. Motives were assessed and investigations conducted on the possible suspects. The bourgeois audience lapped up the daily stories and speculated about the mysterious justice-maker. He was hailed for avenging the 'small-town girl Sheetal Sachdeva, student of the BA Programme, Ms. Fresher 2012, fashionista, blogger, and aspiring model'. The debaters came on news channels once again, this time to discuss the growing crime against women and how perpetrators of sexual violence hardly ever received adequate punishment. They also discussed the growing anxiety regarding the perilous state of the city.

But the mystery deepened as four more men were found castrated in the following month. All four had once been charged with sexual assault and let off. It was obvious that all of these attacks were linked.

The city was in a flurry. People didn't know whether to be appalled by the barbaric attacks, or laud them. Was it excessive? Or was it justice? It began to be said that when the legal system in the country was so inefficient, it was inevitable that retaliation would come from other quarters. A civilian taking the mantle of responsibility for punishing criminals who had been let off lightly by the state was needed in times of such fear and violence. It was comforting to think that there was an invisible crusader watching over the neighbourhood, and punishing those who managed to escape the law. Killing off the rapists was the only way. Nothing else satiated the thirst for justice of the wronged. The victims of abuse whose attackers had been castrated, felt triumphant, and openly declared on social media that they support the unknown avenger. The unknown man was branded as a self-styled vigilante who brought justice to the rape survivors and their families.

But the identity of this person remained undiscovered despite the journalists' and police's best efforts. Who was this subaltern hero? There were no clues or witnesses so far. Nobody knew what to expect.

✦

Jugal was running out of ways to find out about more rapists in the area who had been let off with light punishments, or who hadn't been convicted yet. It was easy to track the four men he had castrated because they were recent cases, but after that, there were no more to be found. He had exhausted his resources and did not know anyone who could give him more information.

Then one day while he was double checking with one of the rickshawwallas who plied around the area about a woman named Gayatri Sharma who had been raped in the neighbourhood two years ago, someone said he should look it up on the internet instead of badgering people with incessant questions. Apparently, it was possible to get almost accurate information of all kinds on the computer, and it didn't even take much time.

Jugal was fascinated by the idea. The internet sounded like the best way to get a lead on obscure rape cases. All he had to do was go to a cyber cafe and use the internet to find information. But he did not know how to operate the computer—he didn't even know how to read. He would have to find someone to help him. Someone who could read and write and could use a computer.

Then one day, he saw Devika, one of the girls who were his regulars, who went to the same college as Sheetal. She was walking to the metro station late in the evening, with her arms wrapped around a bundle of books, and her head bent slightly as she walked. She looked preoccupied and in a hurry. Jugal knew she would help him. All he had to do was to explain the situation to her, and somehow win her trust.

Jugal hesitated. He was sure to scare her off with his story. He didn't even know how to narrate it properly. The whole incident, since the rape of Sheetal Sachdeva, was quite mixed in his own head. He didn't know how he would begin because it might come out completely garbled. And if asking her for help backfired, then he would have to flee the area.

But he knew that if didn't ask her, he would reach an absolute dead-end. He had to take the risk.

To his surprise, Devika was not only open to listening to his story, but also far more enthusiastic about helping him than he had expected. She went to the cyber cafe with him several times and helped him chart out names and details of the perpetrators he wanted to go after.

It took a month to dig up all the data. Devika kept him in the loop while doing her research, often making time to meet him and discuss things in the musty old basement cyber cafe near the college. They met in the district park too—the same park where Sheetal Sachdeva was raped—and went over the information she had procured over and over again. She always carried around a thick file where she kept printed pages of articles, photographs, reports, which she brought for his benefit. She would read and translate all the written things, and show him pictures if there were any. Sometimes if it got late, she allowed him to feed her, and they went to the momo or chaat stalls that she liked to eat from. She knew he did not have too much money, and ate just to give him satisfaction. And she made it a point to bring him home-cooked food as often as she could.

✦

Jugal had castrated seventy rapists in Delhi within eight months, but his desire for revenge had still not ebbed. He constantly thought of his wife and daughters, and how his little girls had been brutalised so mercilessly so many years ago. At night, he cried himself to sleep, and in the morning, he hardly had the energy to work. His money was fast running out and he knew he would be kicked out of his shanty soon if he did not pay the rent in time.

But Jugal knew he had to do the work. If he backed out, who would do it? He pushed himself harder and harder, until it started to make him go crazy. The seventy severed members lay in a box in his room. Sometimes at night, he could hear rats trying to cut through it, and he would yell loudly and brandish a stick to drive them away. The image of the seventy rotting penises haunted him in his dreams. He was sickened by the sight of coagulated blood and hair, and the screams of the men rang in his ears until he fell asleep in exhaustion each night.

Devika's enthusiasm gave him courage. She was tireless and brave, and did not let him falter. She later told him that she had been molested by an uncle when she was a child.

Jugal knew that even if he grew tired of the work and quit, he would not be able to find peace. It was better to keep at it than be guilty forever. Perhaps he would gain redemption after some time. But until then, he had to keep going.

✦

The mystery of the castrations deepened. It had been a year, and so far, a hundred and eight cases had been filed. Eighty five of them had survived the attacks, but the rest had succumbed to the injuries.

Strange stories began circulating through the neighbourhoods of Janakpuri. People reported sighting a thin, lean man with shaggy hair, wearing nothing but a loincloth, and wielding a penknife at night. He seemed to be wearing a heavy garland but nobody could tell in the dark. Then one day, a youth on a bike managed to photograph him.

The photo showed the man looking straight into the camera, his eyes widened in surprise, and his mouth half agape. He was dark and ordinary looking, but it was difficult to distinguish his features due to his thick mass of beard. What shocked everybody was that he seemed to be wearing a garland made of human penises. The photo had captured clearly, the dozens of penises sown together and hanging around his neck.

In no time, the picture could be seen everywhere. The police put up beware posters bearing the photograph, while some groups from the general public enlarged the photograph and made it into posters which they hung around Janakpuri as a mark of respect for the man who protected their daughters and avenged women who had been violated. The Hari Nagar Ghanta Ghar displayed this picture for a week straight. People in the neighbourhood put flowers around it and began distributing langar in his name. Then a local kitty party decided to hold a fundraiser for the unnamed hero, and even conducted a jagran for his benefit. Locally, he was being called 'Lunduriya'. But now it didn't seem proper to refer to him by such a title. He deserved more. After all, he was no less than their saviour.

The police was baffled at the goings on. They could not trace the man, no matter how much they tried. Besides, if they did catch him, there would be a lot of opposition from the middle class populace. No one was willing to help them conduct investigations.

Then one day, a local MLA visited the district for his election campaign. Amongst the several issues he touched upon in his public speech, he mentioned a 'Lundur Baba' who was the custodian of the neighbourhood. Soon after, the new title went up with the posters showing the severed penises of more than a hundred rapists. People even began making offerings and charities in name of Landur Baba.

The rest of the city, baffled by the hullabaloo in West Delhi, looked towards Janakpuri with interest as the cult gained popularity and attempted to enter other parts of Delhi. Social media was flooded with the spine-chilling image of the man with the garland of penises. People began circulating WhatsApp messages about him. A CCTV video showing him castrating a man at night even went viral on Facebook. It was replayed on news channels, with the warning of 'explicit content'. The tabloids were going berserk.

✦

Jugal was growing tired despite his success. He wanted to put an end to it. But tracking and attacking culprits gave him a sense of satisfaction which was hard to resist. He could not stop just yet.

Then one day, the rape of a minor girl in Mayapuri by a boy in his teens caused a huge furore all over the city. The girl had to be hospitalised after the incident.

When Jugal heard about it, an unspeakable rage welled up inside him. He was in the market at that time and he gripped the handles of the rickshaw so hard that the rubber handles cut into his palm. He dropped off his passengers, and cycled home. He decided to go out that night and track the boy responsible for it.

✦

As it happened, the boy who had committed the rape was the son of a rich man, and the parents of the victim could not even manage to file an FIR.

There was tremendous confusion in the following days. People had begun discussing Lundur Baba. Would he bring justice to the girl? They hadn't heard any news about him in very long. Nobody knew.

A week later, the parents, relatives, and neighbours came to the streets to protest. An angry mob marched through Pankh Road, holding up banners, and crying for justice. Suddenly, they began chanting the name of Lundur Baba. The system had failed them. They needed a surrogate of justice.

The morcha turned from Nanak Pura and towards the road leading up to the Clock Tower. For a moment, nobody saw anything unusual. Then when they reached the tower, a wave of shock swept through them. Standing atop the tower, before the east-facing clock, was the lean darkened form of Lundur Baba. The crowd cheered: 'Jai Lundur Baba! Landur baba ki jai!'

Jugal looked down at the mass of people, cheering not for him but the deliverer that they saw in him. The teen boy who had committed the rape was unconscious at his feet. His naked body twitched but did not move. With one swoop, Jugal gathered him in one arm and held him up for the crowd to see. A collective gasp went up at that.

'Kya chahte ho?' he asked, looking down at the faces.

A rhythmic chant began rising from them. 'Maar do! Kaat do!'

Jugal breathed heavily. The people looked crazed. They wanted him to extract the revenge they couldn't for themselves. It was not anger towards this boy alone. It was the impotent, suppressed fury of the whole of society against a system that had failed them.

The blade flashed in the street light. The crowd cheered. Jugal held up the organ and flung it to the ground, at the crowd's feet, then disappeared.

✦

Several months passed and the cult of Lundur Baba lost its novelty. The media moved to other subjects, occasionally printing small pieces about him. But he no longer generated hype, and eventually lost his status as a TRP-fetching figure. Only the small neighbourhood of Janakpuri still discussed the incident at Hari Nagar with the same interest as before.

Then one day, a young IPS officer, Prakash Narain, who was visiting Delhi for a few days, decided to take the matter in his own hands. He had heard of Landur Baba before, but when his aunt who lived in Ashok Vihar, told him about his bhakts, he made a few calls and visited the police station in Janakpuri where his friend was the SHO.

It didn't take him more than a month to catch Lundur Baba. As it turned out, there hadn't been an actual attempt to catch him before. After a while, the CBI got involved in the investigations, and they scanned the room where Jugal Kishor, aged fifty-seven, lived. The infamous garland of penises was recovered. The organs were in a state of putrefaction and were found covered in maggots.

The court pronounced judgement speedily. Jugal Kishor was sentenced to fifty years in prison, for fatally attacking thirty-six men, and sexually injuring another ninety-eight. The case of Lundur Baba was finally closed.

DREAM GIRL

It was an unexpectedly cool night. Bhola slowed his rickshaw as he turned from the Kalka Marg on the sloping road, and cycled towards the Rickshawwalla Colony. Cars went by occasionally, as he pedaled towards the dumpster, beyond which lay the enclosure. From a distance, he could see cows and buffaloes lounging on the road, sitting in the garbage that had spilled well into the middle of the road. He rang his rickshaw's bell as he manoeuvred through the filth. The light from the colony was illuminating the street and he could see familiar posters as he rode up. The tall lamp post they had erected right in the middle of the colony shone from above like a lighthouse lighting up the whole colony and the street leading to its entrance.

Bhola spat out his gutka and cycled inside, through the gateway they had built a few months ago. The government had made several improvements in the colony over the past one year for the people's safety and well-being. They even had a 24x7 dispensary of their own now. A new school was going to be built at the end of the year. Everybody was happy with this new sarkar. The area had transformed completely. The jhopris had nearly disappeared as every family was given a house in the buildings that were constructed for them. The entire neighbourhood was much cleaner than it used to be. The best thing was that the drainage system was overhauled completely. Everyone had their own toilet and bathroom in their homes. Bhola was given a room with a kitchen and balcony because he was young and would start a family soon. He was amazed by the sagacity of the sarkar.

The fluorescent light from the tower cast long shadows as he dismounted from his rickshaw. He flicked out his supari and stuffed his mouth as he made his way to the water basins. A few shops on the street were still open. He could hear shutters being dropped one by one. Some boys were laughing in one corner, huddled around a scooter. One of them was holding a cigarette which they passed around as they peered into a mobile phone, laughing boisterously. He walked past them, towards his house in the East D-4 section. The twelve feet posters hanging on the dispensary walls lifted precarious in the wind as he walked around it towards the basins. The smaller posters on the trees and lamp posts also rustled hard. Bhola gazed reverentially at the grinning face of the neta who had implemented changes in the colony, as he filled his bottle from the tap. From where he stood, the neta's face was everywhere, pasted on walls or hanging from streamers. Some artists had even made his caricature portrait on the wall of the four-storied building in the West A-3 side. TV people had come with cameras to film it when it was being painted.

Bhola bent down and washed his feet quickly. Somewhere a dog began howling and soon a ruckus ensued as many dogs came running from different directions, barking at each other to protect their respective territory. He flung a stone at them and they howled as they retreated. He was hungry and wanted to get home quickly. He began walking again.

A rumble of a vehicle made him turn as the headlights swept through the alley. A white Innova pulled up directly in front of the mandir on the street across. Bhola paused. It was unusual for cars to come around at this hour. Around him some of the shopkeepers who were about to leave also looked surprised.

A man came out of the van and pulled out a speaker. Another announcement? Pramod had told him that people had come a week ago to make an announcement about a tower being constructed there…was there another construction they were being told about now?

'Bhaiyo aur beheno, sarkar ki nayi Intarrnet-For-India yojana ke tehet, aap sabko ye bataya ja raha hai, ki kal se, aap sab mein baatein jayenge esmart phones, yaani ki mobile phones, aur saath mein di jayegi free internet ki suvidha…bhaiyo aur beheno, sarkar ki nayi Intarrnet-For-India yojana…'

The shrill speaker-voice followed him as he turned around to go into his building. By the time he lay on his mat to sleep, the announcements had stopped.

✦

The market was bustling with shoppers as Bhola went around ferrying passengers all day. It was intensely humid, but at least the sky was overcast. The shoppers seemed to rejoice in that because the market was unusually crowded even though it was the middle of the week. The word 'SALE' was plastered on every wall and every billboard. It was on banners hanging down from stores, on windows of showrooms, on posters stuck on auto-rickshaws. SALE was always good. The market was always full during this time and he hardly had trouble finding work.

It was beginning to drizzle. The shoppers and pedestrians ran for cover even as the thelewallas swiftly dismantled their displays to save their wares from the rain. He had just dropped off two ladies at KFC, so he parked behind the parked cars and waited. He watched as e-rickshaws zoomed by, undeterred by the rain. The young boys who were riding them, laughed and cussed as they rode wildly, gliding between the cars stuck in the jam.

He had been fantasizing about an e-rickshaw for several years but hadn't been able to save enough. He had begun to feel that maybe he never would be able to afford one. When he started working at the age of fourteen in a college canteen in north campus, he was known as chotu. After a few years, he had saved a little money and then he commenced on his rickshaw-pulling career. He couldn't even dream of getting an e-rickshaw so soon. His wife was pregnant. What would happen when the child was born? He would have no money to feed it. Of course, he would be earning more. But who knows how long that would last. What if they bring some new rickshaw in the market and everybody wants to ride in that and not the old ones? He laughed to himself as he imagined flying AC rickshaws, zooming around the marketplace carrying fat Delhi aunties.

The honking of cars jerked him out of his reverie. He yelled at the driver and pulled his rickshaw out of the way. The drizzle was already subsiding.

✦

Bhola and Rinky were married for about six months when they found out that she's pregnant. At that time, they had begun constructing a tower. When the child was born, they announced that it was completed. It was just weeks after the 'Internet for India' scheme was first announced.

Finally, a few months after the child was born, the yojana was being implemented as the surveyors came knocking on doors to do a headcount. The people in the colony rejoiced. It was heard that mobile phones would be distributed for free soon. The sarkar was finally doing what it had promised for so many years. After all, the MLA who had visited them the other day had proclaimed that internet was a basic human right in today's time. He said that even the poor should have access to it. Everybody was jubilant. This sarkar was certainly much more progressive than the previous one and should have no problem in winning the upcoming elections. No other government had done something so significant for the common man. When the MLA visited next, he was met with a mad, cheering crowd in the colony.

Soon, there were posters all over the city saying: 'Internet For India: Entertainment Hai Sabka Adhikaar'.

Pictures of ministers hung about, wearing garlands and waving in the distance. The health minister was involved. It was to be an experiment towards the progress of the nation. Mobile phones were supposed to be instrumental in bringing change.

Bhola did not understand so much. He did not care for mobile phones much. But Rinky wanted one. So he signed up.

✦

It wasn't long before the white Innovas started coming every day.

'Bhaiyo aur beheno, sarkar ki nayi internet-fo-raall-yojana ke tehet, aap sabko ye bataya ja raha hai, ki kal se, aap sab mein baatein jayenge esmart phones, yaani ki mobile phones, aur saath mein di jayegi free internet ki suvidha aap ke entertainment ke liye…bhaiyo aur beheno, sarkar ki nayi internet-fo-raall-yojana…'

Rinky said that her ears rang with the words all day. She laughed and said that even the baby had memorised the lines. She said she was having dreams about the smart phone.

✦

It was the first day of Dussehra and Bhola had just woken up. He was still sleepy when he walked into the balcony as the sun rose over the eastern horizon. The other half of the sky was overcast which indicated it would rain that day.

He was about to go back in when he heard the buzzing of people talking excitedly. Automatically he looked towards the tower. In the middle of the settlement where people generally gathered during any event, some trucks and vans were parked. It had surely something to do with the yojana. Rinky had told him that the government had announced the phones would be distributed in the next few days.

By the time he came out of the house to go to work, he saw that they were unloading the trucks, even as the local boys hung around excitedly. Bhola smirked. He knew just how much those boys wanted those mobile phones. They wanted to watch naked American girls all day.

It was still early, but the workers had unloaded the trucks. There were rods and tent material. Were they making a shamiana for some event? They were already beginning to set the poles on the ground.

Bhola turned around to get his rickshaw. He couldn't be less interested. What was a mobile to him anyway, except for a way to make Rinky happy?

That night when he returned, Rinky told him that men and women in green uniforms went around talking to the women in the colony about the internet yojana. There were to be screenings every day for the residents of the colony. It was mandatory for adolescent boys and men to attend. The government had initiated the scheme for them specifically. Rinky told him that entertainment is important for everyone. The uniformed people said that the labour class should have equal access to it, and she couldn't agree more.

Rinky told him to come home by 9 p.m. next day so they could go watch the show together.

'What show?'

'The show they will be screening,' she said. 'They will probably show us some Shah Rukh Khan movie.'

✦

The entire area from the dumpster to the arid land beyond the colony was lit up. The tent they had made covered the maidaan area of the settlement and there were police vans everywhere. The whole place was bustling as people gathered. It seemed like it was a mela, not a government scheme. Bhola looked up to see the colourful streamers zigzagging the sky. They must have a huge budget for the colony. There were cotton candy and kulfi stalls here and there. Plastic horns were being sold and there was a cacophony in the air as people pushed about, laughing, happy, excited.

As Bhola and Rinky walked up towards the entrance, they saw that there were desks lined up by the wall of the tent. There was a long queue already. Rinky pulled his arm and said, 'Bhola, jaldi! The line is getting longer!'

They walked along the wall of the tent where the line ended and stood waiting. Rinky was almost bouncing next to him, her jewellery jingling as she turned this way and that, waving to the neighbours and chatting with the other women in the queue.

All of a sudden, a jeep drove up and parked at the head of the queue where the desks were stationed. The uniformed personnel walked around busily. The CRPF men rearranged themselves, watchful. A man came forward and turned on the speaker. He picked up the mic and blew into it.

Immediately the noise around him dropped. People jostled each other, still laughing, but mutely, as they ran towards the queue. Those who were already standing in the queue shoved each other around. A CRPF officer walked up to him and the men in front of him quietened down. Within a few minutes everybody had joined the queue. He was amazed at the discipline with which everyone stood in line, like good school children. Bhola watched as the uniformed men walked up and down the queue to maintain order. A few cops roughed up a man in front of the queue when he didn't stand properly and he was taken away.

'Kitna high security hai...' someone said behind him.

'This is happening everywhere in the city, do you know?'

'Very hi-fi!'

'For our protection only...the public is too unruly...'

'Yes, yes...after all, they have so many expensive phones. This rowdy public can go to the extent of looting them.'

'Yes, people should understand and co-operate. Sarkar is doing so much for us. People should also become more civilised.'

'Yes, brother. Why will the government do anything for us if indiscipline and gundagardi occurs? We should all respect procedure...'

'If the government is giving us technology then we should value this initiative and behave well.'

'I agree, who has ever done anything for us before this?'

The man holding the mic was finally ready. He got on one of the tables and looked around.

'Bhaiyo aur beheno...'

The CRPF men and cops were walking up and down with their rifles in hand, elbowing men who were misbehaving. Soon, the low hum of excited chatter died down.

'Internet For All: Entertainment Hai Sabka Adhikaar!' came a voice from the speaker. Everyone erupted in loud cheers and whistles pierced the laughter and clapping. 'Bhaiyo aur beheno,' he continued. 'Sarkar ki nayi internet-fo-raall-yojana ke tehet, aap sabko ye bataya ja raha hai, ki kal se, aap sab mein baatein jayenge esmart phones, yaani ki mobile phones, aur saath mein di jayegi free internet ki suvidha aap ke entertainment ke liye...'

A few uniformed men were making their way up the queue. They reached him and pointed to Rinky, talking between themselves in English.

'Kya hua?' Rinky asked quizzically. Up ahead, they saw that the ladies were leaving the queue. 'Kya, hum nahi lag sakte line mein?'

'Bhayi, kya ho raha hai?' Bhola asked.

A woman in uniform approached with a clipboard and said, 'Ye yahan nahi lag sakti, ladies ki line dusri side pe hai.'

'But...'

'Jaldi karo,' she snapped. 'Itna time nahi hai.' She moved away, waving at her subordinates.

A man was walking ahead, stopping to talk to every man standing in the queue. 'Literate or angootha chaap? Literate or angootha chaap? Literate or angootha-chaap?'

'Angootha-chaap,' Bhola told him when it was his turn.

Just then there was a cackling of the loudspeakers again.

Everybody looked around, craning their necks to see what was happening.

There were murmurs. People began fidgeting in the queue. A few men left talking boisterously among themselves. The sanctity of the queue was broken.

'Jaldi shuru karo, oye!' someone yelled from behind.

'Haan, jaldi!' More voices poured in.

'Mobile phones kaha hai?'

'Mobiles kaha hai!'

There was a scuffle near the end of the queue. Bhola turned to see what was going on when the shoving began. He fell down.

There was dust everywhere as the men began to push each other, shouting, laughing as some fell down because for them it was both a funny and happy situation they were in. The prospect of getting mobile phones was still very exciting. The commotion only added to the excitement.

Bhola got up and pushed back a man who was falling on him. He looked around to see what the uniformed people were doing. They were scattered, trying to control the mob with the CRPF men. One of them came up to where he was standing, and slapped a young boy because he was hooting. Bhola watched as three of the four men were taken away. The man who spoke on the mic stood on the table, although the laughter and hooting did not stop.

'Please maintain order. Those who will create a ruckus will be locked up for the night.'

Just then the men in front of him in the queue began shouting, 'Internet For India: Entertainment Hai Sabka Adhikaar! Internet For India: Entertainment Hai Sabka Adhikaar!'

Other men joined in.

'Internet For India: Entertainment Hai Sabka Adhikaar!'

'Internet For India: Entertainment Hai Sabka Adhikaar!'

'Internet For India: Entertainment Hai Sabka Adhikaar!'

'Internet For India: Entertainment Hai Sabka Adhikaar!'

Bhola stayed quiet. This was madness.

✦

It was midnight by the time the crowd was seated inside the tent. There were several announcements about the yojana being made and they were told they could collect their Aadhaar and ration cards before leaving. Those who did not have IDs were issued a special laminated card to include them into the scheme.

The rule was that they were to attend the screenings every day for a month. Their attendance would be marked. Whosoever came every day, will be given the mobile with free and unlimited internet after thirty days. They would be served chai and glucose biscuits inside the tent.

✦

No one objected to the movies they were shown. They were about Indian men pursuing foreign-looking women who were extremely voluptuous and beautiful. They had beautiful large breasts and a slim waist and full hips that were absolutely round. They had golden hair and big eyes and thick lips. Their noses were slanted and cheeks angled.

Bhola was both appalled and attracted by the beauty of the actresses. On the first day of the screening, as the sex scene began, Bhola sat with his eyes fixed on the screen as if he was hypnotised. Before he knew it, he had an erection. Around him men were laughing and whistling and hooting at the screen. One boy stood up holding his crotch. But the CRPF men were all around, he could not dare to misbehave.

But the men were horny and excited. They knew it was okay to sing and dance a little, during such movies. In the dark, Bhola raised his leg lightly to be able to move freely and wrapped his shawl around himself. Nobody could see he was rubbing his organ underneath. The man sitting next to him did the same and Bhola ignored him, watching the actress seduce the actor, displaying her huge bosom. He was aware of the panting around him as the men grew hard and began masturbating.

There was grunting and heavy breathing all around. It was getting hot and sticky inside the tent. Bhola closed his eyes as he ejaculated. He knew men around him were also reaching their climax.

✦

It wasn't long before the mobile phones were distributed. There was a workshop held to demonstrate how to use them. Only men were given the phones, but no one complained. Bhola discovered almost immediately that the mobile phones did not have free internet for everything. They could only watch the same 'entertainment videos' that were screened for them for a month. But it was okay. All the men of the colony had become absolutely besotted by the girls they were shown. They did not understand what was being said because the dialogues were in English but the voices and accents were enough. The foreignness of it all was so appealing. The anchor of the show had told them each time that the heroine was 'Dream Girl'. They were the best kind of beauty there was in the world.

Very soon, it was just the 'Dream Girl' they saw around. Photos of Bollywood actresses and models were taken down from around the city. All they saw were images of blonde beauties with figures that were so perfect that they were almost magical.

One day Bhola brought home a blonde wig for Rinky to wear in bed at night. She was reluctant but she knew if she refused then he would beat her up. She wore it and came to him. Their infant was miraculously asleep in the corner at the time.

He ordered her to talk to him.

'Kya bolu?' she asked and sat there awkwardly in the blonde wig which was attached clumsily on top of her hair, in frilly bra and panties, and waited for him.

'Talk and make me hard, you bitch,' he told her.

Rinky looked scared.

'Talk like...talk like Dream Girl.'

But she didn't know how to talk like Dream Girl. She stammered and stuttered and squirmed uncomfortably. Finally, to punish her, he thrashed her. Why didn't she have a husky, drawling voice like the Dream Girl? He gagged her and fucked her until she began choking, just like the men did in the videos.

✦

One day Bhola was cycling along the Moolchand road late at night when he saw a tall prostitute wearing a blonde wig and white makeup. He stopped near her and observed her as she fixed her skirt. Her legs and arms were brown but her face and neck were painted white. Her lips were drawn red. Her plastic blond hair fell in ringlets around her shoulders. Bhola felt a stirring of desire, but cycled away.

That night he ate dinner and sat down to watch his Dream Girl again. She was performing oral sex on a brown man who looked quite like him, and he felt his organ get harder and harder. She was showing her breasts and dancing around. The man pulled her close to him and began fondling her. She was growing restless and tried to resist him, but too weakly. He knew she wanted it just as badly. He was rubbing her vagina and she was moaning softly.

Bhola took out his organ and began rubbing it. The Dream Girl was lying next to him on the charpayi. He bent down to lick her between the legs. The Dream Girl turned around and bent over, and he sucked her as she cried out in pleasure.

'Oh, Bhola…Bhola…' she was saying, holding up her hair. She had parted her legs for him. He pushed his penis inside her and fucked her. She was pleading him to go harder.

'Yes, yes, yes!' she was yelling out.

Bhola ejaculated, holding the phone in one hand. His arm grew limp as he fell asleep, half undressed. Rinky was asleep in the corner.

✦

Rinky left with the baby soon and Bhola began to live alone. He did not mind that she had run away with the child. He was almost glad she was gone. Now he could spend all the money on himself without having to worry about a wife and a child. In any case, she was becoming too intolerable. Her ugliness revolted him and he only found respite in the videos he watched on the smart-phone. He even made her bleach her hair blonde but that only worsened matters. She gave him no pleasure. She was too brown—she was not like Dream Girl.

✦

After a year, the free mobile phones that were given out began to malfunction. Bhola had to go out and purchase one at an 'almost free' price. Posters of Dream Girl holding up smart phones were plastered across the city. Bhola knew he had to buy a phone otherwise he wouldn't be able to masturbate.

There were five towers in the colony now. The mobile company that gave free internet for a year was charging 199 rupees/month—a nominal fee. The men in the colony did not mind. It was a small price to pay in comparison to keeping wives. Most of the men had driven their wives away and had more money to spare now. They all enjoyed Dream Girl's escapades and were happy masturbating to her. She was so beautiful that it did not matter she was on a screen and they could never actually make love to her. She was too life-like even in the videos. Who needed a real woman who was so inferior to her in beauty?

✦

'ID number 228372' called out a dull monotonous voice.

The camera focused on the doorway where a number of men were standing in a queue. The next man in the queue walked up. He wore a patched pair of trousers, frayed around the ankles, and a vest which was torn in places. He walked in hesitatingly, clutching his smart-phone. The uniformed men waved him on and he sat down at the table in one corner. Around him were several other tables where men like him sat nervously, holding their mobile phones, looking hungry, sunken. There were CRPF men standing all around, alert, watchful. One of them had their eyes glued to him. In the background, the same dragging voice called out more ID numbers as the queue progressed.

'Year of issue?' the official asked the man brusquely.

'2015' he replied.

'Colony?'

'Rickshawwalla colony.'

'Flat number?'

'A-232.'

'Family members?'

'No one.'

'Mobile phone?'

He held up the phone.

'Children?'

'One…'

'Place it in the box.'

He obeyed. Everybody knew they were going to take the phone away and the man was prepared. Several men had been jailed for not bringing in their phones. There were tracking devices installed in them so all of them got caught.

'Fingerprint.'

He pressed him thumb onto the device screen where the official indicated. The printer behind him screeched as some printed sheets came out and he filed them immediately.

'Next!'

The man got up hastily. A uniformed man holding up a staff directed him towards the exit. There was a commotion as someone tried to take back his mobile phone and Bhola heard some shouting as he left the tent.

That was the first scene of the documentary. The camera lost focus and the screen dimmed.

The next scene was a close shot of the man. The camera focused on his eyes—wide, unseeing.

The camera focused behind the man. There was a window with bars. Just under it, there was a mattress. The camera turned to give a view of the rest of the chamber. It was large, with at least twenty to thirty mattresses lined up along the walls. The camera came back to the man. He was sitting on his haunches.

'What is your name?' the interviewer asked.

'Bhola,' he replied.

'What do you do?'

'I pull rickshaws.'

'How many years have you been doing this job?'

'Eleven years.'

'Do you know why we are interviewing you?'

He smiled without saying anything. It seemed like an innocent smile.

The interviewer tried again, 'Did you have a mobile phone given to you by the government?'

'Ji, madamji.'

'For how long did you have it?'

'About seven years.'

'How old are you?'

'Thirty-nine.'

'Were you married?'

'Yes…'

'How many children did you have?'

'One…a boy.'

'Did you leave him?'

'No, my wife took him…she left me several years ago.'

'Do you have any other partner?'

He hesitated.

'Do you have a mistress or a new wife?'

'No.'

'Do you want a woman as your partner?'

He thought for a moment and then said, 'No.'

'Can you tell me about the colony you lived in?'

'They removed us from there?'

'Why?'

'They said that it was to be emptied for the next batch of residents as we had been supported for enough number of years.'

'How many years did you live there?'

'Five.'

'Where did you go once you were removed?'

'I began working in East Delhi. But the money wasn't good. So I came to Camp.'

'What about your mobile phone?'

'They took it back.'

'How do you feel now?'

He laughed drily and didn't respond.

'How do you feel now that you don't have access to the internet.'

'I feel...I don't know...I am not able to understand anything...'

'Are you lonely?'

He didn't respond.

'Do you feel the need to use the videos?'

'Yes...but now I have memorised them...'

'So you can imagine the videos?'

'Yes...and sometimes more.'

'Is that satisfactory?'

'No...the mobile phone was better.'

'Better than real relationships?'

'Yes.'

There was a pause as the interviewer processed the response. The camera kept recording. From the window they could hear the traffic swelling as the day progressed to lunch time.

'Bhola, tell us about the first time the yojana was implemented.'

He thought for a while. 'They built a tent in our colony, like a mela, and screened the films about Dream Girl.'

'What did you do when you first saw it?'

Bhola smiled, looking embarrassed.

'It's okay, you can tell me.'

He didn't say anything. He wiped his brow with a cloth and looked down.

'Bhola, why did your wife leave?'

'She didn't like...the videos. She threatened to leave...I told her she could go.'

The interviewer paused. 'Now what do you think will happen? Now that you have been brought here?'

'I don't know...'

'Do you know why you have been brought here?'

'They told us that the videos had a harmful effect on us… so to rectify it…'

'Do you think you will ever forget…the Dream Girl?'

Bhola did not know how to explain. He hadn't even been interested in any of it when the phones were distributed. But now the Dream Girl was always on his mind. How could he ever forget her?

He stayed quiet. The camera kept rolling and the video ended with a close-up shot of his eyes, staring into the lens vacantly.

ACKNOWLEDGEMENTS

I offer my sincere appreciation and gratitude to Kanishka Gupta and Sayantan Ghosh, for reading and feeling the stories as I wanted them to be read and felt. It was because of their passion for stories, and I suspect, a little madness in them, that this book of madness came about.

I cannot express enough thanks to my supervisor and mentor, Prof. Nishat Zaidi, for being patient with me throughout the journey of this book, and for indulging in my lapses into fiction-writing as I worked on my doctoral thesis alongside. It is only due to her firm guidance, unfaltering faith in me, and sheer maternal affection, that I had a sense of direction in the most important years of my life.

My love for literature wouldn't have been born had it not been for Antara didi and Dadu, Mr A.K Nanda, who told me since I was a child, that I must always write. It is because of their enthralling story-telling that two children became readers so many years ago.

Anamta Rizvi, I must thank you first and foremost, for bearing with all my moods and phases. Thank you for infusing positivity and optimism in my life when I was at my lowest. Vaibhav Wadhwa, I am ever grateful to you for reading and re-reading my stories, for loving them, and for always buoying me up when I needed it. I thank Bipasha Nath, for always being the first to read my writing, for her brutally honest opinions, for always helping me find the right word, for walking and exploring with me when I needed a companion... and most importantly, for never tiring of my stories.

I do not know how to thank my parents, Dr Tushar Kanti Nath and my mother Capt. Sabita Nath (Retd). It is a great comfort to know that you always believe in me. You have always fuelled my passion to write, you gave me the time and space to be consumed by stories especially as this project came about, and most importantly, for always being so certain that everything will turn out well.

This book is dedicated to all of you.